The Postcard was a wonderful story of ⟨...⟩ enjoyed the storyline from David's poi⟨...⟩ from the beginning with his whole stor⟨...⟩ ⟨...⟩ to see Josh reappear in this story. Laura Hilton just keeps providing wonderfully crafted stories for us, her fans.

—Cindy Loven
Coauthor, *Swept Away* (Quilts of Love series)
Author, *Dianna's Wings: The Parables of Trevor Turtle*

I have read all of Laura V. Hilton's Amish fiction books. She is one of my very favorite authors. She has a way of telling a story that, when it comes to an end, leaves me wanting more. Her books are filled with God, Scriptures, prayers, and faith. That is important to me. I also love that she writes clean romance. I would never be ashamed to pass her books along to a friend or church member.

—Judy Burgi
Reviewer, ChristianFictionBookReviews.org

The Postcard by Laura V. Hilton transported me away to Jamesport, Missouri, with the first two words, "*Kiss me….*" I was immersed into the lives of Rachel, David, and their families. Rachel seems to have her head in the English world with her books, but seems happy in her Amish community. Who among us have not dreamed of traveling and seeing those far off places? Rachel takes her trips through the postcards she receives in the mail. I immediately sensed that she was a kind and caring person. Who else would read the paper to find people who need encouragement? David is a mystery and often referred to as "a stray." He is far from home and I could sense hurt in his past and confusion as to his future. The story did not get old; there were surprises I did not expect. I love the fact that Laura keeps writing believable stories that never once seem silly. She makes her characters come alive, as if the reader is allowed to take a peek into their world. Are you ready to meet some new friends? Then get your copy of *The Postcard* as soon as you can.

—Christine Bronner
Reader

From David and Rachel's first face-to-face meeting, I was engrossed in this story. The characters are easy to relate to. The story progressed at a nice, steady pace, and provided surprises and food for thought along the way. I finished it in one day but hated to see it end. I hope we haven't heard the last of these two characters and their families. Thank you, Laura, for another Amish story that shows less of how we differ and more of how we are all human.

—*Carol J. Written*
Pastor's wife and reader

Laura V. Hilton conjures fresh, unusual Amish plots. A *gut* Amish author, a fun series. *The Postcard* contains adversity contrasting sharply with *Gott's* calling in a love story quite distinctive, yet believable.

—*Alan Daugherty*
Columnist, Angelkeep Journals, *Bluffton (IN) News-Banner*

The Postcard is a story of redemption, forgiveness, new beginnings, faith, and love, with a little humor thrown in for good measure. The author captures your attention from the first page. Once you pick it up, you won't be able to put it down until you've reached the end. The characters are real people facing real issues, so much so, that the reader can easily put him or herself in their place and feel what they are feeling and experiencing. The ability to immediately grab your attention and to create authentic and relatable characters is the mark of a great writer—and Laura V. Hilton is just that. She is a master at hitting that mark, and she definitely hits it with *The Postcard*.

—*Dali Castillo*
Reviewer, Goodreads

The Amish of Jamesport

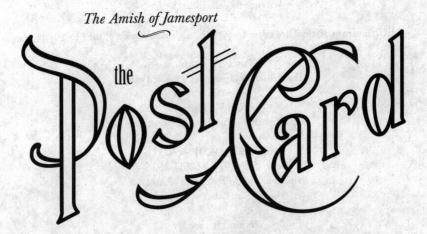

the PostCard

LAURA V. HILTON

WHITAKER
HOUSE

THE POSTCARD
The Amish of Jamesport ~ Book Two

Laura V. Hilton
http://lighthouse-academy.blogspot.com

ISBN: 978-1-62911-359-3
eBook ISBN: 978-1-62911-360-9
Printed in the United States of America
© 2015 by Laura V. Hilton

Whitaker House
1030 Hunt Valley Circle
New Kensington, PA 15068
www.whitakerhouse.com

Library of Congress Cataloging-in-Publication Data

Hilton, Laura V., 1963-
  The postcard / Laura V. Hilton.
    pages ; cm. — (The Amish of Jamesport ; Book Two)
  Summary: "Two Amish pen pals turn into something more when they meet face-to-face and discover the true depths of their affections for each other"— Provided by publisher.
  ISBN 978-1-62911-359-3 (alk. paper)
  I. Title.
  PS3608.I4665P67 2015
  813'.6—dc23
                                        2014045610

1 2 3 4 5 6 7 8 9 10 11 ᴜᴊ 22 21 20 19 18 17 16 15

Dedication

To Aunt Marcia. Thanks so much for sharing my books with all your friends and our relatives.

Acknowledgments

Thanks to Lisa Lutz for telling me the real-life story of a race-horse. And to Barbara Ann Beers for picking out the name of the horse.

Thanks to Whitaker House and their amazing team for taking a chance on me and publishing my stories, and to my readers for buying my books! I couldn't write them without you.

Thanks to Tamela Hancock Murray, my hardworking agent, for believing in me all these years.

Thanks also to my husband, Steve, and daughter Jenna, for being my first editors, and to all my amazing critique partners for pointing out helpful suggestions for rewording, for asking questions to make the story better, and for telling me when something didn't work. Special thanks to Kate, Michele, Barbara, B J, and Kathleen. And to Candee for making me look deeper.

And, as always, to God be the glory for the things He has done.

Glossary of Amish Terms and Phrases

ach	oh
aent(i)	aunt(ie)
"Ain't so?"	a phrase commonly used at the end of a sentence to invite agreement
boppli	baby or babies
bu	boy
buwe	boys
daed	dad
danki	thank you
dawdi-haus	a home built for grandparents to live in once they retire
der Herr	the Lord
dochter	daughter
dummchen	a ninny; a silly person
ehemann	husband
Englisch	non-Amish
Englischer	a non-Amish person
frau	wife
Gott	God
grossdaedi	grandfather
grosskinner	grandchildren
grossmammi	grandmother
gross-sohn	grandson
gut	good
"Gut morgen"	"Good morning"
"Gut nacht"	"Good night"
hallo	hello
haus	house

"Ich liebe dich"	"I love you"
jah	yes
kapp	prayer covering or cap
kinner	children
kum	come
maidal	an unmarried woman
mamm	mom
maud	maid/housekeeper
morgen	morning
nacht	night
nein	no
onkel	uncle
Ordnung	the rules by which an Amish community lives
porcupine jelly	the Amish term for jelly made from wild grapes
rumschpringe	"running around time," a period of adolescence after which Amish teens choose either to be baptized in the Amish church or to leave the community
sohn	son
süße	sweetie
to-nacht	tonight
welkum	welcome
wunderbaar	wonderful

Chapter 1

Awareness darkened his eyes.

"*Kiss me....*"

Rachel Miller read the words near the end of the novel with a sigh. If only some man would gaze at her with awareness. Of course, she wasn't sure what that would even look like, but she didn't think Obadiah ever had. Not even when he proposed. But he was much too practical for that.

So was she, for that matter.

Might as well just enjoy the rest of the story. Nein point in entertaining silly daydreams. She turned the page as heavy steps clomped across the wooden floor outside the employee break room in the discount grocery and bulk food store where she worked. She bolted to her feet, slid the bookmark in place, and quickly exchanged the romance for her notebook from her black bag, tossing her coat over the top to hide it. The steps passed by.

She was on her fifteen-minute break, but the manager—a rather strict Amish man named Joel Lehman—would be unhappy catching her reading an Englisch novel. It was historical, set in the dream-inspiring countryside of northern Michigan. The descriptions of the landscape were so detailed, she could almost see the blowing snow, the pillowy drifts, the ice-covered lake. The handsome hero.

The draw was too great. She started to reach for her bag again, but the footsteps returned, pausing outside the door. Instead, she snagged her pen—pink—and opened her notebook to a blank page. Joel might frown at a pink pen, but he couldn't fault her for writing a letter. Round-robin letters were encouraged, and she quite possibly could be writing one of those.

Except she wasn't.

She glanced at the door as he entered the break room. He set the windup alarm clock on the table for fourteen minutes, so she would know when her break was over. The fifteenth minute was for putting her things away. Joel was strict about making sure his employees didn't break for a single second longer than allowed. And Rachel tended to lose track of time.

Should she mention that she'd gone on break a bit early—early enough to read a chapter in her book?

Was Joel this big of a control freak with his frau and kinner?

She smiled. He was so predictable with the alarm clock. He quirked an eyebrow at her and left the room, carrying something. She hadn't seen what he'd picked up. But that didn't matter. Her book was safe.

The store owner, an Englisch woman, didn't care. She'd even taught Rachel how to use the computer in the small office at the back of the store. Encouraged her to use it so that she could order books online, anytime she wanted to. If only she had an unlimited income, she'd buy boxfuls of paperback entertainment. Enough to last a month or two.

Rachel shook her head. She was wasting her break with silly thoughts. Joel avoided the office—and he would frown on her sneaking in there. He left the computer work for Billie Jo. A funny name for a woman.

Rachel uncapped her pink pen and began to write.

Dear David,

Everything is changing—except my life. Sometimes I wonder if it'll always be the same old, same old for me. Even though I'm marrying Obadiah next fall, I know that little will change. He wants me to continue working. Sometimes I wish something would happen to shake up my life just a bit. But that is just wishful thinking.

My cousin Esther eloped with Viktor Petersheim this summer. I never dreamed that would happen. He whisked her off to Florida for a belated honeymoon. Can you imagine? She's going wading in the ocean—Viktor said "Swimming" with a chuckle and a rakish grin—but here the autumn chill is already

in the air. I begged them to take me. I've always wanted to go to
Florida. Well, anyplace, actually. But it doesn't matter. Esther's
in Florida. I'm not. At least she promised to bring back some
postcards.

Have you ever lived anywhere other than the outskirts of
Seymour, Missouri? Do you ever think of seeing something new?
I think I asked you this before—or maybe I just meant to—but
I don't remember if you answered.

She couldn't keep from smiling as she wrote. Funny how a man she'd never met managed to stir her heart in such a manner. If only she and Obadiah could communicate like this. She would miss writing David when they were married. But since they both were promised to someone else, their correspondence would kum to an end sooner or later.

The alarm rang. She jumped, her pen leaving a pink squiggly line on the page.

Rachel replaced the cap on her pen, closed the lined notebook, and returned it to her tote bag. The book snagged her attention again, and she started to reach for it, wanting to read about *the kiss*, but she forced herself to put it back. Break was over. She could read to-nacht after she finished her chores. She needed to get back to work so her cousin Greta could take her break.

Leaving the small room marked "Employees Only," she went into the main area of the store. She waved at Greta to let her know she was back. Joel wasn't anywhere in sight. There weren't any customers waiting at the lone cash register, so she started "fronting" the aisles, making sure everything was arranged neatly and within easy reach of customers—Amish and Englisch alike. She crouched down to rearrange jars of peanut butter on the bottom shelf, sorting them by brand and size.

The chimes on the door rang as it opened. Rachel looked over her shoulder. An Amish man entered. Nein beard, so he wasn't married. But she'd never seen him before. Odd, considering almost everyone in these parts made it to the Amish Country Store sooner or later. Not to mention, the unmarried ones usually attended singings and frolics—especially those where they could meet maidals from other districts. It expanded the dating pool considerably. That was how Rachel had met Obadiah, two years ago. He lived in a different district than she.

The stranger pulled off his straw hat, revealing light brown hair and dark brown eyes. He glanced at her, and a slight smile formed as his gaze skimmed over her. Something inside her jumped to life. Her stomach fluttered.

Wait. She shouldn't be so excited about a stranger. She was already taken. But there was nothing wrong with appreciating a customer. A tall, handsome customer with a nice body. Strong-looking. Except for his eyes, there was nothing dark about him.

His smile widened, and he slowed to a stop. It was then that she noticed the wooden cane he carried but didn't use.

What had happened that he needed one of those? An accident of some sort?

Rachel stared at the cane, then blinked. She was being rude. She looked away and resumed straightening the bottom shelf. But his presence loomed behind her, making her more aware of him than she wanted to be. She really shouldn't fill her mind with romance if this was how it would affect her. Her imagination worked overtime.

The floor creaked behind her. "I'm looking for Rachel Miller. I was told she works here." The stranger's voice broke the silence.

Rachel's heart stuttered. He knew her? Well, obviously not, or he would've recognized her. But he knew her name? And the way he said it…mmm. Like fresh butter melting on a hot biscuit right out of the oven. She smiled, enjoying the warm, husky sound of her name sliding off his tongue. She glanced over her shoulder.

"Do you know her?" he asked. "Is she here today?" He moved in her direction again, and this time she noticed his limp.

Who did she know who limped? Nobody came to mind. Ugh. She hated when someone knew her and she couldn't think who he might be. It made conversation so awkward. Except, he obviously didn't know her....

Rachel rose to her feet and wiped her sweaty palms on her apron. "I'm Rachel Miller."

The man's face lit up. His brown eyes—no, this close, they appeared to be a greenish, golden brown—twinkled with his smile. Something undefined flashed between the two of them, making her heart thud. Awareness flickered in his eyes—just like in her novel. Or maybe that was her imagination at work again.

"You're even more beautiful than I imagined." His smile faded as red crept up his neck and colored his checks. "I didn't mean to say that. I'm sorry."

She stared at him, ignoring her increased heart rate and the flutter in her stomach.

And you're more handsome than I imagined, even though I don't know who you are.

Nobody had ever called her "beautiful" before. Nor had a man ever acted so flustered around her.

"I'm David Lapp."

He said it as if it meant something. It didn't.

The only David Lapp she knew lived in southern Missouri. The other side of the state. He was the one she'd started writing to during her break. Never mind that she'd just written him yesterday. And the day before. And the day before that. Almost daily for the past two months. And he wrote her just as often, usually including a postcard. Feeding her desires for a change of scenery.

He was her special pen pal. But she'd imagined him as being plain and ordinary, maybe even looking like a monster due to all the injuries he'd suffered from a buggy accident. She hadn't pictured him as being attractive, by any means.

This man definitely wasn't the David Lapp from Seymour.

"From Seymour." A concerned look crossed his face, as if he'd begun to wonder about her sanity. Or as if he suspected there were two girls by the name of Rachel Miller who worked here.

Her eyes widened, and she barely controlled her gasp as her hands grasped her apron, twisting it tightly. "What?" The room swayed. She released the fabric and grabbed at the shelving. "It's *you?*"

Her dream man had just walked into the store, and he was everything Obadiah wasn't. Only he was two years too late.

He moved even nearer. "I came to meet you. I fell in— Uh, I mean…. Well, closed buggies appealed to me, and…."

                                                 ~

David stammered to a stop when Rachel's face turned an alarming shade of red, then faded as white as Mamm's freshly bleached pillowcases. He looked away, his gaze going to the other young Amish woman who'd kum up behind Rachel and now stood at the end of the aisle. The wide, frantic look in her eyes, like a startled deer, mirrored Rachel's. But this woman appeared ready to bolt. Unlike Rachel, who held on to a shelf with a white-knuckled grip.

He frowned. He should've warned her that he was coming. Asked her if it was okay. What he'd done was chase a pipe dream to the rolling hills of northern Missouri. He'd fallen in love with the heart of the woman with whom he had corresponded for the past year, their letters having become increasingly personal, not to mention more frequent, as he'd shared his life with her on paper and, in turn, read about hers.

And with the woman he'd courted since before his near-fatal accident pressing him to pick a wedding date, all the while scolding him because of his irrational fears and lingering disabilities, it was time to admit the truth: He didn't love Cathy. He loved a woman he'd never met.

It was time to leave home. Time to embrace the future. A future that stared at him like he was out of his mind.

And maybe he was.

Rachel's lips parted. "It's you," she whispered again, only this time it wasn't a question. Color began to return to her cheeks, just enough to take away the whiteness.

At least he'd stopped shy of blurting out his declaration of love for her two seconds after discovering her identity.

"You're too late," she said, still whispering.

Too late?

A pipe dream.

But he'd burned his bridges behind him, both in Pennsylvania and in southern Missouri. He had nothing to return to—nothing he cared to return to. He couldn't be too late. Because everything he ever wanted stood right in front of him.

Rachel was beautiful. Even with her modest maroon dress, he could tell that she had a great figure, with curves that— He stopped that train of thought from traveling any further. Medium blonde hair, hazel eyes—eyes that looked rather terrified at the moment. As if he was a stalker.

Kum right down to it, he was.

"I'm sorry," he said again. "I shouldn't have...." David cringed as he backed away. He needed to make his exit and seriously think about looking for somewhere else to live. He didn't have a job here or anyplace to stay. Only enough money to last him a matter of days.

He'd hoped to find a job quickly. The local bishop, Joe Weiss, had offered him the hayloft of his barn until he found someplace suitable to stay. And he had indicated that maybe, just maybe, if David's references checked out, there might be an opening at the schoolhaus for a teacher—on a temporary basis, since the regular teacher had fallen from a barn loft and broken her ankle as well as her arm.

But he'd probably ruined his chances by stalking a local girl. Especially since the bishop's comments were so ambiguous to start with. Using words like "might," "possibly," "maybe," and stressing the temporary nature of the position.

Rachel shook her head and glanced around, as if she looked for someone who might kum to her rescue.

David scowled as he took another step back. He'd killed any chances he might've had by frightening this strange girl. A beautiful girl, but a stranger nonetheless. Even if he did know her heart from her letters. Or *thought* he knew her heart.

He certainly hadn't expected her response to be virtually mute, other than the whisper of "It's you."

He eyed her as she released the shelving and wiped her hands on her apron again. Uncertainty crossed her face. She took a step toward him, the beginnings of a smile forming on her mouth. The bell on the door rang, and she hesitated, her gaze darting past him.

He shook his head. "I'm sorrier than you know," he muttered to the two girls standing there, wide-eyed and silent, then turned away. He almost ran into the barrel-chested Amish man with a full beard who'd just entered the store. The bishop.

David shut his eyes.

Could this day get any worse?

⁓

David Lapp. Rachel hadn't dreamed he'd be someone who made her heart pitter-patter like a toddler running barefoot across a wooden floor. She wasn't supposed to have this reaction to him. They were just friends. Best friends, via the U.S. Postal Service, but still just friends.

Not lovers.

Obadiah filled that slot. Except that he'd gone out East a year ago to live with relatives in Ohio and apprentice for a trade to support them once they married. They planned for Rachel to continue working until the kinner came or his business was built—whichever came first. He was learning cabinetry, and the Englisch seemed to always want their kitchens remodeled, so they anticipated that his business would thrive.

But Obadiah never caused these strange flutters in her stomach. Not even when he kissed her after singings or held her hand in the darkness during the buggy ride home afterward.

David hadn't even touched her. Yet his mere presence....

She couldn't even think. Couldn't focus on anything. Not when he was there, in front of her, too handsome for words. And too late.

Much too late.

He shifted, the wooden cane sliding forward a bit. His head bowed, his shoulders slumped, as he faced Bishop Joe's stern expression. Rachel could sympathize. She'd been on the receiving end of his frown a time or two, such as when she and Greta had gone to confront the bishop about his unfair treatment of Esther Beachy. And to tell him about the erratic bouts of temper exhibited by Esther's ex-fiancé, Henry Beiler.

"Bothering these two girls, are you?" The bishop glared at David. "I had a feeling you were up to nein gut. That's why I followed you. You'll state your purposes for coming here—truthfully now, ain't so?"

Rachel turned to glance back at Greta, hoping for some emotional support, but she'd fled the scene. *Figured.* Her cousin didn't handle drama well.

Rachel firmed her shoulders and looked back at the men. Bishop Joe tapped his foot as he waited for a response. David muttered something she couldn't understand. Whatever it was made the bishop's eyes widen, and he glanced her way. Then he grasped David by the arm and steered him outside.

With nothing to do, unless she wanted to stare out the window at the two men talking—and Joel would frown at that—she needed to get busy.

But he—the man of her dreams—was right outside. She moved closer to the front doors, tempted to find her voice, go out there, and tell the bishop that David could stay. That she wanted him around. That....

Joel wandered by and cleared his throat.

Rachel spun around and started straightening the nearest shelf. Except this one was higher and closer to the door, allowing her to keep an eye on the two men talking outside.

What had David said to the bishop? Her imagination worked overtime trying to kum up with possibilities. Maybe he had declared his love for her. Requested permission to court her. To eventually marry her…. She felt her heart leap.

Ugh. She shouldn't have read those few pages in her romance novel. Now she had marriage on her mind. Not a gut thing when her beau was a couple of states away. Not when a stranger produced more flutters than her intended did.

Romance wasn't—shouldn't be—based on feelings. Love was a decision. And she'd made a decision to love Obadiah. To wait for him.

Which meant David couldn't stay here. Writing a man she didn't know—really—in order to encourage him during his recovery from an almost fatal accident was vastly different from encouraging a friendship with him in person.

Especially when he was handsome and obviously unmarried, and thought she was beautiful.

She glanced out the window again. Two buggies pulled away from the parking lot—one closed, the other open, driven by the bishop.

Did David feel safer in a closed buggy? She should've asked. Should've cared enough to thank him for coming all this way to meet her. Shouldn't have stared at him in utter astonishment. He'd probably misinterpreted her response for fear, or even repulsion, due to his limp and the cane.

She owed him a lot more than she'd given. Her behavior had bordered on downright rude.

Why hadn't he mentioned that he was coming? Why show up without warning? She could've mentally prepared herself. Made arrangements to have him over for a meal, maybe play a game or two at the table, before he returned home to Seymour.

Nein. That would have fed her infatuation.

He had to go back. He couldn't stay here.

Her heart lurched.

He simply had to go.

Chapter 2

In the large closed buggy he'd borrowed from Bishop Joe, David followed the man's open pony cart out of the parking lot, through town, and finally to the dirt road where the bishop lived. To his surprise, Bishop Joe pulled his cart into the schoolyard. The school that, according to the bishop, was closed until a suitable teacher was found.

Hope flared. *Maybe....* Maybe they'd ask him. Could it be that the bishop was stopping here to show him the schoolhaus and invite him to stay? Admittedly, that would be a rather sudden turnaround, considering the unkind comments the bishop had just made in Rachel's hearing. Or had he believed David's hushed explanation, even if his frown had gotten fiercer?

That seemed doubtful after the stern talking-to he'd received in the parking lot of the Amish Country Store. The reprimands for stalking Rachel Miller. Coming up here without a plan, because he'd fallen in love, sight unseen, with the woman through her letters.

He probably shouldn't have spilled his heart to the bishop.

After Bishop Joe had tied his pony to a hitching post, David parked his borrowed buggy next to him.

He'd hate to give it back.

Painstakingly, he clambered from the buggy, balancing on his cane for support as he maneuvered himself from behind the wheel. One benefit of the open buggies in Seymour—they were easier to get in and out of with a cane.

The bishop watched him, not offering to help—not that David needed assistance—then turned and led the way up the few stairs. He unlocked the door and opened it, revealing a long, narrow room filled with rows of scholars' desks, as well as a larger one for the teacher. A modern whiteboard hung on one wall, an assortment of multicolored dry-erase markers arranged on the ledge beneath. Across another wall was a display of drawings by the scholars, attached with wooden pins to a clothesline.

"This is our school." Bishop Joe looked at David with pride. *Pride!*

David swallowed hard. If only this meant he would be allowed to teach. He'd always loved school, and this would be a wunderbaar job while he continued recovering. But he didn't want to appear too excited. He fought to keep a smile at bay. "A very nice school. Clean. Orderly. Well cared for."

"Jah. It'll be kept this way, ain't so? Supplies are in that closet." The bishop pointed to a folding door. "Follow me."

He nodded and trailed the man to another door to the left of the teacher's desk.

"Indoor lavatory."

David studied the white porcelain seat and sink. There was a narrow counter but nein tub. Nein shower, either. Just the bare necessities.

"Kum."

What was the point of this? Why give him a tour, unless he had the job? David resisted the urge to pump his fist triumphantly in the air as he followed the older man through the narrow stretch behind the desk to another door, this one on the right, that opened to a tiny room barely big enough for the cot and the hard-backed chair that furnished it.

"Adequate?"

It'd be the smallest, as well as the plainest, room he'd ever stayed in. Nein colorful quilt. Nein blanket or even sheets on the cot. Nein rag rug to warm the floor. Nein curtains or shades on the single window. Just a cot. And a chair.

It'd be a place to sleep. Not home.

David pulled in a shallow breath. "Jah. It's gut."

"Beats the barn, ain't so?"

He'd stayed in the bishop's barn the previous nacht, after some Englischer had driven him from the bus station to the bishop's haus and left him there, unheralded, unexpected, and unwelkum. At least the loft had been comfortable—a bed of hay with a ratty old buggy blanket and a purring calico cat for a bed partner, named, appropriately enough, Calico. He hadn't been offered an evening meal, but at least he'd been fed breakfast while he shivered on the front porch.

He swallowed. "Sure appreciated staying in your barn last nacht."

Though, with the temperatures dipping into the upper twenties, it had gotten rather nippy.

"Think you can teach?"

He had just as much of an education as the women who usually taught school. Eighth grade. Plus, he had the advantage of being an avid reader, which had expanded his education. "By Gott's grace, jah. Appreciate the chance."

"School will reopen tomorrow. I'll send my dochter down with your stuff."

His "stuff" consisted of a duffel bag filled with another pair of work clothes, his gut clothes for church, his black coat and hat, a lantern flashlight, a few personal items, and supplies for tying flies. Not to mention the important things—his Bible, a notebook, every letter he'd received from Rachel, a supply of postcards, a handful of money, and two books. "Danki."

"A supply of wood will be delivered. You are responsible for your meals, laundry, et cetera."

David glanced at the woodstove again. Nein kettles or dishes. Nein tub for taking a bath or washing clothes. As a man, he'd always been out in the barn or the fields with Daed, leaving the hauswork for Mamm and his sister. He didn't have the slightest idea how to do more than build a fire. But he could live on sandwiches. Maybe an occasional can of soup could be heated on the stove. He definitely needed to make a trip back to the store for foodstuffs, toiletries, and other supplies.

"I get my horse and buggy back," the bishop told him. "You're responsible for your transportation."

Translation: He'd be walking everywhere. He looked down at his bum leg. At his wooden cane.

Bishop Joe wasn't the friendliest or most considerate fellow.

"Appreciate—"

"I like your spunk, bu. Coming up here on nothing but a whim, just because some maidal caught your fancy by mail." He chuckled. "At least we get a teacher out of it for a while. Be interesting to see how quickly it takes for your hopes to be squashed."

They already were.

Lord, what now?

Gott had spared his life for a reason—not once, but twice. And he'd thought that the plan included Rachel.

"They that wait upon the LORD *shall renew their strength; they shall mount up with wings as eagles...."*

Jah, he had nein choice but to wait. At least this quiet place would give him plenty of time to think in the evenings.

David turned to stare out the window. Almost directly across the dirt road was a big white haus with a clothesline where laundry flapped in the breeze. In the corner of the front yard, where the road intersected with another, stood a phone shanty.

Close to the school. Handy.

The door to the schoolhaus shut. A moment later, the bishop, still chuckling, tied the pony and cart to the big buggy, then drove off and disappeared down the road.

At least David hadn't been thrown out on his backside.

Yet.

⁓

After work, Rachel dropped Greta off at her haus, then continued home. Bethany Weiss, the bishop's daughter, approached in her little pony cart, a dull green tote bag beside her on the narrow seat.

Had Bethany been hired as a mother's helper? Rachel tried to think of anyone might have need of a maud.

"Whoa," Rachel called to her horse, Buttons. "Hallo, Bethany."

Her friend climbed out of the cart. "Did you just get off work?"

"Jah. Glad to be home, for sure." Rachel looked at the laundry still clinging to the line. It always worried her to leave clothes hanging out on particularly breezy days, afraid she'd be chasing her undergarments all over the countryside. It had never happened.

"Daed asked me to drop this by the schoolhaus." Bethany held up the tote bag. "A wanderer appeared last nacht, and would you believe it, Daed hired him as the new teacher. You might want to tell your mamm. School is open tomorrow."

"*Him?* The teacher's a *him?*" Something fluttered in Rachel's stomach. She looked at the schoolhaus. Could the new hire possibly be David? She shook her head. *Nein.* Gott wouldn't place this source of temptation so close to her. Or continually force her to face her lack of fluttery feelings for Obadiah and the consequences of reading too many romance novels.

Well, she supposed He might ask her to deal with her fetish for romantic fiction. Daed told her such novels were sinful. Frivolous. A waste of time.

"Jah, he came from down south somewhere. Told Daed he looked to make a fresh start and needed someplace to stay. Daed put him up in the barn last nacht. I think he said his name was…." Bethany scrunched up her nose. "David? Maybe."

Nein, nein, nein. Rachel's stomach roiled.

"He's really cute, but he walks with a limp. He told Daed he'd been in a bad buggy accident and spent a long time recovering in the hospital. That he was blessed to be alive."

Rachel looked at the school once more. How convenient—for him—that she lived right across the street.

"I don't know how Daed expects him to live in the schoolhaus. There's just that small cot for the scholars who get sick during class. And Daed told him he'd be responsible for all his own meals and laundry." Bethany shook her head. "Maybe I'll spread the word around. Someone will offer to take care of him, I'm sure."

Rachel gathered her courage. "We'll take care of him. He can join my family for meals. And it won't make one bit of difference to add his laundry to ours. One more person won't be an issue."

Bethany smiled. "He'll think you're a Gott-send for sure, Rachel. I'll tell him the gut news." She grasped the pony by its harness and started leading it across the street. "Are you going to the frolic tonight?"

"Lily's birthday party?" Rachel stifled a wince. She'd had to put up with Lily for far too long when she'd stayed with Esther at the Petersheims' during the summer. "Nein, can't make it."

"I hear she's hoping to meet someone to settle down with—nein surprise there, ain't so?" She giggled. "Maybe I'll invite David."

This might be the perfect solution to Rachel's problem. If David was going to live in the area, then it'd be gut if he found a nice girl.

Lily wasn't a nice girl.

Rachel glanced toward the barn. "I'll ask Sam to run over and invite him."

"Oh, I don't mind asking," Bethany said with a wave of her hand.

Rachel clicked at Buttons, then drove the buggy to the barn. As she climbed down, she glanced back at the school.

David stood in the doorway, taking the bag from Bethany. Then she turned and pointed across the street. He looked toward Rachel's haus and nodded. Then his gaze locked on hers.

At least, that's how it seemed to Rachel. She froze. And for the longest time, they stood there, unmoving.

"What's wrong, Rachel? Why are you just standing there?"

Someone tugged on her apron, and she glanced down at her youngest sister, Jenny.

"They hired a teacher and are opening school tomorrow," Rachel told her. "Run and tell Mamm we're hosting the new teacher for supper." Rachel glanced across the street again.

He was gone.

⌒

David closed the door and leaned his forehead against it. *She* lived right across the street. *She* had invited him to kum over for dinner—according to Bishop Joe's dochter. *She* had offered to take care of his laundry.

"Danki, Gott, for providing for my needs this way." And by *her* hand. *Wow.* He pulled in a deep, shuddery breath. He had a second chance. He couldn't blow it this time. Nein, he'd need to be cool, calm, and collected. He couldn't scare her.

He turned away from the door and surveyed the room. He'd found books both in the teacher's desk and in the storage closet. He had nein idea where the scholars were in their lessons, but he'd figure that out fast enough. In the meantime, he needed to familiarize himself with the teacher's materials: the grade book, the roster, and whatever else he could find.

He hoisted his bag of belongings—all he owned in the world— and carried it back to the tiny room that would be his home for the next few…days? Weeks? Months? Who knew? He dropped the tote on the cot and scanned the area. Maybe he could get permission to put up a small shelf for his belongings. Or someone could donate a small dresser. Though where he'd put it, he wasn't sure. Maybe beside the door.

And perhaps he could catch a ride into town so he could purchase a pillow, a sleeping bag, and a set of towels.

He hung his hat and coat on a hook, shook out his gut shirt, and draped that over another hook, then took out his books and set them on the chair. Next, he dug deep inside the bag for Rachel's letters.

He probably should head over to her haus for dinner soon. But first….

He slid the rubber band off the stack and sat down on the cot to read, starting with her first letter.

Hi, David,

You don't know me, but I read about you in the Budget. It must've been terrifying to be in such a bad buggy accident. I'm glad you survived.

I live in northern Missouri, near a town called Jamesport. I like to write letters to the sick and injured who are listed for

*prayer needs, in order to encourage them. I'd love it if you'd
write back to let me know how you are and how I can pray for
you. Even just a postcard with a picture of the area where you
live would be great.*

   I'm praying for you every nacht.

Rachel Miller

He'd needed those prayers.

He'd written her back, enclosing a couple postcards from
Springfield, Missouri—all that the Amish driver could find in the
hospital gift shop.

Had he been foolish to kum here where she lived?

He put down the letter and reached for his Bible, then reread
the passage that had struck him first in Pennsylvania and again in
Seymour: Genesis 12:1–2.

*Get thee out of thy country, and from thy kindred, and from thy
father's house, unto a land that I will shew thee: and I will make
of thee a great nation, and I will bless thee, and make thy name
great; and thou shalt be a blessing....*

Gott had said "Go."

He'd have to trust.

David's stomach rumbled. He hadn't eaten since breakfast.
Hopefully, the Millers would have plenty to share. He checked his
pocket watch. He didn't know what time they ate, but it was nearing
five o'clock.

Lord, help me to be on my best behavior.

He closed the Bible, stood, and went for his shoes and hat.
Finding a smile, he grabbed his cane and headed for the door.

Rachel waited.

Well, maybe she didn't. But he couldn't wait to see her. To hear
her voice. To spend time with her in person. To meet her family.

To feed his stomach.

And his crush.

Chapter 3

It felt as if a whole flock of Canada geese were flying through Rachel's stomach. She pressed her hands against the quiver to settle it. Strange that David Lapp would cause this reaction—almost as if she were entertaining her beau in her home for the first time. Or introducing him as such to her parents.

Foolish thoughts. Especially since David wasn't her beau. Obadiah was. And David was someone else's intended. Rachel hesitated a moment, trying to remember the name he'd mentioned in one of his letters. Cathy? That seemed right. Cathy who lived in Seymour, Missouri. It might be a gut idea to remind him of her. Hopefully, he'd realize how much he missed her and would go home. Sooner rather than later.

Rachel swallowed the lump in her throat as she checked the table. Everything was ready, including the fresh-baked bread, already sliced, with butter Mamm had churned that morgen, before she'd gotten caught up in sewing and quilting.

Mamm tended to lose track of time when she started her needlework.

There was porcupine jelly made from wild grapes they'd picked in the woods. The water glasses were filled with ice, the table settings in place—

Someone knocked on the door. Rachel jumped. She hadn't even rung the dinner bell yet. The Canada geese returned, and she clutched her stomach again.

Mamm came into the room, rubbing her back. "I wonder who that might be." She moved toward the door.

Rachel gulped. "Mamm, wait. I, um, invited the new teacher to join us for dinner. Well, not just for dinner. To take all his meals here. Bishop Joe is putting him up in the small room at the back of the schoolhaus."

"Did you? Gott bless you, dochter. What a kind thing to do. Jenny mentioned school would resume tomorrow." Mamm flung the door open. "Welkum! I'm Preacher Samuel Miller's Elsie."

"Nice to meet you. I'm David Lapp. I'm...uh, that is—"

"Don't worry, Rachel already told me. You're the new teacher. We'll be more than glad to provide meals for you, as well as anything else you may need. We're the closest to the school, after all." Mamm stepped back. "Kum in."

David entered, taking a moment to slip off his shoes and put them in the tray by the door. When he straightened, his gaze lit on Rachel, and he smiled.

Those annoying geese took flight yet again.

"Rachel, nice to see you. Danki for inviting me." He inched closer. "I.... It.... I...." He stumbled to a halt, his face flushing a light shade of pink. "I'm looking forward to teaching the young scholars."

"You'll have a few of mine in school," Rachel's mamm said. "I'll make sure they bring your lunch with them. Breakfast, too, unless you'd rather kum over in the morgen and eat with us." Mamm waved him farther into the room, then stepped onto the porch and rang the dinner bell.

"Go wash up before the stampede." Rachel gestured toward the sink.

David followed her directions, lifted the bar of lye soap, and scrubbed his hands the way Daed and her brothers did after doing hours of filthy work. He grabbed the towel on the rack beside him and dried his hands, then turned as Mamm came back into the kitchen.

His gaze skittered from Rachel to Mamm. "I'd love to join you for breakfast every day. It'd save your kinner the trouble of carrying extra meals over. And that way, I can take my lunch myself. I really do appreciate this."

Figured. Rachel would see his handsome face almost first thing every morgen. She turned away to check the food keeping warm on the stove.

"We're so glad the bishop found a replacement teacher," Mamm reassured him. She scanned the table, then indicated a seat. "Sit here. Rachel, find out what he wants to drink. I'll be right back."

Mamm disappeared into the living room. Seconds later, the steps creaked as she headed upstairs.

Rachel caught the strong scent of peppermint. She forced a smile and turned to face David. He stood closer than she'd expected. The next thing she knew, his fingers gently brushed her cheek. Unexpected sparks shot through her. She leaned away from his bold touch.

"I'm sorry. It's just so nice to finally meet you." He lowered his hand. "To see you in person. You're so beautiful. As I said, you're far prettier than I dared dream."

Disbelieving his brazen statement, she stared at him, eyes wide, lips parted. She tried to find something to say. Anything.

Nothing came to mind. Or maybe the problem was that she had too many things to say and needed to sort through them, so she wouldn't smother him in an avalanche of words.

"I'm scaring you." David's lips turned down. "I don't mean to. It's just...well...."

"Cathy. What about her? How does she feel about your coming here to meet me? What will she think when she finds out you took a job?" The words tumbled over each other in her rush.

David's brow furrowed with confusion. "I don't see why that matters, but she'll be glad to know I'm gainfully employed. She was concerned that I'd get fat and lazy from sitting around weaving baskets and tying flies."

Tying flies? "You catch flies and tie them together?" She winced at the sarcasm in her tone.

He chuckled. "Fishing flies."

Daed's boots clomped heavily up the porch steps, followed by the not-much-lighter footfalls of her brothers. The door opened. Rachel jumped back, as if she'd just been caught with her hand in the cookie jar.

David turned away from her with a smile as her family came into the room. Daed hesitated in the doorway and looked David up and down. "You the new teacher?"

"Jah."

"Aw, man!" Eli whined. "I thought it was just vicious gossip."

Daed frowned at the use of Englisch slang but didn't say anything. He and the buwe dropped their shoes and boots in the plastic tray, where they landed in a messy jumble. Then the group paraded across the room to the sink, as usual.

Sam peered at David. "Welkum to the area. But you'll overstay your welkum real fast if you try any hanky-panky with my sister. Got it?"

David's face heated. Out of the corner of his eye, he noticed Rachel's face flame red. She pivoted on her heel and went back to the stove.

"Got it." He nodded, then grinned when he caught the glare that Preacher Samuel aimed at his sohn. Both buwe would have words spoken to them in private, no doubt. Probably Rachel would, as well, if her daed had heard her comment about tying flies together.

He lowered himself into the seat that Rachel's mamm had indicated. Soon the other chairs and benches filled, and Elsie returned to help Rachel put the hot food on the table. Then the women slipped into the two empty chairs. Rachel settled across from David, in between two younger girls.

After the silent prayer, Rachel hopped up. "Ach, David, I forgot to see what you wanted to drink. We have—"

"Water's fine." He motioned to the filled tumbler at his place. Nobody else had anything else in their glasses.

She nodded, then sat and served herself a spoonful of steaming mashed potatoes. A pat of butter melted in the middle of it. His mouth watered at the sight.

As if on cue, his stomach rumbled loudly as the platter of falling-apart-tender roast beef came his way. One of Rachel's sisters giggled.

"So, David. Let me introduce you to everyone." Rachel's daed passed a bowl of peas and pearl onions to his right. "I'm Preacher Samuel. That's my frau, Elsie, and you met our dochter Rachel."

David nodded.

"The other two girls are Jenny and Mary. The buwe are Eli, Andy, Luther, and Sam. Both Luther and Sam are finished with school. This is Andy's last year."

"So, I'll have Andy, Eli, Jenny, and Mary in school." David aimed a smile across the table at the two young girls. Neither smiled back. They both stared at him with solemn expressions. He guessed Jenny was a beginning scholar. Or maybe in her first year. Mary appeared to be about eleven.

"So, what brings you to our district, David?" Preacher Samuel aimed a look at him that seemed a little wary. As if he knew—or thought he knew—that David was up to "nein gut," to quote the bishop.

David squirmed, trying to avoid glancing at Rachel. He didn't want to lie to her daed, but he wasn't about to announce that he'd fallen in love with her during the course of their correspondence. His only explanation was his "irrational fear," as Cathy called it, of open buggies.

He frowned. "Ach, I thought maybe closed buggies might be safer than open. I was in a buggy accident, and—"

Sam made a scoffing sound. "Buggy accidents happen with closed buggies, too."

David looked at him. "I was thrown from the buggy. Almost died from complications. And—"

"So, it'd be better not to be thrown from the buggy? To be pinned inside and killed outright?"

"Ach…." How was he supposed to respond? "I guess I didn't consider that." It was the truth. He really hadn't thought much beyond wanting to be near Rachel, to get to know her in person, to woo and win her….

"Such talk," Elsie scolded. "Let our guest enjoy his meal. David, is there anything you'll need to stay comfortably at the school?"

"Um, I'll need a ride into town for some bedding and towels, and—"

"Nonsense. We have plenty. I'll have Rachel help you carry what you need. Sam and Luther can bring over some kindling and logs in the wheelbarrow."

"Bishop Joe said something about having wood delivered."

Elsie waved her hand dismissively. "If he didn't mention it to the hospitality minister right away, it'll take him a few days to think of it again. This will just be enough to tide you over, take the chill out of the school in the morgen."

David forked a bite of the roast. "Appreciate it more than I can say." He could see where Rachel had gotten her gift of mercy, which had been evident in her reaching out to him to encourage him after his accident. He put the bite of roast in his mouth and almost groaned. It was every bit as delicious as it smelled.

The family fell into relative silence as everyone ate the meal. Afterward, Mary went to the window where a couple pies waited, retrieved one, and set it beside David. "Dutch apple pie—my specialty," she told him with a nod. "Mamm helped me with the bottom crust. That takes a special touch, ain't so?"

David grinned at her. "I'm looking forward to trying it."

She used a pie server to slice the dessert, then slid a piece onto his plate. Then she stood there expectantly.

David wasn't sure what to do. Should he take a bite and tell her how wunderbaar it was? Or pass the pie to the next person at the table? It'd be rude to eat before the others had been served.

"Mary, go sit down." Preacher Samuel solved the problem.

The girl sighed as she obeyed.

David passed the pie to his left. After everyone had a slice, he took a bite. And almost gagged. It was way too salty. Somehow he managed to swallow.

Luther dropped his fork and ran from the table, choking.

Sam spit his bite into his napkin. "What'd you do, Mary, Mary, Quite Contrary? Mistake salt for sugar?"

Mary burst into tears and dashed from the room.

Andy snickered, then broke out in a full-fledged guffaw.

Preacher Samuel frowned.

Rachel stood and went to the counter. She peeked inside one of the canisters. "Jah, someone filled the sugar canister with salt." She lifted the saltshaker, shook some into her palm, and tasted it. "This is filled with sugar."

"She was getting too prideful," Andy said in his own defense.

"Sohn." Preacher Samuel rose to his feet, nodding toward the door. Andy groaned but obeyed.

"Rachel, kum with me," her mamm told her, rising from the table. "We'll check on Mary, then gather whatever David needs to be comfortable."

David tried very hard not to watch Rachel go. But the swing of her maroon dress against her legs caught and held his attention. The gentle sway of her hips. The—

Sam cleared his throat.

David's face heated. He looked at the ruined pie. Laid his fork on the edge of his plate.

"I warned you, nein hanky-panky," Sam hissed. "I'm going to be keeping an eye on you."

David blew out a frustrated breath.

So much for behaving himself.

⌒

Rachel followed Mamm upstairs. Her face still burned from Sam's multiple warnings to David. It was nice of Sam to look out for her and Obadiah. But the fact that he'd noticed vibes between David and her seemed to make them more real and less likely to be a mere figment of her imagination.

When they reached the top of the stairs, Mamm opened the bedroom door. Mary lay across the bed, sobbing into her pillow. Rachel's heart ached for her little sister. Mamm shut the door, then sat beside Mary and began rubbing her back. "Hush, honey. Everyone makes mistakes in the kitchen."

Mary sniffed. "But I wouldn't have if someone hadn't mixed up the salt and the sugar." Her voice was muffled. "And he's so cute. Since Rachel's taken, and I look like her, I thought maybe he might be interested in me…." Her voice broke into another wail.

Mamm lifted her gaze to meet Rachel's. She flattened her lips. "Well, there'll be other opportunities to show him you know how to cook." She patted Mary's back, then stood. "You have a few years before you're old enough for courting, anyway."

"Only four. I'll be twelve on my birthday." Mary sat up and rubbed her eyes. "I intend to join the church and get married when I'm sixteen, so I need to start looking now." She swiped at her eyes again. "At least I'll be in school with him every day. I'll let the other girls know I get first dibs. I can't wait until classes start tomorrow."

Poor David wouldn't know what hit him. But having a preadolescent student with a crush on him might drive him back to Cathy faster. And it might keep him from joining the family for future meals.

Rachel hugged Mary. "I'm sorry your pie was ruined. I'll make sure to tell him you can do better."

"Kum, Rachel." Mamm opened the door. "I know just the quilt I want to give him."

Rachel followed her across the hall into the sewing room. It was really another bedroom, but with all the buwe in one room and all the girls in the other, it made sense to have one just for sewing and quilting.

Mamm reached into the hutch Daed had built and pulled out the top quilt—the one they'd finished tying off yesterday. It had a tumbling block pattern and was made to fit a twin-sized bed. They'd planned to offer it at the sale to raise money for medical expenses in the community.

Rachel ran her hand over the top of the quilt.

"Having nothing is a need, ain't so?" Mamm asked.

Rachel nodded. "I just bought a new pillow, but I haven't used it yet." She hurried across the hall and grabbed it, still in its plastic wrapping.

Mary straightened her kapp. "I'm going to wash my face and offer to show David the new kittens. I think he'd like to see them. I'll even give him one. But the kitten can live here, since I don't think they'd let a cat in school."

"Gut idea." Rachel smiled. "I'm sure he'd love a kitten."

"Jah." Mary gave her a hug. "Gut thing you're taken, Rachel, and I'm the next girl in line." She dashed from the room.

Chapter 4

Mary bounded into the kitchen. "Want to see the kittens, David?" she asked in a chipper voice. Apparently her crying spell was over.

The littlest girl—David couldn't remember her name—jumped to her feet. "Ach, they are newborn. So cute."

"You need to stay here and do dishes, Jenny." Mary set her lips.

Jenny shook her head, her eyes pooling with tears. "It's your turn to wash, Mary. I get to dry. And I want to see the kittens, too."

"You both can show David the kittens." Daed rolled his eyes at David.

"You can have one as soon as they're old enough to leave their mamm," Mary offered as she slipped on her shoes. "But we'll keep it here for you."

David rubbed his hand over his chin. He really needed to get back to the schoolhaus and finish looking over the books to get ready for tomorrow, but he figured it wouldn't hurt to humor Rachel's sister for a few moments. He put on his shoes and grabbed his cane, then followed the girls outside.

The barn smelled of animals and sawdust. David also picked up the odor of varnish. He paused in the doorway and inhaled deeply. He'd missed that smell. Daed had a small wood shop in the corner of their barn, and David loved doing the finishing work on the furniture.

A Border collie came around the corner of the barn. It sat just outside the door and lifted a paw. He leaned down and shook it.

"Are you coming, David?" Mary called to him from the dark recesses of the barn.

David followed the sound of her voice, the dog on his tail. He found Mary and Jenny crouched beside a box of mewing newborn kittens lying in a heap. The mother cat sat beside them, grooming them with her tongue. She peered at him suspiciously.

"She doesn't want her babies held yet, but aren't they precious?" Mary looked up at him. "Which one do you want?"

He doubted he'd be able to tell them apart in an hour. David shook his head. "I'll let you pick one for me when they get older."

Mary grinned, as if he'd given the best possible response. "I'm glad you're here, David. Can I be your helper tomorrow at school?"

"I want to help, too." Jenny's eyes filled with tears again.

"Uh, sure. I'll probably need a lot of help. But you'll need to call me Mr. Lapp, ain't so?"

Jenny grinned. "I like you."

Hopefully that would still be the case once he tried his hand at teaching. He smiled. "I need to get back, so let's go see if your mamm found what she needed."

Fifteen minutes later, David crossed the dirt road to the school, a fluffy pillow and thick quilt under his free arm. Rachel kept pace beside him, carrying a couple towels and washcloths, a few toiletries, and a set of bedsheets. He really didn't know what else they'd packed for him.

If only he didn't have to use his cane for stability when walking across uneven surfaces. He did well on level floors, and stairs were okay if there was a railing. He glared at the school steps as they approached them. Maybe the bishop would agree to add a rail.

He glanced at the vision beside him. So beautiful. He studied the curve of her cheek, longing to touch the softness again. He shouldn't have done it in the first place.

His gaze moved to her cute little ear, to the rebellious curls that had sprung out from beneath her kapp. The length of her neck, down to the curve of her—

"Will you stop it?"

He jerked his gaze up to meet her eyes.

"You're gawking. Stop it."

"You're gorgeous. I can't help it."

She stopped in the middle of the road. "Jah, and my beau is in Ohio. Remember?"

David shut his eyes. He'd almost forgotten that not-so-tiny fact. But it really didn't change anything. Her beau—the faceless man whose name he couldn't recall—was in *Ohio*. A few states away.

David was in Missouri. Living across the road from Rachel.

Of course, he had the disadvantage of needing a cane to walk across the road. He sighed, scowling at the polished piece of curved wood in his hand.

The old cliché came to mind: "All's fair in love and war."

He didn't want to give up.

May the best man win.

Rachel carried the items Mamm had given her into the school. David followed her, closing the door and hanging his cane on a hook. Then he trailed her through the building to the tiny room in the back. She'd lain on that cot once when she'd gotten a bad headache during school. Nobody had been home, since Mamm had gone to help an aentie, and her teacher, Mandy Hershberger, had told her to lie down until she felt better. The cot had been hard and uncomfortable. She didn't imagine it had improved at all.

She bustled into the room and hesitated when she spied a stack of letters and postcards she'd written to David, there on the chair. In plain view. One letter was open, as if he'd taken time to reread it before coming to her haus for dinner. Her heart skipped a beat.

She had a similar collection of correspondence in a shoe box under her bed.

There wasn't even a dresser in the room. Granted, there wasn't space for one, either. Not knowing what else to do, she laid her bundle atop the letters on the chair, then quickly made the bed while David stood and watched, his face filled with discomfort. He still held his load, as if he wished he could drop it and run. She took the quilt from him and spread it over the fresh sheets.

He moved farther into the room, bringing along a whiff of peppermint, and picked up the pillowcase, then wedged the pillow under his chin and started yanking the case over it—a rather sloppy job, but it would do. He handed it to Rachel with a smile on his well-shaped lips. If only she didn't notice them so readily.

"Danki." She tried to twist the seam a little straighter without being obvious, but it didn't work. Not wanting to hurt his feelings, she plopped the pillow at the head of the bed.

"Danki to you." His smile widened.

"So." She stepped back, suddenly a bit uncomfortable being alone with him in this small space. The nearness of his strong, broad shoulders seemed to make the already tiny room shrink in size. She searched for something to say. "Shelves would be helpful, ain't so? Maybe in the corner?"

He eyed the space she indicated, as if taking mental measurements. "Jah. Would that be allowed?"

"I don't know. I'll ask Daed. Maybe he could get permission." She looked past him, through the door to the schoolroom. Going out there would get her out of the close confines of his "bedroom." But doing so would also mean brushing against him.

David sighed. She could almost hear his thoughts. She waited, imagining what he might say next. *So nice to be here with you.*

Maybe he'd touch her cheek again.

She shivered.

If David noticed, he didn't react. His gaze skittered to the small window above the cot. "Looks like your brother arrived with a wheelbarrow full of wood. I should help him stack it." He glanced at Rachel, his eyes meeting hers.

She looked away, her face heating.

His chest rose and fell as he pulled in a breath. Then he turned and left the room.

Inexplicable disappointment filled Rachel. As if she'd actually wanted his touch. She hadn't. She walked to the door and watched him stride across the classroom. Willed him to look back. He lifted his cane from a hook, then opened the door and went outside.

He didn't look back.

She took a few seconds to breathe, sucking in the air that had seemed to have been vacuumed out of the room when they were in there alone. Together. Why did she never react that way when she was alone with Obadiah? Was it because they were never in a closed room but usually in a barn or a buggy, in plain view of other people? Must be.

She finished straightening the pillowcase on the pillow, then moved to the window and watched as David rounded the corner of the schoolhaus. Sam, hefting a log from the wheelbarrow, looked up and nodded at something David said. Then he set the log on top of the woodpile, dumped the rest, and pushed the empty wheelbarrow away. David propped his cane against the woodpile and bent to lift a split log, his shirt pulled taut by his back and arm muscles.

Rachel's heart skipped a beat.

He may walk with a cane, but he was far from "fat and lazy," as Cathy had apparently called him. *Ach, wait.* He'd said that Cathy was *worried* he'd become fat and lazy from sitting around tying flies.

Still not something she understood. Of course, she'd never gone fishing. Her brothers did, at their stocked pond, but they didn't use flies. They used gut old-fashioned worms.

She'd need to look up fishing flies on the computer at the store when she had the chance.

David turned to lift another log, and she moved away from the window. She'd delivered the bedding and toiletries he would need; she shouldn't dawdle to watch him work. If he caught her, he might think she was as attracted to him as he'd openly claimed to be to her. Disconcerting.

But true. She was attracted to him. She just couldn't let him know.

Never mind that Obadiah had written her only one letter since he'd left, a year ago. Just one. And he hadn't responded to any of her notes, not even with a phone call. She got all his news from his mamm.

Rachel sighed. She'd write him to-nacht. She'd planned to finish her letter to David, but since he was here, that seemed silly. Nein, she'd write Obadiah. And she wouldn't mention David. He was nothing to her.

Nothing at all.

She sucked in another breath, one filled with the scent of peppermint. The school already seemed permeated with the smell, thanks to the jar of red and white candies on David's desk. There was a bottle of men's body wash/shampoo, peppermint-scented, sitting on the floor beside the chair in his room. A tube of peppermint toothpaste sat beside it.

Would his kisses taste like peppermint?

Her belly clenched.

Ach, her wayward thoughts. The sooner David left town, the better.

David hoisted the final log onto the woodpile as Sam pushed the wheelbarrow around the corner of the school once more, this time with a load of kindling balanced precariously atop the split logs in an apple box. David glanced toward his bedroom window. Was Rachel still in there? Maybe watching?

"She went home," Sam growled, apparently reading his mind. "Doesn't need nein wanderer coming around and making a play for her."

A wanderer? He supposed there was some truth in the term. He'd been part of the man-swap to Missouri, leaving Pennsylvania behind for greener pastures. And then, he'd left Seymour for Jamesport.

Sam's eyebrows shot up. In challenge? Or was he waiting for David to agree?

David had nein intentions of staying away from Rachel. They'd been friends well before he came here, writing to each other for more than a year, and he hoped to rekindle the friendship in person. To fan the flames into something more, if der Herr willed it.

And if He didn't? Then he'd pray about it and see where der Herr led him next.

He hefted the box of kindling from the wheelbarrow and took a step toward the woodpile to set it beside the stack. As he did, he stepped in a hole, and his ankle twisted.

And he went down.

Chapter 5

After helping with the dishes from supper, Rachel carried the bucket of food scraps outside to the hog trough. As she did, Sam came jogging across the yard, pushing the empty wheelbarrow. The metal creaked and whined as if in protest of such rough treatment.

"Get Mamm! The new teacher fell. Not sure if he broke his leg or not. I'm going to help him into the school." Sam abandoned the wheelbarrow in the yard. "Put that away in the barn."

Blinking, Rachel dropped the pail and ran back to the haus.

Mamm looked over her shoulder as she dug through the freezer. "I heard. Run and get the medical supplies." She turned to Mary. "Could you finish feeding the hogs? Or did you finish, Rachel?"

"Nein, I— The bucket's just outside the pen."

"Can't I go take care of him?" Mary put her hands on her hips.

"He'll need you, honey, but not now." Mamm smiled. "I need to go see how bad he's been hurt."

Rachel grabbed the box of medical supplies. "I'll go ahead and take this over, Mamm. Maybe I can help Sam get him inside." She didn't wait for a reply but hurried across the street. She rounded the corner of the schoolhaus and found Sam helping David around the building, one arm wrapped around his waist, with David's arm slung across his shoulders. David seemed to lean heavily on Sam, but at least he was up and walking.

Rachel whirled around and went to open the door. She set the box of medical supplies on a desk and came back to the doorway. "Can I help?"

"I think we got it, Rachel. Can you get a chair?" Sam grunted.

David's face was contorted with pain.

She grabbed the wooden chair from behind the teacher's desk and carried it over. "Where's your cane?"

"Woodpile," David muttered.

Once he was seated, she went to retrieve the cane. By the time she returned, Mamm had arrived, and David's right shoe and stocking were off. His foot was already swelling and starting to bruise.

Mamm glanced at her. "It looks like a bad sprain, but I think he'll be okay, as long as he keeps it elevated and iced. And stays off of it as much as possible. You can bring his meals over in the evenings, and I'll have Mary bring breakfast and lunch." She winked at Rachel.

Rachel nodded. Mary would be happy, getting to wait on him. At least until she got over her infatuation.

"You can stay and eat with him, then bring the dishes home." Mamm returned her attention to his foot and began wrapping it in a long bandage.

David sent Rachel a smile that didn't seem tinged with any pain.

Her heart thudded to a stop. Alone with him, every evening…. Gott was punishing her for her love of romance novels, for sure.

Time to talk about something else before she turned into a simmering sentimentalist.

"Did you continue stacking wood after your fall?" Rachel moved her hands to her hips.

"I helped him up first," Sam spoke up. "He said he was fine." He spread his arms and shrugged. "It was painful only when he tried to walk, so I handed the wood to him, and he stacked it." He lowered his arms and glared at David. "Mamm, I don't think it's a gut idea to send Rachel over with his food, because…." His gaze skittered between David and Rachel. "Well, it's just not a gut idea. That's all."

Mamm waved his suggestion away. "It's fine, Sam. Don't worry so much."

Sam pressed his lips together.

Rachel gazed into David's brown eyes, still fixed on her. Still smiling. Her stomach fluttered. Sam was definitely right. It would be dangerous to spend too much time alone with David.

Mamm finished wrapping David's foot and stood. "I think you'll live. No unneeded pressure on it. Stay off it as much as possible, and keep it iced. I'll send ice packs over routinely."

"Danki." David broke eye contact with Rachel. "Really appreciate everything you're doing."

Mamm gave another flick of her wrist. "I'll send Rachel back over later with some pain medicine and a fresh ice pack. At that point, you can let her know if there's anything else you need."

David nodded. "Danki again." He shifted, then winced. "I'll be fine."

Rachel gathered the unused medical supplies. "I'll see you later, then."

"Looking forward to it."

Her heart leapt.

And she'd thought writing David Lapp would be safe.

He was anything but safe.

⌒

Gripping his cane with one hand, David used the other to push the chair back to the desk at the front of the room. At least it was the already weak leg he'd injured. Not his gut one.

School started tomorrow, sprained ankle or not. He needed to be somewhat prepared. His injury throbbed, protesting the movement.

His day had swung back and forth between gut and bad far too much today. Maybe tomorrow would be more settled. Although that was doubtful, considering he didn't know the first thing about teaching a classroom of students.

What a dummchen he was. He swallowed hard. He'd kum here wanting to win Rachel's affections—or even just her friendship—and instead he'd made an idiot of himself. And injured himself, as well. If he were a dog, he'd tuck his tail between his legs and run home.

The idea was tempting.

Did he ever have such a hard time at home?

Of course, he'd never taken many chances. Never done such crazy things.

With a sigh, he lowered himself into the chair and propped his leg on the desktop. It wasn't comfortable, but he needed to keep his ankle elevated, and he didn't have the energy to finagle a different setup right now. He'd just have to adjust.

He positioned the ice pack against his ankle and opened the nearest textbook and read by the light of the setting sun slanting in through the window.

When it became too dark to read, David shut the book. The ice pack was no longer cold, and his ankle still throbbed. He struggled to his feet and went to get his lantern flashlight. As he returned to the classroom, the main door opened. Rachel stepped into the dimness of the room carrying a drinking glass, a bottle of pills, and another ice pack.

"What are you doing up and about?" She hurried across the room and set the items on the desk, then reached for him. "Here, lean on me."

David didn't argue. He slid his arm around her shoulders, reveling in her softness. Her nearness. He could've stayed there all nacht. He tightened his grip, pulling her closer. She didn't object but curled her arm around his waist. Probably because she thought he needed her support.

"Where were you going?" There was a huskiness to her voice.

"Back to the desk." David set the lantern on the edge of a bookshelf and flipped the switch to turn it on. "Need to prepare for the school."

"Do you want to put it off for a day?" Her arm tightened around his waist. "Kum on. You need to get off your feet."

He allowed her to guide him to the chair, but he wasn't in any hurry to get there, despite the pain in his ankle. Who knew when he'd find himself in Rachel's arms again? It probably wouldn't be anytime soon.

Unfortunately, he couldn't think of a gut reason for her to stay that close once he'd reached the desk. And his traitorous ankle was more than ready to be elevated. With ice. And a pain pill. Rachel had both. He lowered himself into the chair with a sigh. Hoisted his leg up on the desk.

Rachel positioned the ice pack on his swollen ankle, then popped the lid of the medicine bottle. A moment later, he chased down a pill with several sips of cold water.

She sat on the edge of the desk. "Will you be okay getting to bed? Maybe Sam could kum back over and help."

Sam was the last person he wanted to help. David shook his head. "I'll be fine." Still, he hoped Rachel would leave that bottle.

In the next moment, she picked it up and dropped it into her apron pocket. He cringed, but it was probably wise. He'd flirted with an addiction to pain medicine during his recovery in the hospital. He'd shared that with Rachel, if he remembered right.

"Okay. If you're sure. Mary will bring your breakfast and a fresh ice pack in the morgen."

He nodded. "And you'll bring supper."

"Jah." She smiled, then slid off the desk. "I should go."

He grabbed her hand. Sparks shot up his arm. Wow, he loved touching her.

"Nein—wait." He took a deep breath. Released her hand. "Stay. Talk to me awhile. Please?"

Shrugging, she settled herself on the desk once more. "Maybe for a little while."

"I'm not usually so clumsy." He nodded at his ankle.

She reached down to adjust the ice pack. Even the movement of the frozen bag hurt.

"What made you decide to kum to Jamesport?" She arched an eyebrow. "And when are you going back home to Seymour?"

⁓

Rachel held her breath, waiting for his response. She probably shouldn't have been so bold, but the sensations he awakened within her made her desperate for distance between them.

David shifted with a grimace. "Seymour isn't my home, you know."

Rachel frowned. "What do you mean?"

"I'm originally from Lancaster County, in Pennsylvania. A small town called Bird-in-Hand. I signed up to be part of a man swap to Seymour...." He shrugged and looked away. "I guess it's been over a year now."

"A man swap." Rachel swallowed a lump that had lodged in her throat and stared at David. Something she couldn't identify—jealousy, maybe—filled her. "You mean—"

"Jah. I agreed to marry someone and live near Seymour, Missouri. I did intend to. But things changed. I found a girl—"

"Cathy." She barely forced the name out. What was wrong with her? She knew all about her. He'd been open about the fact that he was courting a girl. And she'd been equally open about having a beau.

"Jah, Cathy." He looked down. "She could be really vindictive. I didn't realize it at first. She played some cruel pranks on people. Anything to cause them discomfort or to make them feel bad about themselves. I was warned, but I never saw it. Not until after my accident." He lifted his head and stared at his injured ankle.

Silence fell for a long moment.

"Did she treat you unkindly after the accident?" Rachel prodded when he seemed to get lost in his private thoughts.

David shrugged. "She was injured in the accident, too. She broke her arm, had a cast for about six weeks, and that was it. She claimed her injuries were worse than mine, even though...well, I don't want to sound like a victim. She was hurt, too." He fell silent again, his frown deepening.

"Even though you had to undergo surgery, *died*, and were resuscitated, then had months of therapy? Ach, David." Rachel blew out a breath. "It's terrible that the woman you love would do such a thing." He deserved a better frau than that.

"Love? I don't know." David's brow furrowed. "We agreed that I'm not what she wanted in an ehemann. And you were writing me.... She didn't like that I was pen pals with another maidal. Accused me of cheating." His lips tightened. "After much prayer and discussion with Bishop Sol about whether I should stay or go, I felt Gott leading me here. To you. And so did Bishop Sol."

What would it be like to be able to talk like that with the bishop? And to pray with him? She couldn't imagine doing such a thing with Bishop Joe.

And would Gott really lead someone somewhere specific, just like in Bible times?

If only Gott would lead her like he'd led David.

Something flared inside Rachel's heart, warming it. Maybe it was the idea that Gott had led David here. Or maybe it was the hope that Gott still led His people today. She wasn't sure. Still....

"That couldn't be," she protested, "because I'm— Well, there's Obadiah. And...."

David shrugged. "So you say." His eyes darkened with pain as he lowered his leg from the table. "There's more. But I'm feeling tired. Maybe—"

The door opened so forcefully, it banged against the wall. Rachel jumped up and turned around as Sam charged inside and skidded to a stop halfway across the room.

"Rachel. Go home. Now."

Chapter 6

David stood to his feet as quickly as he could, given his bad ankle. He glanced at Rachel. Anger and something else—embarrassment?—flashed across her face. She spun around to face her brother and tripped over David's extended leg. He grimaced, barely swallowing a howl of pain. She fell forward, arms flung in front of her, and he reached out to grab her.

He automatically wrapped his arms around her and held her, pulling her nearer, enjoying the feel of her body against his. So close, he could smell her shampoo. A green apple scent. He sucked in a shuddery breath.

Rachel squirmed, and every nerve ending in his body sprang to life. Sam made a noise that resembled a growl.

David loosened his grip, sliding his hands down to lightly grasp her waist. Still steadying her. But she was free to step away whenever she wanted to. He hoped it wouldn't be soon. A few stray tresses distracted him, tempting him to touch them, to see if her hair was as soft as it looked.

Another growl escaped from her brother's lungs, and David forced his attention away from Rachel, looking to Sam. He could almost see steam pouring from his nostrils.

Rachel scrambled back from David, and he dared to breathe once more as he lowered himself into the chair again.

"Mamm told me to bring him a pain pill and an ice pack." Rachel kept her voice low and controlled, but David could hear the anger simmering just below the surface, even though he didn't know her well. He could definitely sympathize. Sam had derailed their pleasant conversation, and this episode might put an end to future meals alone together. On the other hand, if it weren't for Sam, he wouldn't have had Rachel in his arms....

"Maybe so, but she didn't tell you to sit on his lap. Seriously, Rachel. It's dark outside, and the lantern is lit. Anyone driving by could see you—"

"I wasn't sitting on his lap!" Rachel stepped backward, stumbling on David's injured foot. He winced. This time, she caught herself before losing her balance. "I was sitting on the desk until you came in and scared me. Ain't so?" She turned to David for confirmation.

David nodded, though it really wasn't necessary. Sam had to know the truth. He'd gotten a clear view of them.

But she could sit on his lap anytime. He wouldn't object.

"And we were talking about his buggy accident until you so rudely interrupted us." With a huff, Rachel folded her arms protectively over her chest. She still stood close enough to David that the slightest movement caused her skirt to brush against his knee.

"Buggy accident?" Sam raised his eyebrows. "As if that really happened." His gaze leveled on David, mistrust in its depths.

Sam didn't believe he'd been in an accident? How then would he explain David's limp and use of a cane? Or maybe he needed glasses....

"Jah. Buggy accident," Rachel reiterated with some heat. "I'm going home. Gut nacht, David."

David watched her skirts sway as she stalked toward the door. Then he glanced at the windows. There were shades. Tomorrow, when she came to deliver his dinner, those shades would be drawn. And he'd make sure to lock the door after she entered.

Sam swung around to follow her, then hesitated. He turned to glare at David, a scowl curling his lips. "You need help getting to bed?"

David's face heated. "Nein. Danki." He would take care of himself. It might take a while, and it might be painful, but at least it wouldn't be humiliating.

Sam nodded. "I'm going to lock the door on the way out." A smirk twisted his lips. "Sweet dreams."

David gave him what he hoped was a passive stare. But "Sweet dreams"? Really? After Rachel had been in his arms?

That was a given.

❧

Rachel marched across the street. She ignored the sound of the school door slamming shut, then the pounding of running feet behind her. "Rachel. Wait."

Brothers were annoying. Irritating. Maddening.

Sam grabbed her arm and forced her to a stop. "Hold up a minute, would you?"

"I'm not talking to you." She blinked back the tears stinging her eyes. How dare he interrupt her pleasant visit with David? He was a friend, even if they were just getting to know each other face-to-face.

"It's for your own gut," Sam insisted. "He's obviously into you. And he's a wanderer. You don't know anything about him. He might be one of those Amish who use those drugs that cause hallucinations. He might mean you harm." He let out a sigh. "You just don't know. He looks familiar. Amish kum from all over, and—"

"I wrote him after his buggy accident."

"What?" Sam frowned. "You mean, one of those needs in the *Budget* you felt obligated to respond to?"

Rachel nodded.

Sam exhaled. "What did Obadiah say about your corresponding with another man? Or did you bother to tell him?"

Rachel shrugged. "It wasn't any of his business. I just wanted to encourage David in his recovery. I didn't know he would show up here."

Sam smirked. "Jah. Exactly. You should've told Obadiah, because now it's his business. Another man pursuing his girl? You're going to tell him now, ain't so?"

"There's nothing to tell." But maybe there was. David had openly admitted that he'd kum to Jamesport because of her.

"I see how he looks at you, Rachel. Believe me, there's something to tell. I'd want to know if someone looked at my girl like that."

Rachel sighed. "You're sweet to be concerned for me, Sammy. But David knows about Obadiah. He knows I'm getting married sometime. Okay? There's nothing to worry about. And Mamm asked me to have my dinners with him. She asked me to take an ice pack over to-nacht. She trusts me. Can't you?"

"It's him I don't trust."

Funny. She didn't trust herself.

⌒

David's ankle and foot were still swollen and badly bruised the next day. He pulled a sock on over the bandage but couldn't get a shoe over it. He shrugged. He could teach with one shoe on and one shoe off. He brushed his teeth and straightened his bed, then entered the schoolroom.

The space was chilly, but he couldn't light a fire unless he brought in some kindling and wood. But he couldn't go outside in a stockinged foot, or with his sprained ankle. It was hard enough walking around inside. He had to hang on to furniture or the wall with one hand, his cane with his other, and he winced with every step.

Nein, he was stranded in the building. Gut thing there was a half bath in there.

His efforts to woo Rachel would now depend on her coming to him. Not on his following her around.

The front door jiggled as someone tried to get in. It was still locked from last nacht. David hobbled toward the door. "Coming!"

When he flung it open, Mary and one of her brothers stood there. The bu had an armful of wood.

David smiled with relief.

"I have your breakfast." Mary grinned at him and held up a tray of food. "Cinnamon rolls with caramel topping. Rachel made them, but I helped. And a bowl of oatmeal with brown sugar and a pat of butter. I made the oatmeal. There's also a glass of orange juice. Mamm sent over some instant koffee and a mug, too, but that stuff is nasty. Stunts your growth, is what they tell me."

David blinked at her energetic rambling. "How do you know it's nasty?" He raised an eyebrow. "Did you sneak some?"

She dipped her head, her cheeks turning red.

He reached to take the tray, then thought better of it. He wouldn't be able to walk while holding it. "Could you put it on the desk for me, please?"

"Jah, and then I've got to run home and get lunch for you. Mamm packed it in a cooler." Mary brushed past him, her shoes tapping all the way across the room. Her brother followed with the wood. He stopped in front of the stove and started building a fire.

"Danki." David turned and shut the door, then started the long trek back across the room. "You have a pain pill and an ice pack, jah?" He was more than ready for both.

"Sammy was supposed to bring them by before he left for work," Mary told him. She picked up the melted pack from yesterday.

"Oh."

"He didn't?" She frowned. "I'll tell Mamm when I get home. Maybe she'll send one over in your lunch cooler." She darted for the door.

David reached the desk and dropped wearily into the chair.

The bu looked up from where he crouched in front of the stove. "Mamm says you need to keep it elevated. And stay off of it."

Right. David forced a smile. "Would you get a chair for my foot, please?" It would be hard to eat with his foot propped on the desk. Hard to teach, too. It would be difficult enough teaching while seated. But he wasn't about to ask for another break in classes. Not with the bishop's attitude. He'd be out of a job faster than he could stand.

The bu—what was his name?—left the stove doors open. "Should catch. I'll add more wood in a bit and shut the doors." Then he picked up a chair and carried it to the desk.

David cringed as he lifted his foot to prop it on the chair.

"Should I get your pillow to cushion it a bit? I had a sprained ankle before, and I know they hurt something fierce."

"That'd be gut. Danki."

David set the empty mug and the powdered koffee off to one side. That would have to wait. If there was an older girl there once school started, he'd ask her to get some water heating on the woodstove for his koffee. Otherwise, he'd have to live without it.

The bu returned with the pillow from David's room and helped him raise his foot higher. "Danki."

The door banged open as Mary ran in with a metal lunch box and an ice pack. "Sammy must've taken the bottle of pills and the other ice pack. I guess he forgot to stop on his way to work. That happens sometimes."

Why did David have trouble believing that it'd been a mere case of forgetfulness?

Of course, the door had been locked over-nacht. Maybe Sam had kum but couldn't get in, and had gone when David hadn't answered the door.

Even so, David was sure he would have heard a knock at the door. The pain medicine he'd taken yesterday hadn't made him that oblivious to the world around him.

Why did Sam seem to dislike him so much? He didn't even know him.

Something inside him chilled.

Did he?

Chapter 7

Rachel joined her family at the kitchen table and bowed her head for the silent prayer, then stood and filled a series of paper plates and bowls with food, meanwhile trying to ignore the glares she was getting from Mary and Sam. She set the paper dinnerware on a tray, which she covered with a towel that she'd heated beside the woodstove, then stepped out on the porch. It was gut to escape her siblings' scrutiny.

The October air was brisk, a stiff breeze ushering in the colder temperatures forecasted for that evening. Daed had said something about a hard freeze, so Mamm had asked Mary and Jenny to bring in all the green tomatoes and store the ones they hadn't fried for dinner in the cellar. They would probably make relish or jam out of them tomorrow. Or maybe green tomato pie. Rachel's mouth watered.

As she crossed the street, she eyed the smoke rising from the schoolhaus chimney. Her fourteen-year-old brother, Andy, had done a gut job keeping the fire going. She would make sure to build it back up and bank it for the nacht before she left.

Balancing her load in one hand, she knocked on the school door, then pushed it open. David hobbled toward her, leaning on his cane.

"What are you doing up and around?" Rachel shut the door with her foot, then steadied the tray with both hands.

David frowned. "I'm ready to be off of it, to be sure. But it's impossible to teach and keep control of the scholars while sitting. I tried, believe me."

"But it won't get better if you keep aggravating it. Wait—I think Sammy has some crutches out in the barn. They're adjustable. He had to use them after he was in a car accident a while back."

"A car accident?" David's brow furrowed. "Then why…?" His frown deepened, and he shook his head. "Never mind." He continued toward the door.

Rachel put the tray on the desk. "Where are you going?" She watched, confused, as he flipped the lock on the door, then turned and started working his way back, pulling down each window shade as he came. "What are you doing?" Sam's warnings replayed in her head. Maybe she should be a little concerned. Though, given his current condition, she'd be able to get away easily if need be. That was, if she wanted to get away. Her stomach fluttered.

"Privacy." David's cheeks reddened. "It'll be dark soon, and I don't want any curious eyes watching every move we—I make."

"What?"

His face flamed brighter. "I don't want to risk ruining your reputation."

"By my being seen eating dinner with you? Ach, jah, that'd fuel gossip, for sure." She decided to play dumb. Use sarcasm.

David smiled as he made his way toward the desk. "Nor do I want your brother scaring us like he did last nacht."

Sam had been rather rude. But his intentions had been gut, even if his concerns were unfounded.

"Do you want me to get his old crutches?" she asked.

"Later is fine." He hesitated, looking down at his foot. "I'm… hungry." The color had faded from his face, leaving in its place a sickly pallor.

"You're in pain, ain't so? When was the last time you took a pill?"

"Last nacht."

She frowned. "Look, I know all about men and their tough-guy attitudes. But you need—"

"Jah, I know. But nobody brought me any pills today. And I'm not exactly in a condition to go get them."

"Sammy was supposed to bring the bottle by this morgen." She lifted the towel off the tray.

David lowered himself into the chair at his desk. "So I heard." He raised his leg to another chair situated nearby and reached for the ice pack on the tray.

"What?" Rachel planted her fists on her hips. She couldn't believe her brother's negligence. "I'll be right back," she told David. "But don't wait for me. You can go ahead and eat."

He dropped the ice pack on his ankle with a grunt, then gave her a wobbly smile. "And after I went to all that work to lock you in."

Rachel laughed. "I'll get the crutches, too. You stay put."

～

Stay put. As if he was going anywhere. She was the one who had the freedom to kum and go as she pleased. And as much as he wanted to pursue her, to woo and win her, it seemed those plans were on hold. Unless she happened to be attracted to a helpless convalescent.

The cane had been bad enough. But at least it hadn't kept him from working. Now, he was nothing. Had nothing. Except his brains.

Maybe Cathy had gotten a glimmer of prophetic insight when she'd claimed that he would become fat and lazy.

Nein, he wasn't ready to admit to that. His ankle would heal. Eventually.

David sighed as the coldness of the ice pack seeped into his bruised, swollen skin. Crutches would definitely help. A weekend of rest—still a few days away—would help more. He'd have to find out the church schedule. Although, unless someone gave him a ride, he wouldn't be able to attend until his ankle healed.

If he missed too many services, it would warrant a visit from the gut bishop or one of the ministers. As a teacher, he'd need to be above reproach.

He should've used that as his excuse for pulling the shades instead of Rachel's reputation.

Granted, he hadn't been thinking too clearly, beyond how wunderbaar it would be if she ended up in his arms again—he pulling her close, passionately kissing…. His body heated.

A sharp pain shot through his ankle, as if to remind him that kissing Rachel was a moot point.

He leaned forward to readjust the ice pack. As he straightened, he noticed the plates of food on the tray. He hated to be a wimp, but the pain was so severe, it didn't seem possible for him to eat anything. Maybe the pill would work fast. He made himself reach for one of the sturdy paper plates and positioned it on his lap. It was piled high with mashed potatoes covered in peppered white gravy, country-fried steak covered with the same, fried green tomatoes, string beans, and a biscuit that had been sliced open, dabbed with butter, and drizzled with honey. He glanced at the tray. Applesauce waited in a bowl, as did a smaller plate with a big slice of apple pie. Despite the ache in his ankle demanding attention, his stomach rumbled.

He said a silent prayer, then managed a few bites of food before the door opened again. Rachel reappeared, holding crutches in one hand, a bottle of pills in the other. She took the time to latch the door, then aimed a mischievous grin in his direction. "There. I'm locked in again."

He smiled. "That you are." His stomach fluttered.

"I think you're familiar with crutches after your accident, ain't so?" Rachel carried them across the room and rested them against the wall behind David. Then she turned around, opened the bottle, and shook a couple of pills into her palm. "Hmm. Not all these pills look the same. A variety of shapes and colors in here. Someone must have combined the contents of several almost-empty bottles." She handed him two pills. "Here you go. These two are the same. Now you'll start to feel better." She picked up the two paper cups from the tray and went to fill them with tap water. "Sam says he's sorry he forgot to kum by this morgen."

David stared down at the pills in his hand. Not only was he convinced that forgetfulness had nothing to do with Sam's failure to bring the pills by, but now he wondered whether he should take them at all. The pain might be worse than whatever side effects would result from taking the wrong pills planted there by Rachel's brother.

Rachel handed David a cup of water, then pulled a chair up to the other side of the desk. "Aren't you going to take them?" She nodded at the pills.

"Just one for now. I'll take the other when I go to bed." He swallowed one and returned the other to the bottle.

Rachel bowed her head briefly for a silent prayer, then reached for her plate. "So, you're originally from Pennsylvania. Is that where your family lives? Do you think you'll ever return home?" She knew a lot about him already, but she hoped the distraction of questions would keep his mind off the pain.

David shook his head. "There's nothing for me there. My parents sold the farm after my buggy accident, since they figured I'd never be able to manage the work. My sister's husband bought it." He shrugged. "I'd planned to settle in Seymour, anyway, but I never dreamed my parents would sell the farm if I didn't take over. Apparently they wanted the freedom to become snowbirds to Florida." His mouth lifted in a tiny smile. "There's a thriving Amish community down there, believe it or not. Mamm said they play shuffleboard and go for walks on the beach. Someday, I'd like to see that."

"Me, too." Rachel sighed. "My cousin Esther's on her honeymoon down there with her ehemann, Viktor, and I finally got a postcard from her today. So beautiful. The picture was of a sunset—streaks of orange and yellow over this great expanse of water. Someday, I'd like to—" She fell silent and took a bite of her dinner. Hopefully her fanciful dreams wouldn't push him away, as they did Obadiah. He always scowled whenever she mentioned travel. She chanced a peek at David. Nein scowl.

"Honeymoon in Florida?" He lifted an eye brow.

Rachel giggled. "I would hardly call my cousin's trip a honeymoon. They took Viktor's großeltern with them and rented a two-bedroom bungalow. But Anna and Reuben needed the vacation, too. Reuben is healing from a back injury, and Anna—"

"I meant, do you want to honeymoon in Florida?"

Rachel's cheeks heated. "That'd be up to Obadiah. But he's all about tradition. We'll probably stay with my family the first nacht, then visit different relatives before setting up housekeeping—the way it's usually is done. He scoffed at the idea of 'going somewhere alone' when I mentioned it." *And drained all the joy from the idea.*

His gaze slowly traveled over her. "Going somewhere alone sounds very gut to me." His voice was husky.

Her face flamed.

"Didn't mean to be inappropriate." He turned his attention to his meal. But the slight quirk of his lips indicated he was anything but sorry.

Rachel finished chewing a bite of chicken-fried steak. "Did you have a girl back in Pennsylvania? Before you courted Cathy?"

"I courted a few." He shrugged. "Nobody special. I thought I was serious about Cathy. But, like I said yesterday, der Herr made it more than clear that I needed to move on." His gaze skimmed over her again.

Something inside her came to life. Her stomach clenched. Why did he affect her this way? It made nein sense. She was probably just responding to his blatant flirting.

Flirting that meant nothing.

She needed to remember that.

And find a way to ignore it.

Easier said than done. Besides, she liked it. She enjoyed the flutters, the warmth, the awareness...and even his casual touch the one time he'd brushed her cheek. The feel of his strong arms wrapped around her when he'd caught her and kept her from falling. The way he looked at her as if she were the only woman alive.

What harm would it do for her to flirt a little in return?

Chapter 8

David managed to finish his dinner, though he had to set aside the piece of pie for later. Rachel polished hers off, then tossed their empty paper plates into the cookstove. After adding another log to the fire, she picked up the tray and carried it toward the door.

He watched her, dread building. "Leaving already?" *Please say nein.*

She lowered the tray to the floor and propped it against the door. "Not yet. I just didn't want to forget it. We can talk a bit more." She aimed a smile in his direction. It seemed different, somehow. Flirtier than any of her previous smiles.

His pulse increased.

"Gut. How about you—have you always lived here? Would you like to live somewhere else?"

"Born and raised right across the street," she said with a tilt of her head. "Never been anywhere else. But…." She shrugged. "You know I'd love to travel. Some of the Englischers who kum into the store have huge motor homes. They live in them and travel all over the United States. They've seen Mt. Rushmore and the Great Lakes, Niagara Falls and the Liberty Bell…all these places I remember reading about in school. I think, 'Someday, maybe…'" She sighed. "But then, Amish don't travel the country in motor homes."

He understood her wanderlust. He'd traveled only twice, from Pennsylvania to Seymour. And from Seymour to Jamesport.

Her skirts swayed as she sauntered toward him.

He watched her approach, his heart thumping. She came around to his side of the desk. He started to spread his arms to welcome her into his lap, but she sat on the desk, as she had last nacht. So much for holding her. He pressed his lips together to suppress his sigh of disappointment and pretended to stretch, just in case she'd noticed him reaching for her.

She was right in front of him. Within touching distance, if he leaned forward. So close.

And yet so far away.

Her mouth quirked, as if she knew just what she was doing to him.

"I've bought a few coffee table books, as they're called. I have one about the Adirondacks and one about Mackinac Island. A couple of others. But most of my knowledge of other places comes from post-cards I receive from other Amish I write to. If they bother to respond."

He struggled to remember his original question. Something about whether she'd always lived here.

She swung her legs back and forth. On her shapely feet, she wore flip-flops, despite the chill in the air. He watched, transfixed, as her delicate ankles moved near, then away.

"Some never do."

What? Ach, they were talking about…? He tried to remember the topic at hand. Writing back, maybe? He wasn't sure. Her legs hampered his brainpower.

"Did it surprise you when I wrote back?" He forced his gaze away from her legs and up to her face.

"Nein, I was just glad you did. But it did surprise me when you dropped everything and moved here." She slid back a bit on the desk. The movement pulled her dress a little higher, revealing more leg. David's gaze returned to the newly exposed skin. He swallowed, feeling a sudden urge to touch her soft-looking flesh. That would be much too bold.

A sharp pain shot through his foot, as if to punish him for his errant thoughts. He readjusted the ice pack. Again.

Rachel tugged on the hem of her dress, returning the length to just above the ankle.

"So, tell me more about you. Where do you see yourself in ten years?" She tilted her head slightly to the side.

He was almost positive she didn't want to know what he thought. But he couldn't think of how to avoid giving a direct answer without lying. He strove to tell the truth, always.

He raked his fingers through his hair, probably leaving it disheveled, since her gaze rose with an expression of alarm.

"Ten years? Hard to say, since Gott's in control. But I'd like to be married"—*to you*—"have some kinner, and"—he laughed—"this will sound funny, but I think Gott is prompting me to be a preacher. I feel the call. But unless He directs the lot so that I draw the correct one, I don't see how that will be possible, given the confines of the current perimeters." He pulled in a deep breath. *Unless I leave the faith.* To be completely honest, that was likely what would happen if he didn't draw the right lot. He couldn't ignore the call just because of the dictates of a man-made system.

Rachel blinked at him. "Wow. You sound so…teacherish."

He chuckled. "Teacherish? Do you mean 'scholarly'?"

"Nein, I mean teacherish—using phrases like 'confines of the current perimeters' when you aren't talking about geometry."

He shifted, trying to decide if she was making fun of him, and noticed that the movement didn't hurt as much as usual. The pain pill must be taking effect. The throbbing in his ankle had gone from a severe, steady pounding to something almost tolerable. Unfortunately, the medicine had also begun to affect his head, making him feel heavy. Fuzzy. Weird.

It reminded him of the one time he—

Nein. He grabbed the bottle of pills, jolted to his feet, and almost crumpled to the floor as his full weight came down on his injured foot.

⌒

All attempts at flirting fled as Rachel jumped down from the desk, grabbed David around the waist, and hauled him against her chest. She ignored his sharp intake of breath as she shoved a crutch under his right arm. Gut thing she was a strong farm girl. "What are you doing? Are you a *dummchen?*"

"Drugs." He shook the bottle, making the pills rattle. "Drugs."

"What?" She reached for the other crutch.

"Whatever you just gave me was not a pain pill."

She shook her head and released him. Silly that she missed his warmth against her. "I told you, someone combined—"

"Combined, substituted, contributed…I don't care what word you use. I'm going to use one word: *illegal.* Make that two words: *illegal* and *dangerous.*"

Her lips parted as she drew a long, slow breath. She stared at David in disbelief. "Are you accusing Sam of trying to drug you?"

His brows furrowed. "Not trying to. Succeeding." He took the other crutch from her and moved toward the bathroom. "Gut thing I took only one."

"What are you going to do?" She trailed him into the bathroom but stopped just inside the door, her face heating, and immediately backed out.

He didn't respond, but she soon had her answer. He opened the bottle and dumped the contents into the toilet. A second later, he pulled down the handle and flushed. The colorful array of pills disappeared down the drain.

He tossed the bottle into the trash, then turned to her. "I am *not* taking anything more from Sam."

"But he couldn't have meant—Someone combined the different pills. They must have interacted somehow. Sam wouldn't do something like this. Certainly not intentionally."

Or would he? These pills did look different from the ones she'd given David last nacht. The bottle had been with Sam all day, and… nein. She didn't like the direction her thoughts were going.

David speared her with his gaze. "Then who? You? Trying to be rid of me by getting me high and then running to tell your bishop I'm a user? Or, worse, hoping I'll overdose?"

"Nein! I don't even know what some of those words mean."

A muscle ticked in his jaw. "If you want me to go, just say so. I'll leave." His voice had turned hard. Curt. Cold. His eyes were angry.

She didn't know what to say. She didn't want to admit that, at first, she'd wanted him to return home to Seymour and to Cathy. That was before this crazy attraction had awakened within her. Before she'd begun to get to know him in person. "I want you to stay."

He swayed slightly and closed his eyes. "I want you to go. Lock the door behind you, please." His hand reached for the edge of the sink. He missed. Tried again.

She needed to bank the fire. Either that or let the school grow chilly until Andy came to rebuild it in the morgen. And was David okay to be left on his own? She eyed him as he swayed again. Maybe she should send Sam or Andy to check on him during the nacht. She wouldn't mention it to Daed. As one of the preachers, he might feel obligated to tell Bishop Joe.

David opened his eyes. Something she'd never seen before glittered in their depths.

"Go. Now." His voice had lowered into a tone that indicated he meant business.

Right. "I'll see you tomorrow."

Silence.

Okay, then. She strode to the door, fumbled with the lock, grabbed the tray, and stepped outside.

Sam giving illegal drugs to David?

Just not possible.

⁓

David fought his way through the fog that had enveloped him. He sat up in a strange room, staring at the walls that, last nacht, had seemed to crawl, moving around as if alive. Demons had danced in the windows. He didn't know how many prayers he'd raised, how many pleas of desperation, or even if they'd made sense.

After his accident, the doctors had discovered he had low drug tolerance and had ordered the usual doses cut in half.

Tears burned his eyes. What a fool he must have appeared to Rachel He shouldn't have accused her brother—or her—of intentionally mixing powerful prescription drugs with regular over-the-counter pills, but....

It seemed everything went against him in Jamesport. So far, his move here had been the opposite of the easy fresh start he'd made in Seymour. At least there, he'd been welcomed. There'd been excitement about the new buwe arriving from Pennsylvania. So many maidals checking him out...the anticipation as they waited to see which one of them he'd choose....

And now, here he was, a *wanderer*. Sam's label had stuck in his mind. And he was right. David was a wanderer with everything to prove. And everything to lose.

The challenge seemed insurmountable.

Suddenly he became aware of noises in the classroom. He heard the squeak of the woodstove doors. He held his breath and listened. There was the sound of paper crumpling.

Rachel must not have locked the door last nacht.

And he hadn't checked. He'd assumed she would do as he'd asked.

Either that, or someone had a key—or had mastered the art of lock-picking.

All three options were believable. Especially after the mixed-up pills. Too bad he couldn't trust an Amish family.

He pushed himself out of bed and quickly dressed, then grabbed the crutches and stumbled out of the room. He needed to shave, brush his teeth, and prepare to take on the day. He didn't feel anywhere near prepared for the task, physically or emotionally.

Mary stood at his desk, arranging food on a tray. She glanced up and smiled sweetly. "Gut morgen, David. Rachel made biscuits and sausage gravy before she left for work. I poured the juice. Want some koffee? I can start water heating on the stove. Andy went to get more wood."

"Danki, Mary. Wait one minute." David slipped into the bathroom and shut the door behind him.

"You aren't very talkative in the morgen, ain't so?" Mary called after him.

Nein, he wasn't. Especially after being drugged the nacht before. Especially when he still fumed from those he suspected of orchestrating said drugging.

But he had nein proof.

And his response to Rachel had been unkind. Shame gnawed at him. He owed her an apology. Sam, too.

David finished up in the bathroom and opened the door. Andy glanced over from the stove, where he was crouched, loading in wood. There was nein sign of Mary. She'd probably run home to get their lunches or to finish her chores before school.

"Enjoy the trip, teacher?"

David's gaze jerked toward the entrance. Sam leaned coolly against the doorjamb, a smirk on his face.

Chapter 9

After work, Rachel drove her buggy directly to the gravel parking lot in front of the school. A thin film of smoke rose from the chimney. The temperature had fluctuated all day long, rising from the hard freeze the nacht before to somewhere in the mid-forties.

She sat there a moment, gathering her courage. Hopefully, David would be in a better mood. Back to his normal, friendly self.

Her heart rate increased at the thought of seeing him. She climbed out of the buggy, grabbed the plastic bag off the seat, climbed the schoolhaus steps, and knocked.

Silence for a few seconds, and then a thump. "Coming."

"I'll let myself in." Rachel twisted the knob and opened the door. David was standing a couple steps away from his desk.

"I owe you an apology," they both spoke at once.

David chuckled. "Me first, please. I said some unkind things last nacht. I'm sorry. I had nein right to accuse you like that." He paused, his eyes taking on a wary look. His lips formed a thin line. "I shouldn't have accused your brother, either. Not in front of you."

Rachel nodded. "I'm sorry for accidentally drugging you. You had a rough nacht. Sam came over to check on you, and you were crying out and flailing, he said." She still had nein clue where the pills had kum from. The bottle had been with Sam all day. And if not Sam, then who? And how?

"Ach, lovely." David's voice was full of self-derision and something else. Anger? He looked away, a blush rising on his face. "Low drug tolerance."

She held out the plastic bag. "I bought you a brand-new bottle of pain medicine. Unopened. And a few other things."

"Danki." He took the bag from her, reached inside, and pulled out the pill bottle. Followed by a bag of peppermint candies and a small canister of hazelnut-flavored koffee.

Her face heated as she glanced at his candy jar. "For your supply."

He smiled. "Danki. For everything."

She nodded and started backing up. "I'll see you later, then."

"Nein, wait." David came around the corner of the desk.

Rachel watched him approach. For a second, she was tempted to flutter her eyelids at him, until she remembered what her manager, Joel, had said when Lily had batted her eyes at a man while shopping in the store that day: "The moment a maidal starts batting her eyes at a man, that's what she becomes—fluttering lashes." Coming from Joel, the comment held weight. Rachel didn't want to reduce herself to that. She wanted to be more.

David stopped in front of her. "Danki again for bringing me a new bottle of pills." His gaze searched hers. "I'm sorry for being a jerk. And danki especially for catching me last nacht when I almost fell." He looked down. "I wanted to stay in your arms." That comment was just a shade above a whisper. Red colored his neck.

Her breath lodged in her throat. She wouldn't admit she'd wanted to keep holding him, too. Her face heated. Her heart pounded. "I...I need to go home. Have chores to do."

"And then you'll kum back to spend the evening with me, ain't so?" he asked, his voice husky. He moved closer. And then nearer still. She breathed in the scent of peppermint. Unfamiliar shivers worked through her, sending tingles up her spine.

With his fingertips, he gently brushed her cheek, and then his hand opened to cradle her jaw. He moved a little closer, his gaze dropping to her lips.

A strange longing filled Rachel with an intensity that scared her. She leaned toward him, wanting—needing—what he offered. It'd been so long since she'd been kissed....

His thumb touched the corner of her lips and slid toward the center. His smoldering gaze rose to meet hers. "Rachel—"

What was she doing? She'd promised to be true to Obadiah! She jerked away from his touch. "I really need to go. Got a boyfriend. Got...got...." She swiveled on her heel and fled.

So much for being a flirt. She obviously didn't have what it took. How could she hope to give as good as he gave?

She couldn't. Not unless she was ready to drop her resolve to keep her heart uninvolved.

He had to go. Somewhere. Anywhere but here.

Of course, if he left, she'd think about him forever, wondering what if....

Nein, she wanted him to stay.

She would send Mary to eat supper with him tonight. Rachel had trouble breathing around him. She longed for things she couldn't—shouldn't—have.

Maybe it was time to write another note to Obadiah. Or to visit his mamm to get the latest news on him.

Jah. That was what she'd do.

And she'd stay far, far away from the man who challenged everything she thought she knew.

∽

David watched Rachel sprint across the road, leaving her horse and buggy forgotten in front of the school. He hadn't meant to scare her away. But she probably had been wise to leave. Because he would've kissed her until he was senseless, until his knees buckled and toes curled, and he would've been praying she'd respond in the same way, clinging to him.... His stomach clenched.

"Someday, Rachel," he whispered. Even so, the words seemed to echo in the silence of the school.

Maybe he would kiss her that evening when she came back with his dinner.

Instant remorse filled him. Why was he burning this way over a woman? Dreaming of things only a married man had the right to dream about his frau? His thoughts were sinful. *Forgive me, Gott.*

David turned and made his way back to his bedroom, such as it was. He propped the borrowed crutches against the wall, then dropped to his knees beside the cot and buried his face in his palms.

Ach, Gott. You know my thought, and my desires….

That reminded him of a Bible passage. He reached for the black leather volume on the chair beside him. Thumbed through it.

There it was—Psalm 139.

O LORD, thou hast searched me, and known me. Thou knowest my downsitting and mine uprising, thou understandest my thought afar off. Thou compassest my path and my lying down, and art acquainted with all my ways.

He must've been on his knees for hours as he prayed over the entire chapter, lingering especially over the final verses:

Search me, O God, and know my heart: try me, and know my thoughts: and see if there be any wicked way in me, and lead me in the way everlasting.

The school door opened and closed, ushering in the aroma of fried chicken. His stomach rumbled in response. He rose, the sprained ankle protesting every move.

And all the thoughts he'd tried to pray away returned as the swish of skirts approached his room.

Another verse flashed through his memory: *"I made a covenant with mine eyes; why then should I think upon a maid?"*

His heart pounded as he flung open the door, and looked—down—at Mary.

He glanced past her, at the tray sitting on his desk. Scanned the rest of the room. Empty. Then he looked back at Mary with raised eyebrows.

She grinned. "Isn't it great? Rachel went to Obadiah's parents' haus for dinner, so I came over for our first date."

❧

Rachel opened the door of the Beilers' haus and slipped inside. "Hallo?"

Obadiah's mamm, Nita, stepped into the kitchen and wrapped her in a hug. "Ach, Rachel. Kum in. We were just ready to sit down for our evening meal. Can you join us?"

"Jah, danki. Anything I can do to help?"

"Nein, it's all ready. Just let me grab another plate. We're eating light to-nacht. Just some leftover beef stew and corn bread." She gave an apologetic shrug.

Rachel smiled. "Sounds perfect. Especially since I dropped in unexpected." She opened a drawer and took out some cutlery while Nita fetched an extra bowl, small plate, and drinking glass from a cabinet.

"Water okay?"

"Jah." Rachel slipped into a chair as Nita set the filled glass in front of her. She glanced at Obadiah's daed. "Hallo, Peter."

He nodded, then bowed his head for the silent prayer. Much like Obadiah, he was a man of few words. If it didn't need to be said, there was nein point in wasting his breath.

The trait was frustrating at times. Especially since Rachel had grown up in a particularly vocal family. David knew how to communicate, too, in writing and verbally.

She cringed and quickly bowed her head. She'd kum here to *forget* David. Not to compare him and Obadiah.

She loved Obadiah. Really. That was why they were planning a future together.

Silverware clattered against dishes, indicating that the silent prayer was over. And she hadn't prayed. Yet.

Danki, Lord, for this meal, for the fellowship, and for Obadiah. Help me to get over David. Forgive me for being unfaithful in my thoughts. Amen.

Short and sweet, but it'd have to do. She raised her head. "Have you heard from Obadiah lately?"

"I got a letter from him today." Nita patted her apron pocket. "We'll read it after we eat. So, I heard we have a new teacher. First male we've had in our district, for as far back as I can remember. You have siblings in school, ain't so? How do they like him?"

Nita would have to bring up David. Rachel shrugged, feigning nonchalance. "I haven't heard any complaints. Andy says that he's already earned the respect of the big buwe—but I'm not sure how— and my sisters adore him."

"That's gut. Difficult sometimes for female teachers to get the older ones to obey. Have you met him yet?"

"A time or two." Rachel tried not to squirm as she ladled some stew into her bowl, then lifted a square of corn bread out of the basket. "This smells so gut."

"Ach, just some leftovers I threw together to clean out the refrigerator. On such a chilly evening, stew just seemed appropriate."

Rachel nodded, her mind whirling as she tried to think of a way to deflect the conversation away from David. She had nothing. She glanced at Obadiah's daed. "Everything gut with you, Peter?"

He grunted.

Jah, she was desperate.

She looked back at Nita. "How's the gross-boppli?"

"Ach, you should see all my grosskinner. My namesake is already starting school. Anita's the oldest. She loves to help me bake pumpkin chocolate chip cookies. And then there's little Abner...." Nita was off and running. At least she was talking about something other than David. But, not really knowing Obadiah's brothers and sisters, Rachel found her mind easily wandering...to David. How was he doing with Mary there? She should stop after dinner and check on him.

After the meal, Nita cut three pieces of molasses pie and poured a mug of koffee for her husband. Then she pulled the folded letter out of her pocket and shook it open. The paper crackled.

"Dear Mamm and Daed,

"Danki for your last letter. If you see Rachel, tell her danki for writing, as well. I'm very busy here. I'm learning how to use some electric machinery to make grooves and fancy designs in wooden furniture like the Englisch prefer. They are allowed to use electric in their places of business for all the power tools.

"I am doing okay. I've started taking Ab—"

Nita stopped short and scanned a few lines, her face paling. Then she cleared her throat and looked up. "I've started taking Aleve for my terrible headaches. In fact, I'm getting one now. Be a dear and run get me a pill, please, Rachel?"

Rachel stood and moved through the haus to the bathroom, hearing the rise and fall of Nita's voice in the kitchen but not understanding her words.

She opened the medicine cabinet. There wasn't any Aleve to be found. There was only ibuprofen.

Nita's request had been a ploy to get her out of the room while she finished reading the letter to her ehemann. Because there was something Obadiah mentioned that Rachel wasn't supposed to hear.

It didn't take a genius to figure it out: Obadiah was seeing another girl. An Ohio girl.

Rachel stared at the contents of the medicine cabinet, then finally reached for the ibuprofen.

She ought to give Obadiah the benefit of the doubt. Maybe he hadn't written what she imagined at all.

Perhaps he'd written that he'd started taking "absolute" care to set money aside so that he would be able to kum home for Thanksgiving.

That could be it.

Right. That would count as highly classified information Nita wouldn't want her to hear, so much so that she would lie about needing Aleve.

Her spirits sagged.

Rachel mentally shook herself. They were promised. She would hold on to that.

She had to.

Because any other scenario was too impossible to believe.

If David were still in Seymour, she would write him a letter to convey what had just happened and ask for his insight.

She really needed to talk to a friend.

Could she consider David a friend, in spite of his obvious desire to be more?

Chapter 10

David looked up from the checkerboard. "King me."

Mary moved one of his conquered men to cover the piece. "I'm still winning."

"That you are." He wouldn't mention that he'd deliberately made some bad moves. He didn't know how competitive she was, but he didn't want the child leaving in tears.

The school door opened, and Rachel blew in with a burst of cold air. She held her black coat clasped shut with one reddened hand. Her nose and cheeks were rosy from the wind. "I think the temperature dropped twenty degrees since I left home this afternoon. I heard we're supposed to get some freezing rain to-nacht. How was dinner? Do you want me to carry the tray home for you, Mary?"

"Jah, please." Mary didn't look up from the game board.

"Why don't you stay a bit?" David couldn't take his eyes off Rachel, afraid she would disappear as fast as she'd appeared.

"Ach, I don't want to interfere." Rachel glanced from him to Mary, then back again. She released the hand holding her coat, letting it fall open to reveal a green dress that made her eyes appear the same color.

David looked away. There was the matter of it being his and Mary's first date—according to Mary. That still made him uncomfortable. If the bishop got word that he "dated" an eleven-year-old maidal, it would look very bad. But he didn't know how to send her away without hurting her feelings and ruining the gut rapport he had with one of his scholars. Inviting Rachel to stay would be asking for trouble. Especially in front of her little sister, whom he didn't want to upset.

A lose-lose situation.

David made another intentional bad move on the checkerboard, and Mary jumped his final man.

"I need to teach you how to play checkers," Mary grumbled.

He smiled and pretended to yawn. "We should probably call it a nacht, Mary. Danki for eating dinner with me." He cleared his throat. "I enjoyed our 'date,' but I could get in big trouble for dating a student, so we need to be just friends right now, okay?" He pulled the ice pack off his ankle and rose to his feet, then grabbed his crutches. "Let me see you ladies home."

"We can be friends for now." Mary peered up at him. "How can you see us home?"

"I'll stand at the door and watch."

Mary giggled.

Rachel studied him. "I should bank the fire if you're headed to bed."

"Not yet, but danki. I need to prepare lesson plans for tomorrow." He glanced at her, then dropped his gaze and studied the floor at his feet. The pain in his heart rivaled that of his ankle that he'd scared her to the point of prompting her to run to the haus of the parents of her intended. He'd need to tread carefully.

Maybe feign disinterest.

"I'll kum back later then, jah?" Rachel tilted her head at him.

Jah, please. He pulled in a long breath, then shook his head. "Nein, that's okay. Send one of your brothers over to do it. Andy, maybe. Please."

Her lips parted, as if she wanted to say something. A confused expression settled on her face. "Are you sure?"

His heart lurched. But he nodded. "Jah, I'm sure." He looked at Mary. "Danki again for a lovely evening."

"I'll see you tomorrow, David." Mary scampered out the door.

Rachel picked up the tray of dirty dishes. "Jah, tomorrow, David."

He stood in the open doorway, ignoring the chill, and watched them cross the street, climb the porch stairs, and duck inside. He started to shut the door, but a moving shadow on his left caught his attention before disappearing around the side of the building.

When Rachel followed Mary into the kitchen, Mamm and Jenny were still cleaning up from dinner. None of the buwe was in sight. Probably out in the barn finishing up the evening chores. Her cousin Greta looked up from wiping the table and smiled.

Rachel blinked at her. "Hallo, Greta. What are you doing here?" She took the tray of dishes over to the sink. Using paper plates that could be burned afterward was far easier than lugging dishes back and forth across the street. But maybe David would soon be able to start taking his meals with the family, when he was able to navigate the stairs with crutches.

Greta frowned. "I'm spending the nacht, remember? So we can get an early start on the boppli quilts for—"

"Ach, I forgot. And we were going to make green tomato relish, too."

"Jah. I thought you'd be here for dinner, like we agreed on."

Rachel's face heated. "I went to Obadiah's haus to see if his parents had news from him." Her voice broke slightly.

Greta gave her a questioning look.

Rachel shook her head.

"Table's wiped off, Aentie Elsie," Greta told Rachel's mamm. "Is there anything else I can help with?"

Mamm waved her hand. "The girls and I will finish. You two go catch up."

As if she and Greta hadn't seen each other at the store every day this week. Admittedly, they didn't talk much there. Joel would have a conniption if they spent their time visiting instead of working. "Let's sit on the porch," she suggested. She wanted to keep an eye on the school without blatantly spying on David.

She led the way outside, then settled down on the top step as a tall Amish man approached the phone shanty. He waved at her before ducking inside. Greta shrugged on her coat and lingered in the shadows. "Josh," she whispered.

Rachel nodded, but her focus was on the schoolhaus. She gazed through the window and saw David standing at the back, near the door. Sam came around the corner of the building, carrying a load of wood.

"I'm sorry," Greta said, not straying from her hiding spot.

"You can't avoid him forever, you know."

"I can do my best. But let's not talk about him. You went for news about Obadiah?"

Rachel's breath caught again. "Jah. I think he's seeing someone else. His mamm read the letter out loud but stopped short when she reached a certain part: 'I've started taking Ab—' She quieted, then said something about having a headache and sent me for some Aleve. But she didn't have any Aleve. He must be seeing—"

"Ach, you don't know that," Greta said. "Obadiah loves you. Besides, if you break up with Obadiah, what does it mean? There's nein hope for any of us. Did you hear the latest? I heard that Li—"

The shanty door opened again. Greta slipped farther into the darkness as Josh approached.

"Hallo, Rachel." Josh sat next to her. "Curious about something. There's smoke coming from the school chimney...."

⌒

David frowned as footsteps thumped up the stairs outside.

He opened the door and tried to keep his voice pleasant as Sam drew nearer. "Sam. Kum on in."

"Gotta load of split logs for you." Sam carried an armful up the stairs, entered the schoolhaus, and piled them by the woodstove.

David shut the door.

Sam crouched in front of the stove and peered inside. With the metal poker, he jabbed at the logs, then added one. "It's going gut right now."

David nodded. "I did okay getting wood in there after the scholars left." A log or two had ended up crooked, but that hardly mattered. He realized his comment had sounded inane. "Danki for bringing more wood."

"Don't think I forgot." Sam straightened and turned to David, his hands clenched in fists. "I warned you. And you touched her."

David adjusted the borrowed crutches. The desire to lie tempted him. Or he could pretend he didn't know what Sam was talking about. After all, he hadn't touched Mary. Just Rachel. Yesterday. And earlier today. But even pretending was a lie. He firmed his shoulders. "Don't you have anything better to do with your time than to spy on me?"

Sam narrowed his eyes, anger simmering in their depths, and strode toward David.

David braced himself. He was taller, but Sam was stockier. He probably outweighed David by a gut thirty pounds or more. Besides, David had one hurt ankle and lingering weakness in the same leg from the previous accident. He eyed Sam's arm muscles, his stocky build.

Jah, Sam would be gut at wrestling. And David would be pinned.

A knock on the door broke the tension.

Sam's shoulders fell as he appeared to relax. His hands uncurled at his sides. David exhaled and opened the door. A tall, blond, clean-shaven Amish man stood there. His blue eyes studied him warily, with uncertainty. He nodded at David, then looked past him to Sam. "Hallo, Sam."

Had Sam called for backup? Two against one? David wasn't sure where to look. He shifted so he could keep an eye on both men.

Sam was quiet a long moment. Then his stance stiffened again. "Joshua."

Another someone Sam didn't like. David smiled, glad for the intrusion now. He stepped aside to welcome the newcomer, then shut the door behind him. It'd be gut when all the visitors left so the fire could warm the building.

Joshua pulled off his black hat, revealing hair cut in an Englisch style. "I was just using the phone shanty when I felt der Herr leading me to kum here. I wasn't aware anyone lived in the schoolhaus until now."

"Temporary. Very temporary," Sam growled. "And since when did der Herr ever lead you to do anything, Joshua Yoder?" He pushed past them, flung open the door, and stomped down the stairs. Over his shoulder, he grumbled, "Someone will be back to bank the fire, teacher."

"I can do it," Joshua called after him.

Sam acknowledged his comment with a backhanded wave.

David pulled in a breath and shut the door again. At least he wouldn't be recovering from further injuries at Sam's hand tonight. He looked back at Joshua. "*Danki* for stopping by." *And danki, Lord, for sending help when I needed it.*

"My friends call me Josh." He came farther into the room and set his hat down on a desk. "Place hasn't changed at all. Except the peppermints." He crossed over to the desk, picked up one, unwrapped it, and stuck it in his mouth.

David grinned at Josh.

"So." The wariness still remained in Josh's eyes. "I'm going to sound like a *dummchen*, but...." He pulled in a deep breath. "*Der Herr* really did tell me to *kum*."

David nodded. Whatever the Lord's reasons for sending him, whether to protect David from Sam or something else altogether, he was grateful that Josh had listened and obeyed.

Josh took another long breath. "I...uh, *der Herr* also told me you had a close encounter with Him. I want to hear about it."

Chapter 11

When Greta finally ventured out of the shadows, Rachel scooted over so she could sit next to her. She eyed her friend. "What was that about?"

"I know I shouldn't avoid him, but...."

"But you have ever since he came back into town. The second he walked in at the singing in July, you went into avoidance mode. Have you two talked at all?"

"There's nothing to say." Greta looked away.

"You need to forgive him and move on."

Sam came striding across the road, his shoulders set, and disappeared inside the barn. What had he said to David? Had they gotten into a verbal fight? And had Sam really given David illicit drugs? She shifted uneasily. Maybe she should head over there and find out what was going on. As soon as Joshua left.

"I'm moving on, for sure." Greta looked back at Rachel. "I heard that Lily is being courted by Esther's old beau, Henry."

Rachel frowned. "I'd hate to wish that on anyone." She stared at the schoolhaus, watching the two men through the window. What were they talking about? Why hadn't Sam stayed? If only Joshua would leave so that she could go over there.

"I know. His horrible temper and his lying...ach, and that time he slammed down that bag of flour in the store and left me a mess...." Greta winced. "I should forget that. The bishop said he talked to him. Still, I'd hate to marry him, especially after what he did to Esther."

Rachel glanced at Greta. Her gaze was fixed on the schoolhaus, too.

"Have you met the new schoolteacher yet?" Rachel pulled her coat tighter around her.

Greta blew out a noisy breath. "Not exactly, but I did see him when he came to the store, if he is who I think he is. And I'm not going to meet him, so long as *he* is over there."

"His name is David Lapp." She waited for Greta to make the connection.

Silence stretched on for endless seconds.

Then, finally, "David Lapp?"

"From Seymour."

"Ach!" Greta gasped. "He's the one you've been writing, ain't so? Didn't you tell him you were engaged? Or is he ignoring that?"

"I told him. But if Obadiah is seeing someone else, why—"

"Shush! Obadiah hasn't said any such thing. Don't you think he'd tell you?"

Rachel shrugged. He'd told his parents. And if he was interested in another girl to the point where he was giving her rides home, then it meant he wasn't interested in Rachel enough to marry her. At least, that was the way she saw it.

And with David sending shivers up her spine and making her want his touch, it would seem she wasn't interested in Obadiah enough to marry him.

She heaved a heavy sigh.

Greta looked at her.

Rachel shrugged. How could she confess to her cousin that she was more than a little interested in the new schoolteacher?

~

David stared at Josh, not quite sure what to make of him. "Gott told you that I had an encounter with Him?" His ankle had started to throb, so he adjusted the crutches and started for the desk. And the chair.

"Let me start over." Josh took a cavernous breath. "I needed to make a call, so I walked to the phone shanty. As soon as I got there, I felt this urge to go talk to the person in the school, except that I didn't know anyone lived here. I saw smoke coming from the chimney, so I asked Rachel Miller, since she was sitting on her porch. Didn't want her watching me knock on the door and thinking I was an idiot for expecting to find anyone inside." He laughed. "I guess I should learn to trust His leading and not worry what others think of me. But that's an issue I've long struggled with."

David resisted the urge to look outside to see if Rachel was still sitting on the porch. "Sometimes it's hard to follow what you don't understand." He sat in his chair and lifted his foot, propping it on another chair, then reached for the more-liquid-than-frozen ice pack.

Josh nodded. "Listen, you don't know me. And I won't share my life story with you at this point. I'm sure you'll hear the gory details if you hang out with Sam enough—"

"I don't." David looked around for some leftover cookies or a slice of pie—a snack to offer his guest, other than peppermint candy. But there was nothing. "Have a seat, Josh."

"Danki." Josh lowered himself into a nearby seat. "Suffice it to say, I left here angry at the world. My wandering took me to the Appalachian Trail. During the course of my hiking, I was blessed to be used to rescue a man being swept away by a mudslide. He was delirious, but Gott appeared. And nobody in the area left unscathed. Gott met me—us—there. And He led me back here, the last place I wanted to be. I'd burned too many bridges. Hurt too many people." His shoulders slumped. "But Gott made it clear that I was to kum, and that my life's purpose is to serve Him."

David nodded. "Jah, I understand. I feel Him calling me to be a preacher." It was the first time he'd made that confession to anyone other than Bishop Sol and Rachel. He braced himself for the derisive laugh sure to kum from Josh. What Amish man in his right mind wanted to draw the lot to be a preacher? It carried so much responsibility.

David studied Josh. Why would Gott send someone to him? He wanted to ask Josh about his story, but something stayed him. He probably should share his own first. Maybe Gott was providing him a friend in this district, which had been so unfriendly thus far. His heart warmed.

Josh reached for another peppermint. "How did you get the call?"

David shifted in his seat. "It happened because of a double date. The girl I courted in Seymour and I were out in a buggy with her

They begin to interpret it from their perceptions; then they see that it can have six possible meanings. (To see for yourself, try reading the statement six times, each time emphasizing a different word: "*I* didn't say . . . ," "I *didn't* say . . . ," and so on.)

Listeners also often assume that they already know what the speaker is saying or meaning. Frequently an individual develops the habit of interrupting, and of excusing the interruption by asserting, "I knew what you were going to say." That's a remarkable skill! A listener who doesn't interrupt may nevertheless assume he knows the mind of the speaker and fail to really listen. Once, as a graduate student, I sat in a conference room listening to a fellow student's presentation. During the presentation he asked another student, "Do you know what I mean?" and the other student replied, "Yes, I know *exactly* what you mean." I remember wondering to myself, "Does he really know *exactly* what the speaker means?"

The popular game, "Rumor," further illustrates the possibilities for faulty communication. In this fun activity, one person whispers a message to the person next to him, who whispers it to the third person, and so on around the room until the message returns to the one who started the game. The humor emerges in the gross distortion which usually occurs. It is sad that we do not realize what this simple game teaches us about the nature of communication: it is easily distorted and needs constant checking out for accuracy.

But checking out is simply not done in most communication. A husband does not typically say, "Let me tell you what I heard you say. I want to be certain I've heard you correctly." More likely, he assumes that what he thought he heard was what his wife actually meant, not realizing how significantly his internal filters and faulty listening skills have changed the message. Because messages are so often distorted, checking out is vital to insuring accuracy of communication.

Checking out goes beyond accuracy of communication, however, as important as that is. The authors of *Alive and Aware* note:

> Checking out isn't useful only because it helps you, however. Sincere checking out demonstrates your commitment to your partner's well-being—you are letting him know that you're interested in him and care about what he thinks or feels or wants. So check-outs can contribute a great deal to good feelings in your relationship.[1]

A Shared Meaning

I have said that the skill of checking out communication is the foundation upon which the shared-meaning process is built. Through the consistent application of this process, many relational struggles can be reduced and many communication distortions can be straightened out. People who learn to reach a shared meaning will have better feelings about their relationships because they will have achieved greater mutual understanding. Gaining a shared meaning is more apt to build friendships than feuds.

But just what is a shared meaning? I have described checking out as a communication skill that increases the accuracy of communication between speaker and listener. Reaching a shared meaning is a process in which two persons use the check-out skill to reach a mutual understanding about some topic, issue, or concern.

Mutual understanding does not necessarily imply agreement. My wife may say to me, "Norm, I understand that you want to take five hundred dollars out of the bank to purchase a motorcycle. I don't agree that it's a good use of five hundred dollars." It is unrealistic to think that two people will, or should, agree on everything. But we all want to be understood, and to have our feelings respected. In this chapter we will be exploring a process whereby we say about each other: "He (or she) understands."

How to Reach a Shared Meaning

The process of reaching a shared meaning is meant to be used—not just studied. Therefore, I would like to outline the process as clearly as possible, so that you will understand how to implement it in your relationships.

Step 1: The speaker sends the message.

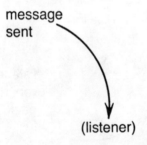

message
sent

(listener)

In step 1, the individual who is concerned about an issue and wants to reach a shared meaning goes to the other person and tells him or her: "I'd like to have a shared meaning with you." (Of course, both partners should know about the process and be able to work through it.) The speaker then describes the issue as clearly and simply as possible, using a factual, self-reporting approach rather than blaming, ridiculing, or accusing the other person.

It is best for the speaker to send the message in small units interspersed with listener check-out. Remember, overload of information is a common communication problem. A rule of thumb is to speak for about twenty seconds and then ask the listener for feedback; it is probably impossible for a listener to feedback a longer message with any degree of accuracy. Some couples find it helpful to have a signal, such as a raised hand, whereby the listener indicates, "That's all I can handle; let me check-out for accuracy.

At the end of the message, the speaker invites a shared-meaning response by stating, "What have you heard me say?" This statement leads to the second step . . .

Step 2: The listener reports back.

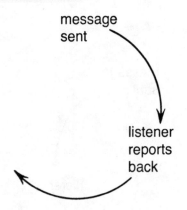

message
sent

listener
reports
back

In step 2, the listener describes as accurately as possible what he has heard the speaker say. His or her goal is to match the speaker's message accurately. The listener will probably paraphrase the information, but must avoid adding his or her own opinion, interpretation, or meaning to the speaker's message. There is no place in the shared meaning process for statements like these:

"You said you love me, but I don't think you mean it."
"I heard you say you want to be more helpful with household
   chores—but you just said that because you feel guilty about
   my being overworked."

sister and her sister's beau. We were going fishing, and we needed to cross the highway. While we were waiting for the traffic to clear, a driver honked his horn. The horse spooked and bolted out into traffic. The buggy was totaled."

A pained look crossed Josh's face. "Wow."

"Jah. By the grace of Gott, nothing happened to the girls. They were treated at the hospital for minor injuries and released. The other man and I were in the same hospital room, but he was being observed for a concussion. I had a broken leg and a broken arm, and..." He pulled in a breath. "That nacht, we talked a lot and formed a friendship. But then, something happened. I got a blood clot. And I died."

Josh's lips parted. "And...?"

David had never shared the rest of the story with anyone. It was too sacred, too wonderful to put into words. His mouth went dry. He didn't know how to begin. Didn't know if Josh would take him seriously. He shut his eyes so he wouldn't see any doubt or derision that might appear on Josh's face. "And I went to this really beautiful place. I saw Jesus. I threw myself at His feet, and I didn't want to leave." His eyes burned. "But He told me that He wasn't finished with me yet, and I needed to go back and tell others about Him. The doctors and nurses who responded to the page in the hospital brought me back to life." That was the short version.

"Wow." Josh's response was filled with awe. Nein mocking at all in his tone.

David opened his eyes and studied Josh's face. He felt relief at seeing nothing but friendly acceptance.

"Just—wow." Josh slowly pushed to his feet and leaned over the desk. "I'll kum back. I'm going to bring a friend. I'm thinking we should have a men's Bible study. You let me know which nacht, and we'll be here."

David's heart leapt at the idea. But his position in this community was still fragile, at best. "Is that allowed?" If not, it might cost him his temporary job and home.

Josh's mouth quirked. "If the current preachers aren't going to teach the Word, then somebody needs to, ain't so?"

The current preachers weren't teaching the Word? Well, based on the bishop's attitude and the hateful treatment he'd received from Sam, maybe not. But maybe he should withhold judgment until after he'd attended his first church service.

⌒

Rachel pulled her coat more tightly closed and got to her feet. "Kum on," she said to Greta. "Let's go across the street so you can meet David."

Greta also stood but made no move to follow Rachel. "Josh is still there. I'll just wait here."

Rachel shrugged. "You have to face him sometime. It wouldn't be like a date or anything. And…." She really needed to talk to David. She had to tell him about Obadiah. Well, maybe not *had to*. Wanted to.

Plus, Greta *needed* to see Joshua. Needed to move past him instead of hiding and holding grudges. To stop living in fear of confrontation, paralyzed by the thought of making waves.

Gut thing Greta was already wearing her coat and shoes. Rachel grabbed her arm and tugged. "Kum on."

Greta resisted, but only a little. Not as much as Rachel had expected.

She led the way up to the schoolhaus steps. As she raised her hand to knock, the door opened. Joshua stood there blinking at them for a moment before stepping back. "Rachel. Greta." His voice softened a little when he said Greta's name. "Kum on in."

"I wanted to introduce Greta to David."

"I see." Was that a flash of disappointment on his face? "I'll be on my way, then." Joshua glanced at David. "I'll kum back in a couple days."

David nodded. "Nice meeting you." He pushed himself to his feet, eyeing Greta with wariness.

"Ach, you should stay, Joshua." Rachel smiled at him.

He glanced over her shoulder at Greta, something akin to longing in his expression.

"You can stay," Greta whispered.

He hesitated a beat. But then he shook his head. "Better go." And he disappeared out the door.

David approached, using the crutches. "What brings you by?"

Rachel pulled Greta forward. "This is Greta, my cousin and also one of my best friends. Greta, this is David Lapp from Seymour."

"Bird in Hand, Pennsylvania, actually," David said. The wariness didn't leave his eyes.

Rachel frowned at David. Why was he acting so reserved?

Greta acknowledged his comment with a nod. "Excuse me for a second." Her voice cracked. She headed back to the bathroom and shut the door.

"Joshua used to court her," Rachel explained quietly. "I made her *kum*."

"I'm not interested in getting to know *other* girls for a relationship at this point, if that's why you brought her by." David held her gaze.

His emphasis on the word "other" caused her stomach to clench. "Nein. I needed to talk to you. You are—were—one of my best friends." Except that he was something other than a friend now. Just what, she didn't know, only that she wanted to know him. Wanted to kiss him.

She sucked in a deep breath. "I think Obadiah is seeing someone else."

David blinked. A slight smile played on his lips.

Chapter 12

Why do you think that?"

David struggled to control his grin and to keep a straight, noncommittal face as Rachel told him about Obadiah. She didn't act heartbroken, and he wasn't sure whether he should mutter comforting platitudes or shout for joy, take her in his arms, and ask if he could court her. Declare his love.

The first choice was probably better, considering that he was laid up with an injury and had nein way to court a girl, much less support a frau.

But it definitely would make things a lot easier knowing she didn't have a boyfriend.

And with her cousin there—though apparently hiding in the bathroom, since she'd been gone awhile—it was probably not a gut idea to—

Rachel moved closer, wrapped her arms around his middle, and hugged him tight, fragmenting his thoughts and sending them scattered in a zillion different directions. He expelled a slow breath, let his crutches fall where they may, and enfolded her in his arms. His mind rang the emergency alarm—the window shades were still open, the front door unlocked—but David ignored it. He would hold her for just a minute. Nothing wrong with a simple hug, ain't so? That was all he'd allow. But, smelling the scent of her…. Feeling her softness pressed up against him…. It was heaven.

She didn't seem to be crying. At least, her shoulders weren't shaking.

Her arms tightened around him. He brushed tiny kisses along her hairline, so subtle that she may not have noticed them, as he tried to think of something comforting to say. But with her in his arms, his mind refused to function, beyond registering every breath she took, every move she made, the very essence of her. *Ach, Rachel….*

She leaned back away long before he was ready, and looked up at him. At least she had the strength he lacked.

This was it—the moment he needed to say something wise. Encouraging. Profound. He released her and opened his mouth. *Gott, speak through me.*

She leaned forward, rising on tiptoe, and her lips brushed across his cheek before landing full on his mouth. His heart thumped against his rib cage. She was kissing him! After a moment of hesitation, he slapped the blaring mental alarms silent and closed his eyes. As she started to pull away, he moved one hand to the back of her neck, his fingers weaving through the few loose strands of hair that had escaped her kapp. With his other arm, he reached around her waist and pulled her closer. She leaned into him.

Heaven....

He tasted a hint of koffee on her lips. A touch of chocolate. Mixed with the scent of vanilla. Wondering if she'd let him, he deepened the kiss. Slowly, cautiously. It was a little like stepping into the deep part of the creek and plunging unexpectedly into a hole, his head going under. David could think of nothing else than his desire to explore it.

He could stay there all day. Nein, he couldn't. She didn't know for sure whether her beau was seeing someone else. They needed to be certain it was over before they started anything.

He needed to rein himself in. And quickly.

He released her and stepped back, opening his mouth again to say what he should. But his brain refused to connect.

"Ach, David," she whispered.

"What was *that* for?"

The question hadn't kum out as he'd intended. Hardly the wise words from Gott he'd hoped to say. But that was what he got for speaking before his brain was fully in gear.

Truthfully, though, she had taken him by surprise. Never before had a woman flung herself into his arms and initiated a kiss.

Rachel's face flushed. "It was because...because...I needed...a hug."

He raised his eyebrows. "Most hugs don't include kisses like that." Not that he'd minded.

"I meant to kiss your cheek. For being such a sweetheart." She shrugged, her cheeks turning a deeper shade of pink. "Do you want me to admit that I wanted to know what it would feel like to kiss you? Because I won't...ach!" Her face flamed red, and she dipped her head.

David needed to see her expression, to read her thoughts. He cupped her chin with his hand, lifting her face, and studied her a moment, seeing the vulnerability in her eyes. The neediness. The—

With no warning at all, Rachel inhaled sharply, then thrust her arms around his neck and yanked him toward her. Her fingers tangled in his hair as her mouth hungrily sought his. Passion flared as their kisses deepened, becoming more insistent. His knees went weak. His toes curled. His heart pounded out of control. He slid his hand slowly down her back, to her waist, and—

Something clanged, and a sharp pain pummeled his head.

The world went black.

⌒

Rachel swayed beneath David's weight as he sagged, then wrenched free from her arms and fell to the ground with a thud. Her eyes popped open, but she had to blink a few times to dispel the passion-induced stars. Greta stood in the bathroom doorway, hand pressed flat against her mouth. Off to the side was Sam, holding the fireplace poker.

Sam?

She looked down at David's body, crumpled on the floor. She dropped to her knees beside him and ran her fingers through his hair, finding a lump at the back of his head.

She glared up at Sam. "What did you do that for?" Her throat clogged with tears.

Sam's behavior was over the top. David's accusations about the drugs suddenly didn't seem so outrageous. Could she even trust her own brother?

"I warned him."

"You killed him!" She didn't see any blood, but he wasn't moving. Was he even breathing?

"I wouldn't be lucky enough." Sam kicked David's leg with his boot, and David moaned. "Not dead."

Rachel tried to straighten his bad leg. "But—"

"But nothing. I told you, the man's trouble. Stay away from him. I figured out where I know him from, and—"

"Tell me later." Rachel waved her hand. "Greta, run and get Mamm. And Daed. Anyone. We need to get him to bed."

"Tell them he fell," Sam ordered Greta.

Greta nodded, wordless, and started for the door. Her eyes were bloodshot, as if she'd been crying.

Rachel decided to delay wondering why. She turned her attention back to Sam. "He didn't do anything wrong. All he did was leave everything he knew to kum here and take a job teaching school. That's all! What do you have against him?"

"He was kissing you, and I warned him. Besides, you're engaged to Obadiah. Remember him? My best friend? Did you even mention him to David?"

Tears burned Rachel's eyes. "I did. But Obadiah's seeing another girl."

"So, he knew about him, and—what? Who? Obadiah…? Nein. He wouldn't."

David groaned again.

"We need to get him to bed," Sam conceded. "Don't worry, I don't think I broke any skin. He'll just have a bad headache for a while." He set the poker by the woodstove and crouched by David's head, reaching for his shoulders. "You get his feet. On the count of three. One, two, three."

Somehow, they got him into the cot. Rachel was going to retrieve his crutches when the door opened.

Mamm bustled in. "That bu is so accident-prone. Where is he?"

❧

David woke with a splitting headache, making the pain in his ankle pale significantly in comparison. He brought his hand to his head and ran his fingers gently through his hair to the sore spot. There was a giant bump there. Then he opened his eyes, wincing against the bright light beaming into the small room. He pulled the padding away from his head and held it in front of him, finding himself gazing at another ice pack. He must have hit his head somehow. Must've fallen, because he was in bed fully dressed. That meant someone had been with him when he'd fallen. Or had found him later.

Josh had been there. Sam, too. Had something happened? Had they gotten into a fight? If only he could remember.

He'd had the most wunderbaar dreams about kissing Rachel. They had to be dreams because she was the one who'd initiated the kisses. And he doubted any gut Amish girl, especially one as practical as Rachel claimed to be, would do such an impulsive thing.

His infatuation with her was making his imagination unruly. He needed to spend more time in prayer and not let fantasy get in the way of reality.

Speaking of reality, what time was it? As bright as the sun was, he probably ought to be up and about by now. The scholars were surely on their way.

He glanced over at the chair to check the time on his windup clock, but it wasn't in its normal spot. Instead, the chair was occupied by a pair of pants, suspenders, a blue shirt, and a beard. Rachel's daed? The *preacher*?

David sat up, cringing at the painful movement. His stomach roiled. He pressed a hand against it, willing the contents—or lack thereof—to stay put.

Preacher Samuel opened his eyes, then rubbed them, slowly straightening his posture. "You okay, bu?"

"Jah. I'm okay." He wouldn't mention the pain. Or the nausea. *Danki, Lord, for the untainted bottle of pills Rachel had brought.* "What are you doing here?"

"You fell." Preacher Samuel rose to his feet and stretched. "You up to teaching school today?"

David sucked in a breath and swung his feet off the cot, fighting a wave of dizziness. Taking his crutches from where they were propped nearby, he pushed to his feet, ignoring the way the room seemed to tilt and weave. "Jah." Not like he could afford to take a day off. He'd been in the position for less than a week.

The preacher surveyed him. "My sohn Sam implied you might be...a 'user,' he called it. Of illegal drugs. Got something to say about that?"

Not really. But he didn't want to lie to a preacher, either.

"I took them, knowingly, once—a couple of years ago. But I didn't like what they did to me."

Memories assailed him—demons dancing in a bonfire that looked just like something out of hell. So closely had that bonfire resembled his mental image of hell that it had scared the liquor he'd also consumed right out of him. He'd fallen to his knees right then and there, at the party, confessed his sins to Gott, and begged to be saved from eternal wrath.

"I gave them away," he went on. "Should've destroyed them, but I was a stupid teenager. Later, after the buggy accident, I took prescription drugs for the pain, but I got off them as quickly as I could." He wouldn't mention Sam's attempt to drug him. Not to Sam's daed. That would put him on the same level as Sam, and his accusations would probably be presumed false, as payback for the alleged lies.

"Hmmm." Preacher Samuel pulled on his beard, looking at him with concern. "You sure you're up for teaching, bu?"

"Positive." Though he still felt light-headed. The room was still weaving. Nausea still threatened.

David adjusted one of the crutches. He couldn't tell from the preacher's expression whether he believed David or whether he would go straight to the bishop and order David to be thrown out on his ear.

At least then he wouldn't have to teach feeling the way he did. But he'd also have nein way of supporting himself. He'd be back at square one. Without so much as a hard, too-short, uncomfortable cot for a bed. Despite its shortcomings, it beat the bishop's scratchy, mice-infested hay and old, ragged buggy blanket.

Not that he wasn't grateful. *Danki, Lord, for providing for my needs.*

"Your breakfast will be over straightaway." Rachel's daed headed toward the door.

At least David would get one last meal.

He cleared his throat. "Did you spend the nacht here with me?"

Preacher Samuel looked over his shoulder. "My frau thought you might have a concussion and said someone needed to look over you. For some reason, Rachel insisted it not be Sam. That left me."

That meant Rachel had probably seen him lying passed out in a heap on the floor. Or being carried like a bag of flour to his cot. Or....

David looked away, setting his mouth. He was tired of being made to look like a wimpy fool in front of her. He tried so hard to be strong, to be capable.

"Are you going to the bishop?" He had to know.

Preacher Samuel cocked an eyebrow. "If you are having epileptic fits and passing out, I should. If you are on drugs and overdosed, as my sohn claims, I should. If you are simply clumsy, as my frau believes, you need to be more careful. And if my sohn walloped you over the head with a fireplace poker, as Rachel insists—and as the evidence seems to support—then I have nein need. But you'll need to be much more watchful."

That little speech made David's mind throb. He filed the information away to dissect later, when his head didn't hurt so badly.

The preacher turned away. He strode across the schoolhaus, opened the door, then paused and looked back with a slight smile. "I must say, you have some interesting and revealing dreams." He shut the door behind him.

David stood there, his heart falling somewhere around his ankles. Had he cried out Rachel's name when he'd dreamed about their passionate kisses?

Chapter 13

Thursday morgen, while Mamm and the little girls did the early chores and fixed breakfast, Rachel and Greta tackled the ever-growing mountain of dirty clothes. They washed them and took them out to dry. Freeze-dry, really. The wind whipped at the garments as they hung them. Gut thing the store was closed on Thursdays. Daed didn't like Rachel driving the buggy in such strong winds. Too dangerous.

The schoolhaus door opened, and Daed came out, yawning. He mustn't have slept well, sitting in a chair all nacht. But then, Mamm had insisted he wake David every few hours due to his concussion. Rachel had offered to stay with David, but that idea had been shot down in a hurry with one stern look from Daed. Nein maidal should spend the nacht alone with a man. At least Sam hadn't blurted out that she and David had been tangled in each other's arms, kissing. Rachel had expected him to, especially after she'd accused him of hitting David over the head with the fireplace poker.

That had earned her a stern look, too. From both Daed and Sam.

Greta had wisely kept her mouth shut. The scene was probably too confrontational for her, with Rachel getting all emotional and Sam being overly defensive when Daed spoke with them. Perhaps that was why Greta had excused herself and gone up to the girls' bedroom, where Mary and Jenny were already asleep in their bunks. Greta had appeared to be asleep in Rachel's twin bed when Rachel had kum in with a pillow and blanket for making a bed on the floor. Rachel had slept there instead. So, they hadn't had a chance to talk about why Greta had been crying in the school bathroom. Or about Rachel's kissing David.

Ach, just thinking of those kisses…. Her stomach fluttered. He affected her a lot more than Obadiah ever had. She glanced toward the school again but didn't see any movement in the windows.

She turned her attention back to the laundry and picked up the next soaking-wet pair of pants. Daed's. Standing in a cold wind with wet laundry wasn't a gut time for serious discussion. Maybe Mamm would get sidetracked by quilting while Rachel and Greta worked on green tomato relish and made a couple green tomato pies, and would leave them alone awhile so they could talk.

Rachel darted another glance toward the school and saw Andy carrying David's breakfast tray across the street for Mary. She trotted along beside him, holding a lunch pail. Rachel forced her attention back to the clothesline. If only she had a reason to go over there. She could apologize for her too-forward actions…. On second thought, after what she'd done, it would be too awkward to face David. And she'd had witnesses! She pulled in a shuddery breath and reached for the last pair of pants.

Greta picked up the laundry basket and turned toward the haus. Rachel hurriedly clipped the pants to the line, then caught up with her.

"So, about what you saw last nacht…."

Greta's face reddened. "I don't think you need to worry too much about Obadiah seeing another girl. Not with you two kissing. How long have you known David, exactly?"

"We've written to each other for a long time. But in person? I first met him when he walked into the store four days ago."

"Four days." Greta shook her head. "I guess you know his heart, since you corresponded for a while."

"He's my best friend—other than you and Esther. Or was. I don't know how I'm going to face him after this."

"What do you mean, face him? He's the one who kissed you, ain't so?"

Rachel's face flamed. "I initiated it."

Greta's eyes widened. "Rachel, really? That sounds like something Lily would do."

"I know," Rachel moaned. "He's going to think the worst of me. And I can't avoid him. I need to take his dinner over to-nacht. He already told Mary nein, because she has a crush on him. I mean, he was nice about it, and I don't know if she understands, but his meaning was clear to me. What if he rejects me now?"

Greta gave an embarrassed laugh. "I don't think you have anything to worry about."

"I just don't know what to do."

Greta shrugged. "It's not so easy to ignore the big issues. Almost like having a horse standing in the kitchen nobody is talking about, ain't so? But perhaps that's what you'll need to do—let him make the next move."

Maybe that was gut advice. Though Rachel wasn't sure she could manage it. When she saw him, she'd probably blush so much, she'd burst into flames.

~

David had to increase his doses of pain medicine, but somehow he made it through the day. At least the scholars seemed to respect him. He had few issues with anyone, except one bu: William seemed easily distracted and intent on teasing the other buwe and girls seated near him. If this continued, David would need to talk with William and see if he could identify the problem.

David tried to concentrate on grading papers while Rachel's sisters and brothers swept the room and wiped the whiteboard. At long last, everyone left except for Andy. He brought in more wood and loaded the stove.

With the building blessedly quiet, David headed back to the half-bath, void of all his personal items, since it was shared with scholars, and hand-washed his face. Then he filled a mug with water and put it on the stove to heat while he went back to his room for his Bible and koffee tin. The pain in his ankle seemed to have diminished a little— or maybe it merely paled in comparison with his still-throbbing head.

The pile of letters he'd received from Rachel caught his attention. They sat on the floor next to his windup clock. Rachel's daed must've moved them. Had he read them, too?

David decided not to dwell on the possible violation of privacy. He was just glad he'd heeded the urge to write her. He'd found a new friend. A best friend. And maybe, if Gott willed, his future frau.

Though being a member of the same family as Sam didn't exactly appeal. Would they ever get past the enemy stage and become friends? That seemed doubtful.

He loved seeing Rachel in person, but he didn't like making a fool out of himself almost every day. And he missed the almost daily letters they had exchanged. Did she miss them, too?

He couldn't send her a letter without involving his scholars, since he'd have to send one of them out to the mailbox with his missive. Unless…what if he put one in the lunchbox when he sent it back?

Nein. That would depend on her being the one who cleaned it out.

At least she didn't know he struggled with inappropriate thoughts, dreaming things he shouldn't. His body heated at the mere memory of the passionate kisses he'd imagined.

If kissing her in real life was half as gut as in his dreams….

If he kept scaring her off, he'd never know.

And his wishful thinking…he'd even imagined her saying something about her boyfriend seeing another girl.

If only.

David sighed and left the letters where they lay. He picked up the Bible and the koffee tin, then turned back toward the schoolroom.

The door burst open, as if from a gust of wind. David set his things on the desk and started for the door, intending to shut it.

Rachel blew inside, carrying a paper plate in one hand, a bag in the other. "My daed and brothers are coming over to install a railing on the steps and shelves in your room. The bishop gave approval. And someone else is coming over with a rick of wood. Greta and I made green tomato pie, and I brought you a slice. Daed and my brothers will be over in just a minute. You do know sleet and freezing rain are in the forecast, right? One hundred percent chance. And there's to be a snowstorm after that. It is only October, ain't so? Or did I miss a month?"

"You're rambling." He smiled.

She snapped her mouth shut.

He studied her, noting the high pink in her cheeks. It could have been caused by the wind. "Why are you so bothered?"

She shook her head, mute.

Okay. Probably none of his business.

David glanced around, looking for a calendar. Being laid up, he'd lost track of time. It could be December, for all he knew.

She bumped the door shut with an intriguing move of her foot and hip, then started toward him. "Bethany came by with some things. She left them with me because she didn't want to interrupt school."

Bethany? He frowned, running the name through his memory banks. Then he nodded. "The bishop's dochter."

Rachel blinked. "You remember her?" A strange expression crossed her face. Jealousy?

He reached for the bag. He could carry that while using a crutch. She relinquished it and followed him to the desk, where she set the slice of pie. He peeked inside the bag, and Rachel leaned over to peer in. Too close. He breathed in the scent of vanilla mixed with other miscellaneous spices that had haunted his dreams. From her baking, maybe? A strand of hair escaped the confines of her kapp. He resisted the urge to tuck it back in.

Don't pay attention to her.

Easier said than done. He wanted to tug her into his arms and recreate his dreams.

They'd known each other only four days—not counting the months they'd written. She'd likely never allow a man to be so forward.

Gott, help me.

He forced his attention to the contents of the bag. Another small tin of koffee, a box of tea bags, a packet of hot chocolate with marshmallows, and another mug. There was also a packet of unopened pens and a couple of large Ziploc baggies. One was stuffed with what appeared to be beef jerky, the other with trail mix. He smiled. "What a thoughtful gift."

Rachel frowned. "I should've thought of all that."

David shrugged. "It was gut she did. She invited me to a frolic the first nacht I was here. I turned her down, since I was going to dinner at your haus." And that was probably where all the trouble had begun. He'd managed to get on Sam's bad side, started lusting after Rachel, and ended up injured—multiple times. "In hindsight, I probably should've accepted."

A hurt expression crossed Rachel's face. "There'll be others, when you're better. Maybe you could go with Sam and me to singing Sunday nacht. We used to give Esther rides, though she and I usually rode home with our beaus, freeing Sam free to take his girl home."

Sam had a girl? Huh. A lot about Sam didn't make sense. And David preferred not to think of him.

"I'd rather not catch a ride with Sa—you two, if you don't mind."

Another pained look contorted her features. "We don't have a spare courting buggy," Rachel said. "Or I'm sure Daed would let you use it."

David shrugged again. "I'm not courting anyone." Just as well. He looked down at his sprained ankle. "Won't be for some time." He picked up the bag and carried it back to his room, leaving it on his bed. He heard footfalls on the front porch, indicating that her daed and brothers had arrived. A railing would be helpful. He turned back to Rachel. "As much as I'd like you to stay, you'd better go before you get stuck here awhile."

"We do have a couple of regular buggies. Maybe you could borrow one of them," she said, dismissing his comment. "You can't stay hidden in here all the time. People will start thinking you're a hermit."

"I'm not hiding, and I'm not a hermit. But I *am* hausbound for now. I'll get to know everyone eventually." If he was allowed to stay around that long.

Rachel studied him a moment. She opened her mouth, then shut it. Her gaze lowered to his lips.

His pulse accelerated. He forced himself to look away, to tamp down the desire that quickly fought its way to the surface of his thoughts. *Gott, help. Please.* He made his way to the desk and sat in his chair.

"Don't you have anything to say?" Rachel's voice had a needy tone.

Why would she ask that? He looked at her in confusion. She didn't meet his gaze. Jah, he had plenty to say. But…. He ran his finger over his Bible. First, he needed to make things right in his heart, in his mind. "Nein, not really. The pie looks gut. Danki."

Disappointment clouded her eyes. "Nothing? Really? About anything?"

Should he have something specific to say? He shrugged again and picked up the plate. "Danki for the pie." He took a bite.

Her lips parted in a show of confusion and hurt.

What did she want him to do? Confess his dreams, after her brother had hit him—knocked him out cold—with a fireplace poker? That still made no sense to David. Seemed he would've seen Sam grab it and would have made some effort to protect himself. He rubbed his hand over the lump on the back of his head.

Rachel flinched.

If Sam had hit him, how would Rachel know? David didn't remember her being there. But then, he didn't remember much of anything from last nacht.

Other than in his dreams. His face heated, and he frowned.

Had Rachel's daed told her about whatever David had spoken in his oblivious state of sleep?

⌒

Rachel tried to force her hurt feelings into a dark spot in her heart. Was she deficient in some way? Not gut enough? She'd definitely been too bold, kissing him like that. It'd probably given him the wrong idea about the kind of girl she was, and now he wanted nothing to do with her. If only she could do yesterday over again.

She'd acted like Lily. *Ach, Lord. Help me not to end up like that.* A maidal all respectable men avoided.

That would explain his cool response. Still, after their passionate kisses, she'd expected him to have something to say. A special look or touch. Something.

Her eyes burned with tears, and she blinked them away.

David polished off the pie and laid the fork on the edge of the plate. "Sur gut, Rachel. Danki again."

She missed her friend. If only she knew how to repair the damage she'd accidentally done. Her shoulders slumped. "I suppose I should go home and fix supper."

David nodded and reached for his Bible. He opened it and started thumbing through the pages. "I need to focus on Bible reading and prayer."

He wanted her to go? He wouldn't try to stop her? "We're having meat loaf, creamed spinach, and baked potatoes."

An eyebrow rose. "Sounds gut."

Pounding began outside as someone wielded a hammer. What, he wasn't even going to say how much he'd enjoy eating dinner with her?

"Look, if I'm not gut enough, just say so. It's not as if I had a whole lot of experience. Just Obadiah. And you." She grabbed the paper plate and the fork.

David's other eyebrow rose, and he looked up at her. "What *are* you talking about?" His confused frown seemed genuine. The nerve.

She gave him what she hoped was a withering stare, then opened the fireplace door, tossed the empty paper plate inside, and slammed it shut.

How could he pretend nothing had happened? She stalked toward the door.

"I'm not sure exactly what's going on, but you...confuse me. I need to figure some things out."

"*I* confuse *you?*" Rachel paused and whirled around, hands on her hips. "How so?"

David sighed, closed the Bible, and stood. "Look. I don't know what to say. It's too soon to admit my feelings for you. Not to mention, you have a beau—"

"I told you, I think he's seeing another girl."

He stilled. "I thought I dreamed that." He didn't reach for his crutches. Nor did he move. But his gaze softened as he looked at her. "Does that mean I didn't imagine the other part?"

"Probably not." Her face heated. "I'm sorry. I shouldn't have done that." She looked down. He couldn't remember? He'd been hurt worse than she'd thought. At least he wasn't deliberately ignoring her.

"Nein, you shouldn't have. Unless you meant it. And if you did, then you should write Obadiah and make sure it's over before we go any further."

"You mean, ask him if we're finished?"

"Or break up with him."

Rachel frowned. "Ach."

David's chest rose and fell. "That's only if you choose to. Either way...." A slight smile played on his lips. "Since I didn't imagine those steamy kisses, this is a very dangerous attraction we've got going here. And I'm smart enough to recognize a fork in the path when I reach it. I'm going to take the high road."

Ach, those steamy kisses.... Maybe she wasn't as inexperienced as she'd thought. And she wasn't alone in wanting to relive that moment over and over in her mind. And in real life. She moved toward him.

But, wait. The high road?

She didn't like the high road very much. And the implication was that their relationship—whatever it was—would be put on hold until she had ended her relationship with Obadiah. She sucked in a breath and backed up. "I'm sorry. So sorry." Whether she was speaking of her unwillingness to break up with Obadiah, and was, by default, breaking up with David, or whether she was referring to her inability to stop kissing him the previous night, even she didn't know.

She spun on her heel and hurried the rest of the way to the door.

"Jah, so am I," David whispered.

Rachel blinked back tears as she marched down the steps, flanked on either side by her daed and brothers installing the railings. Swallowed hard as she crossed the road.

He was leaving it up to her to figure out what she wanted.

How was she supposed to know? Either direction would change the dynamics of her relationship with so many people.

And her feelings for David were such a tangle. Should she give up a sure thing for something that might be a mere whim?

Chapter 14

David gazed out the window as Rachel staggered across the road, looking forlorn. He frowned, running his finger across the cover of his Bible again, then forced himself to look away. He reached for the crutches, stood, and made his way toward the school-haus door. The pounding of hammers ceased when he opened it.

Preacher Samuel set down his hammer on the middle step, then reached for the railing and gave it a shake. It didn't move. He tried again with the other side. It, too, remained steady. He looked up at David with a grin. "Think you can handle these now, David?"

"Let me give it a try." After Preacher Samuel grabbed the hammer, David leaned his crutches against the wall and carefully made his way down the steps. It'd be gut to have one less handicap to deal with. When he reached the bottom, he grinned. "I should be able to kum to your haus for dinner now."

Sam scowled as he pushed a wheelbarrow full of wood to the bottom of the stairs. "Great," he muttered sarcastically.

"Jah, great." But David was being earnest. The beginnings of a smile tickled his lips. Another gut thing—he wouldn't be alone with Rachel, and, with Gott helping him, he might be able to get his sinful desires tucked away. Not to mention, he'd get to know the rest of her family and no longer be the hermit she'd accused him of being. He might also earn the support of her daed and maybe figure out how to mend fences with Sam—for the sake of a future with Rachel.

"Let's get started on the shelves you asked for." Preacher Samuel nodded toward his haus. "Andy and Luther, go on home and get started on the chores. Eli, you tell your mamm that David will be coming for supper, then go help your brothers. Sam, you help me with the shelves."

David made his way back up the stairs. It'd been easier going down.

Preacher Samuel led the way to the small room where David slept. Sam followed his daed carrying a box filled with wood, already cut into triangles, and some other supplies.

"Won't be space for all three of us in here, teacher." Sam dismissed him with set lips and a hard, angry glare. "And I'm helping, since you're..."—his gaze skimmed David from head to toe, and he sneered—"disabled."

Ouch. But that was about the truth of it. David forced his anger into submission, put what he hoped was a pleasant look on his face, and nodded. "All right. I have lessons to prepare and papers to grade, anyway." He started to leave the room, then hesitated and looked back, worried about his belongings, however meager. About Sam sabotaging his letters from Rachel. At least he wouldn't be without supervision. When both men looked at him, eyebrows raised, David floundered for a valid excuse. "Preacher Samuel, I'd like a word with you when you finish, if there's time before dinner."

"Jah, we'll talk." He didn't look back at David. "Maybe after dinner would be better. I'll accompany you back to the schoolhaus, then we can sit and talk."

Sam's gaze speared him. David turned around and left the room. He sat at the desk and reached for his Bible. Maybe he should study some Scriptures on loving your enemies and doing gut to those who hated you before he moved on to the topic of not looking lustfully at a woman.

Or maybe he should pray first. Four days in Jamesport had already taught him that he was nowhere near the man he ought to be. Gott had a lot of work to do—and a lot of sinful thoughts to forgive.

⌒

Rachel finished setting the table, then checked the potatoes baking in the woodstove. They were done, so she grabbed the tongs from the countertop and lifted the foil-wrapped vegetables from the hot coals, put them in a white serving dish, and carried them to the table. Spinach simmered in a kettle on the stovetop, and the meat loaf waited on the warming shelf at the back.

The door opened, and Daed, Sam, and David filed inside. Rachel blinked at David. Eli had yelled something about David joining them when he'd stuck his head in the door earlier, but she was still surprised. She hadn't really expected him to kum.

"Where's your mamm?" Daed looked around.

Rachel glanced at the ceiling. "Upstairs. Greta and I started some boppli quilts as gifts for our friends, but...." She shrugged.

"Your mamm and quilts," Daed said with a grin. "She took over, ain't so?"

Rachel smiled in answer.

Daed headed for the stairs and went up.

David took off his one shoe. Sam started to untie his laces but stopped. "Got plans tonight, Rachel." He pulled out his pocket watch and glanced at it. "Figured it was about five. I'm meeting someone at six. Need to make a quick phone call. I'll ring the dinner bell on my way back in."

David stood quietly behind Sam, not looking at Rachel. When her brother moved out of the way and disappeared out the door, he shuffled over to the sink to wash up.

Rachel's heart ached as she studied David from behind. Did it matter so much that she knew where she and Obadiah stood before she began a relationship with David? As far as she was concerned, if Obadiah had been taking another girl home, then she had the right to explore the possibility of a new relationship. Why did David have to insist on her being completely free?

Because he wanted to seriously court her? Her stomach fluttered.

Maybe breaking up with Obadiah would ease Sam's spiteful attitude toward David.

But Obadiah had spoken of specific plans for their future. David had nein plans. *Just what Gott wants.* How could a man marry and care for a frau and kinner with nothing but faith?

Well, Gott had taken care of David so far. And He would continue doing so. Which made David safer than a man who didn't follow Gott.

If only she had the relationship with Gott that David seemed to have.

She watched David as he dried his hands and turned toward the table. He glanced at her with a nod, but his eyes didn't meet hers. It was as if she were nobody special.

Nobody. Having kissed as they had, she was hardly nobody. But his standards were strict. He was taking the "high road." She sighed. David was a much better person than she.

Impossibly so. She'd never measure up.

Never.

Shaking her head, she reached for the meat loaf. She hadn't expected it to be as hot as it was. The sides of the metal pan burned her hands. She yipped and jerked back, staring down at the marks already reddening her palms.

Strong hands grasped her shoulders, searing her skin through the material of her dress. David steered her over to the sink, then reached around her and turned on the cold water. "Keep your hands under there for a few minutes. I'll get the meat loaf. Do you want it on the platter?" He didn't wait for an answer but discarded the crutches and picked up two oven mitts. Then he lifted the metal baking pan and carried it a couple of hobbling steps over to the counter where an empty platter waited. He hesitated, frowning. "I suppose I should drain the juices first."

"I'll get it." Rachel's voice caught. "I'll be okay. You need to use the crutches."

"My ankle is a little better." David aimed a glance in her direction. "And I'm not totally helpless in the kitchen. Mamm taught me the basics, just in case. I can set the table, make sandwiches...."

"We're not having sandwiches to-nacht. But you'll probably have leftover meat loaf sandwiches tomorrow."

"I think I can figure out how to drain the meat. You keep your hands under the cold water. Either that or tell me where the salve is, and I'll doctor your burns."

Rachel shut her eyes, mostly to keep the tears at bay. "Just inside the laundry room. There's a shoe box on the shelf. It's labeled."

"Just let me put this back on the stove to keep warm, then."

Rachel kept her eyes closed. A few seconds later, she heard the laundry door open. "Found it." The door closed with a slight thud, and then his warm, firm chest brushed against her arm as he leaned over and turned off the water. He grasped her hands with the soft, worn hand towel. "Kum, now."

Rachel opened her eyes as he pulled his hands away, leaving her feeling oddly bereft. He had draped the towel over her hands like a sheet.

"Pat them dry," he instructed her. "Don't rub."

Although she knew what to do, it was nice of him to remind her. Once her hands were dry, she followed him over to the table. He pulled out a chair for her, and she dropped into it. He sat across from her, opened the box of medical supplies, and took out the salve. Then he reached for her right hand.

Sparks shot through her at his light touch, seeming to relieve the sting of her burns. He carefully bandaged her hand, then reached for her left one.

Ach, she loved David's touch. And if she broke up with Obadiah, she could experience it more, and under pleasanter circumstances. She gave herself a silent reproach and then searched for a topic to distract her from the combination of pain and the tempting touch of David's hands on hers. But there was only one topic standing between them.

"What do I say to him?"

He'd probably noticed the huskiness in her voice. Probably knew he took her breath away.

He remained silent for a long, seemingly endless moment. Finally, he looked up, his eyes smoldering. "It's not that hard. Tell him you found your soul mate and you need to be free to pursue the relationship."

"My soul mate?"

Having finished bandaging her hands, he returned the supplies to the box. "Jah. Soul mate. Heartthrob. Love of your life. Choose your own term." He held her gaze for a moment, then looked down and closed the box lid as footfalls sounded on the inside stairs. Seconds later, boots clomped up the porch steps. David got to his feet—well, his gut foot, and the stocking-covered toes of the other—and hobbled across the room to return the medical supplies to the laundry shelf.

Just then, the dinner bell rang. The herd would rush inside within seconds.

David wasn't using the crutches. She watched his not-quite-steady gait as he neared the laundry room. "Is your ankle that much better?" She stood and followed him.

David set the box on the shelf, closed the door, and reached for the pot holders once more. "Jah, it's better. Not perfect, but getting there. Hurts when I put weight on it."

"You still need to stay off of it." Probably. She wasn't sure, but if it hurt, then it seemed he should. She took the pot holders from him. "I'll take care of the meat loaf. You go sit down."

"I'll use the crutches outside for a while yet. The ankle is weak. I should probably wrap it for support, but…." He shrugged and hobbled to the table as the door opened and Sam came inside, followed by a rush of younger brothers, all of whom kicked off their shoes, then pushed and shoved, vying for a spot at the sink.

Mamm and Daed came into the room, followed by Mary and Jenny. Greta had gone home when Rachel had started the supper preparations. Mary grinned when she saw David. "You really are better! I thought your walking had improved at school. You haven't been using the crutches as much."

Mamm gave him a concerned frown. "You need to use them for a while longer. Just because you think you're better doesn't mean you really are."

David nodded and retrieved his crutches. "Don't worry. I won't do anything foolish."

"That's debatable," Sam muttered.

Daed frowned. "Stop it, Sam. Enough already."

Sam didn't say anything more, but Rachel caught the hateful glare he aimed in David's direction.

Once everyone was seated around the table, Daed bowed his head for the silent prayer. After a moment, Rachel followed his lead. She didn't think she could tell Obadiah she'd found her soul mate. And "heartthrob"? She'd never even heard that term. Love of her life...is that what David was? Really? Or was it all sinful? She snuck a peek at him. "Lust of the eyes," the preachers called it.

He was gut-looking. Strong. Capable. Confident. She could list positive attributes all day long. And his kisses.... Her stomach clenched. Wow, that man could kiss. She wondered whom he'd practiced on. Probably Cathy.

A rush of jealousy surged through her.

Silverware clanged against dishes as the dishes of food started their rounds. And she hadn't prayed yet. David wasn't gut for her prayer life.

Danki, Gott. That would have to suffice. She opened her eyes and reached inside the serving bowl beside her for a baked potato before passing it to Mary.

Mary didn't notice. She was staring at David, looking completely enraptured.

David had turned Mary down, yet he had done it so nicely that she didn't seem to have fully received the message.

Kum right down to it, he'd turned Rachel down, too. He told her that she needed to be sure her relationship with Obadiah was over. But, unlike Mary's rejection, hers had been sweetened by the hint of something more to kum.

She pictured herself taking out a pen and a piece of plain white lined notebook paper. In her mind, she began to compose the letter she would write.

Dear Obadiah,

I've met someone new. Well, not really new; I've actually known him awhile, just not in person. And since you've been taking someone else home from singing, I'm wondering if we're calling our relationship quits?

Someone slapped her arm. "What happened to your hands?"

She answered without thought, watching David as he helped himself to a slice of meat loaf.

Someone poked her in the ribs.

Rachel blinked and realized she'd been holding the bowl of spinach while staring, open-mouthed, at David. Probably mirroring her sister's look of fascination.

The heat of a blush warmed her face as she spooned a helping of the green leafy vegetables onto her plate, then passed the bowl to Mary.

She wouldn't look at him again during this meal.

But that was easier said than done, given that he was sitting right across the table, talking with her family members, laughing at some of their comments. He fit right in, while both she and Mary sat in infatuated silence, staring at the man of their dreams.

Pathetic.

Maybe she could walk him home afterward.

She straightened, smiled, and took a bite of food. Jah, that was what she'd do. Offer to walk him home.

Her stomach fluttered as a shiver worked through her.

Maybe, if she locked the schoolhaus door so they wouldn't be interrupted, they could recreate that passionate moment....

～

David leaned back in his chair and tried not to watch Rachel while she and her sisters bustled around the kitchen, cleaning up after supper. He'd also attempted to ignore how she and Mary had stared at him throughout the meal, but he'd failed miserably where Rachel was concerned.

Elsie had made a hasty return to her quilting, saying she needed to finish the project for someone's boppli gift, and Preacher Samuel was enjoying another slice of pie.

"I'm going out to meet some friends," Sam yelled as he ran out the door. A few minutes later, a beat-up car drove out from behind the barn.

David hadn't realized Sam drove a motorized vehicle. He felt a stab of envy. What would it be like to drive a car? It would probably be safer than a closed buggy. Would Sam teach him?

Rachel had told him Sam had been in a car accident and had needed to use the crutches awhile. The thought was quickly followed by a flashback of a car with Missouri tags, crashed head-on against a tree on a riverbank in Pennsylvania. The unseeing eyes of the Amish bu behind the wheel.

David bolted to his feet and reached for his crutches. "I need to go."

Rachel turned to him. "Wait a minute. I'll walk you home."

"Nein, it's okay. I...uh, your daed and I are going to have a talk."

Rachel's eyes widened. "Then I'll see you at breakfast?"

"Um...nein. We'll keep breakfast as it's been. I'll eat at the school." He couldn't start the day by seeing Rachel. Ending the day with her was enough to disrupt his sleep.

Preacher Samuel stood, grabbed a couple cookies from the jar, and headed for the door. He set the cookies on the windowsill while he slipped his shoes on.

David followed suit, except he still wore only one shoe. The swelling in his sprained ankle had gone down considerably, though, so he could probably resume wearing his other shoe.

They crossed the street in silence, except for the crunching of the cookies the older man ate. David opened the door to the schoolhaus and stepped inside, then stopped and stared.

The place had been trashed. The scholars' desks were upturned, the papers from his desk were scattered all over the floor, and his Bible had been thrown across the room, now lying at a weird angle on the floor, the pages creased beyond fixing. He leaned the crutches against the wall, snatched up his Bible, and pressed it to his chest.

Across the whiteboard in angry, black slashes, someone had scrawled, "Go home, loser."

Clenching his jaw, David headed to his room. It'd been ransacked, too. The bedding had been thrown off the cot; his shampoo bottle had been opened and dumped in a giant puddle. Toothpaste had been squirted across the floor and on the walls. And his letters from Rachel were gone.

Unless they were under the blankets littering the floor.

He heard a thud, presumably as Preacher Samuel righted a desk in the classroom.

He put his Bible on one of the shelves Preacher Samuel and Sam had installed earlier that evening. Shutting his eyes, he prayed, *Gott, who would've done this?*

But he knew. Beyond the shadow of a doubt.

David's head throbbed. He reached for the bottle of pain pills, somehow left undisturbed on the chair. He unscrewed the lid, shook out one pill, and then hesitated. This was not the same type of pill he'd taken earlier that day. Someone had made an exchange. Again.

He returned the pill to the bottle, put the lid back on, and pocketed it. Then he lifted the blankets.

And there, marred with a muddy shoe print, and badly ripped, were his precious letters. His eyes burned.

There was another thud from the main room.

He needed to get out there and help. But first, he picked up the letters, hugged them to his chest, and set them on the shelf next to his Bible. His two most valuable possessions—torn, dirty, and mutilated.

With a sigh, he went back into the classroom. Preacher Samuel's mouth was set in a grim line as he looked up. "Mess back there, too?"

"Jah." Balancing on one crutch, David started picking up papers, putting them in a giant stack. Homework, seatwork, pop quizzes, a letter home, and his personal Bible study. He'd sort them later.

"What was it you wanted to talk about?" Preacher Samuel thumped another desk upright.

David swallowed. He never should've mentioned anything about a talk. He'd thought that some accountability might be gut.

And it probably would be.

He dropped the stack of papers on his desk, then went for the nearest scholar's desk and turned it upright. "Your dochter Rachel."

Silence.

For a second, he was tempted to glance at the older man to see if he'd heard. But maybe it would be better if he didn't.

David shrugged. "I'm sure you're aware that I like—am fond of— love her."

No answer, other than another thud.

This was too awkward.

David straightened another desk. "I struggle with my thoughts. Especially since she's spoken for. I've been praying…a lot."

"And you're telling me this because…?" There was a mixture of confusion and amusement in the older man's voice.

David swallowed. "Because I need accountability. I need someone to lift me in prayer."

Another desk thumped upright.

A non-answer.

David straightened the last desk, then headed for the whiteboard. *Go home, loser.* He stared at the masculine scrawl for a second. A minute. An hour. An eternity.

Maybe he should follow the advice. His family would welcome him. He could go back to his old job, working in a greenhaus by day, weaving baskets or tying flies by night to sell to tourists at craft shows.

He had money in the bank in Pennsylvania that he could use to start his own greenhaus, if he chose to—except that he had nein land, because his parents had sold the farm. Because he'd foolishly left—had gone to Seymour and gotten in an accident.

He might've been saved beside a bonfire years before, but he'd drawn significantly closer to Gott because of that accident.

He might be able to find land.

But he'd lose Rachel.

Not that he had her.

All he had was hope. And a vicious enemy. His vision blurred.

A heavy hand rested on his shoulder. Squeezed. Then pulled away. Preacher Samuel picked up the eraser, and the words disappeared from the whiteboard with a couple swipes of his arm.

David shoved his hands in his pockets. His fingers hit something hard, then closed around it. Ach, the pain pills. He pulled them out and held them up for Rachel's daed to see.

"Rachel bought a new bottle. But the person who was here...." He wouldn't accuse Sam. "Look at the picture on the bottle. Then open it up and look at what's inside."

Preacher Samuel took the bottle from him and did so, letting out a long whistle. He closed the cap and slid the bottle into his pocket. "I'll see about getting you a key so you can lock the door when you leave."

"Danki."

"And I appreciate your sharing your struggles. Obadiah started courting her when they were both sixteen. They are all the other knows. Never courted, or was courted by, anyone else." He raised one shoulder, then lowered it. "Does absence make the heart grow fonder? Or is this a case of 'out of sight, out of mind'? I don't know. Rachel struggles. Especially since he rarely calls. Never writes."

"He writes his parents."

"And there you go." The preacher shrugged again. "I'll pray for you." He patted David's shoulder. "Let's go clean up your room."

David shook his head. "It's okay. I can do it."

It hurt that Rachel's brother thought so little of him that he would stoop so low—planting illegal drugs on him, striking him with a fireplace poker, and now vandalizing the schoolhaus. What had he done to make Sam so angry? It couldn't be merely his interest in Rachel, or Preacher Samuel wouldn't have reacted so calmly to David's confession.

His face hurt from the effort required to keep his emotions at bay. To act normal, and not give in to the depression that threatened.

Whistling, Preacher Samuel headed for the smaller room, despite David's insistence that he could manage on his own. "Get the cleaning supplies from the closet. I'll start making your bed."

He bent, picked up the shampoo bottle, and set it upright on a shelf. Then he reached for the tube of toothpaste.

"Those came from your haus," David said. "I'll have to replace your supply." He tried to force his jaw to unclench as he went to get the cleaning supplies. A few minutes later, he returned with a bucket full of water with a squirt of a product from a clear plastic bottle marked "Use to scrub the floor" that had tickled his nose and made him sneeze.

When the room was clean and the bed made, the preacher started for the door but stopped when he reached David. He put a hand to his shoulder again and squeezed, but this time, he didn't let go. David forced himself out of his numbing defeatism enough to turn and look at the preacher.

"You wrote her every day when you didn't even know her. I think you fell in love with the Rachel you knew on paper, and you moved up here on a whim to get to know her in person."

It hadn't been a whim. He'd believed Gott was calling him, leading him, to move here. Bishop Sol had believed the same thing. But now he felt the need to pray for confirmation, since he'd met with so much opposition. Maybe he'd ask Josh Yoder to pray with him.

"What I know of you shows extraordinary courage and confidence. I would be proud to call you sohn. And I will pray for you, as I said."

"Appreciate it." David swallowed the lump in his throat. He struggled to absorb the acceptance and peace he saw in the preacher's eyes.

"My dochter would be a fool to turn you away." Preacher Samuel released his shoulder with a pat. "She let me read her letters to you. And yours to her, up until her feelings started changing. Then she hoarded the notes, as if they were too precious to share. I think she loves you, too."

David's heart pounded. Her family had recognized the change?

"And maybe sometime soon, she'll kum to realize it. If you want Rachel, now is not the time to give up, tuck your tail between your legs, and run home." Preacher Samuel turned and walked toward the door.

Ah, the hope, the beginnings of a confirmation, that maybe—just maybe—Gott had been behind it, after all. David needed to pray and continue to seek His face. His will. He moved a few steps toward his room to retrieve his Bible.

"Then again, maybe you should," came the preacher's voice, "before he decides 'an eye for an eye, a tooth for a tooth,' and—not to add to Scripture, but…a life for a life."

Chapter 15

Dear Obadiah,

I went to your parents' haus for dinner....

Rachel crumpled the paper and tossed it in the trash can. The tone was too cold, too accusatory.

Dear Obadiah,

Why don't you call me? I miss you....

She crushed this second attempt into a ball and threw it so hard, it bounced off the far wall of her bedroom. That line conveyed frustration at his lack of attention—and made her sound like a big boppli.

Obadiah,

I want to end our relationship. I've met another man.

She stared at the words. Too short. Too abrupt. She threw that one away with the others.

If only she could remember the letter she'd started composing in her mind. She tossed the pen on the desk and walked over to the window to stare across the street. Daed had gone over to the school with David, and as far as she knew, he hadn't returned yet. What were they talking about?

David wouldn't be discussing her, would he? Telling Daed about her bad judgment in kissing him the way she had? Confessing that she'd tried to flirt—and failed?

Though, the way he'd responded, maybe he had as much to hide as she did.

Ach, that was vain, thinking it was all about her. About them. David might want to know about the pay he could expect as a teacher, or to discuss transferring his membership to the local community, or to ask about buying a horse and buggy.

Or maybe he wanted to tell Daed about Sam's hitting him, drugging him, running him down....

David seemed above all that.

But her own brother! What did Sam have against him?

She wanted to march over there and listen in. In fact, why didn't she? She could use the excuse of taking something to David. But a glance around her room didn't identify anything he might like. A book? The only thing she'd seen him reading so far had been his Bible and the school textbooks. An old copy of *The Budget*? Nein. They used those to start fires in the woodstove.

Rachel sighed, then sat on her bed again. Picked up another sheet of paper.

Dear David,...

Wait. She was supposed to write Obadiah and define their relationship. It seemed kind of silly to write David when he was right across the street.

But she missed writing him. And he was so much easier to write to than Obadiah.

> *How do you like living here? It's strange to be able to look out my bedroom window and see you moving around the schoolhaus. I'm watching you right now as you carry something across the room....*

She filled two pages, front and back, then laid them aside and picked up another sheet of paper.

Dear Obadiah,

> *I recently went to your parents' haus, and they shared your latest letter with me. Most of it, anyway. Your mamm quit reading where you said something about taking someone home—female, I assume, since your mamm acted very strange afterward and sent me on my way pretty quick.*

I'd already been reconsidering our relationship. There's a man who recently moved to the area, and he fascinates me. I'd like to get to know him.

So, I guess that if you are seeing someone else, and I want to do the same, maybe we should take a break.

She hesitated, running her fingertips over her lips, remembering the way David had kissed her. Hungrily. Passionately. As if he couldn't get enough.

Her pulse increased.

It's been nice getting to know you, Obadiah. And I do miss you. But I want to end the relationship. I'll take the gifts you gave me back to your mamm sometime.

Rachel

That would have to do. She reached for two envelopes addressed them both and affixed a stamp to Obadiah's, slid the letters inside, and then got up. She would walk Obadiah's letter out to the mailbox right now, before she lost her courage. She opened her bedroom door and smiled when she heard Daed say something to someone downstairs. He had kum home. Seconds later, she heard the door open and shut as he left to go to the barn.

Rachel hurried downstairs, slipped her shoes on, and scampered out to the mailbox. Then she ran across the street. She didn't knock; she just stepped inside the school, then shut and locked the door, even though Sam wasn't around.

David wasn't at his desk. She noticed movement in the small bedroom. She shouldn't go back there. Too inappropriate.

She glanced at the open window shades. Should she pull them shut?

David must've heard her, because he appeared in the doorway of his room. He moved stiffly, his hands clenched at his sides, as if he was wary of whoever might have entered.

"Rachel?" His suspenders hung down, and his shirt was unpinned, hanging open and offering a tantalizing glimpse of his muscular bare chest.

Her heart pounded.

David's fingers closed around the edges of his shirt, and he yanked them closed. "I'm sorry. Didn't know you planned to kum over." He secured his shirt with a couple pins, then pulled up his suspenders. "I spilled dirty water on my other clothes."

"I…I'll take them home and wash them."

"What brings you by?" He moved the rest of the way into the classroom and sat on the edge of his desk.

She walked closer until she stood in front of him. "Where'd you learn to kiss like that?"

⌒

"What?" David blinked. "Where did that kum from?"

Rachel's face flamed red. "Ach, I didn't mean to say that. I meant…what were you and Daed talking about?"

"Ah, you're curious." David smiled. "What if I won't tell you?"

"So it was about me?" Rachel's hands went to her hips.

He looked away. "Your name might've kum up. But it wasn't all about you. It was about me and some issues I'm struggling with." And while her daed had seemed supportive of the idea of his eventually courting Rachel, he'd also given him more things to pray about.

But now was not the time to mull that over.

"I didn't mean to ask that, either. I wanted to tell you I wrote Obadiah. I told him I wanted a break. I think. I mean, I really don't remember what I said, exactly. Something like, 'Since you're seeing another girl, I'd like to get to know another bu.' I shouldn't have kum over here. Maybe I should go. Something has me distracted." Her gaze lowered to his mouth and descended to his chest before she jerked her head up and started to turn.

David's hand shot forward almost without his volition and closed around her wrist. "Wait. You did?"

She stilled. "Jah. It's in the mailbox." She looked down at his hand.

He released her. "Gut. Let me know when he responds."

She glanced up at him. "*When* he responds? What makes you think he will?"

David raised his eyebrows. "What if he has a reasonable excuse for taking another girl home, and he's still madly in love with you? In that case, your letter will take him by surprise, and he'll probably write back—or even call—right away. He might even kum home."

"He will?"

David chuckled. "I would."

"You would've kept in contact."

"I wouldn't have left you in the first place." Did she hear the huskiness in his voice? He stood and moved around to the other side of the desk, putting distance between them. Removing the temptation to pull her into his arms.

Well, not removing it, exactly, because it was still there. But at least he couldn't succumb to the temptation unless he jumped over the desk. And that would be difficult to do, given his healing ankle and still-throbbing head.

She studied him quizzically. Her lips twitched with disappointment. As if she'd wanted him to take her in his arms.

Ach, he wanted to. He wanted her.

She wasn't his to have.

And she probably never would be.

An eye for an eye, a tooth for a tooth.

David shut his eyes. Took a deep breath.

A life for a life?

He wouldn't think about that.

Couldn't.

He'd go insane.

∽

"*I wouldn't have left you.*"

He was so romantic, and with that husky voice....

Rachel stared at David, watching as his expression shuttered, shattering her tender thoughts. Had he remembered something unpleasant? Was that why he'd decided to put a huge desk between them?

Yet he had seemed happy to hear that she'd written to Obadiah. *Ending the certain relationship for the uncertainty of David.*

She knew she ought to go, but she really wanted answers. Even to those two questions she hadn't meant to ask. But she didn't know where to start.

Or perhaps she did. Sam had said he thought he knew David. He'd said he'd figured out from where, too. But he hadn't filled her in yet.

She inhaled slowly. "Sam says he knew you before you moved here. Can you tell me where you two met? And when?"

David met her gaze with eyes of unfathomable depth. A muscle ticked in his jaw. Finally, he shook his head. "Believe me, if I knew, I'd tell you. As far as I know, I never met him before coming here. But if we did cross paths, I must have made a very negative impression on him." He swallowed, his Adam's apple bobbing. "And I'm sorry for that."

"Me, too." She leaned closer. "How many girls did you say you courted?"

A smile flickered and died. "Ah, we're back to the kiss."

Her face heated. She looked down.

He reached across the desk, his fingers grazing her chin. He lifted it gently. "Look at me."

She swallowed hard, then obeyed.

"Cathy was the only girl I ever courted. We kissed, but not like that. I have taken other girls home but never kissed them. I've never kissed anyone, in that way, before you. To my knowledge."

She blinked. Wanted to believe him.

But he'd seemed such an expert.

And his last statement—"To my knowledge"—left a huge hole for doubt.

Chapter 16

David stared at the messy stack of papers on his desk—the ones that'd been trashed on the floor. He didn't know where to start. His temples pounded. He rubbed them. His eyes burned. Tension, no doubt. Not like he was under any stress.

At least Rachel had left—but not without asking questions he couldn't answer, even if he wanted to. If he and Sam had met, and had somehow become enemies because of that meeting, surely he would have remembered it. He hadn't thought there were any holes in his memory, but….

He sat down, propped up his throbbing leg, and scowled at the papers in front of him. They needed to be sorted, some of them graded, even though he wanted to toss the whole pile in the wood-stove and have a redo on the first several days of school. Maybe even start his whole stay in Jamesport anew. He lifted the top page. A first-year student's work—the spelling test he'd given a few hours earlier. *Dog. Cat. Hen.* Simple three- or four-letter words. He scanned the terms. All correct. He wrote a comment at the top and set the paper to the side, hoping the little girl wouldn't be too upset to find her page badly wrinkled and torn. Girls usually cared about appearances more than buwe.

At least her page was in better shape than his precious letters.

He couldn't allow himself to go there.

The next paper was half of the letter he'd written home. A jagged tear had ripped it right down the middle. It was also smudged. He'd have to start over. He crumpled it up to feed to the fire and tossed it at the box holding kindling and small logs. *Two points.*

He picked up the third page. Math problems, completed by an older student. William. He'd been a model scholar today, actually seeming to pay attention. Though he'd acted a bit depressed. David glanced over the paper, then marked it with a grade and a comment: *Praying for you.* Then he bowed his head and did just that.

Someone knocked at the door. It opened a crack.

David looked up with a frown, his muscles tensing. He really should've locked the door after Rachel had left.

Josh peeked around the corner. "Busy?"

David smiled, quite possibly for the first time that evening. "Grading papers. Kum in."

"Seems strange to knock before entering the school." Josh shut the door behind him. He grabbed a chair as he approached the desk. "My friend Viktor isn't back yet, but his onkel was at his farm when I stopped by. He said he'd be home this weekend."

David's smile faltered. "Okay." Why would Josh tell him this? Since he didn't know Viktor, his return meant nothing to him.

"He's a new Christian. Figured he'd want to join us for Bible study."

David lowered his gaze to the paper in front of him. But the writing on it blurred. Had he agreed to lead Bible study? He remembered Josh's mentioning it. He'd asked if it was approved....

David didn't think he'd agreed.

"So, what nacht would be gut for you? I'll clear it with Viktor, make sure it works for him." Josh reached for the candy jar on the edge of the desk and snagged a peppermint. "Love these things."

David twirled the pen in his fingers. He had so much on his plate—healing; trying to find his place in this new community; defending himself from a new enemy; adjusting to a temporary job and home. And Rachel. He couldn't forget her. With everything so unsettled, how could he possibly take on more?

Though, if he were truly called by Gott to preach, how could he not?

He swallowed. "Any day is fine. I'll be here." It wasn't like he had any semblance of a life. Being stranded in the same place wasn't what he'd had in mind when he'd kum here. He'd imagined courting his postcard pen pal, making friends....

Okay, to be fair, Gott had placed him right across the street from her haus. David saw her every day. And Gott sent friends to his door.

Maybe the first topic of discussion for the men's Bible study should be…. "Do you think Gott calls us away from our homes?" He hadn't meant to blurt it out like that, without preamble. He'd planned to make a mental note that he would scribble down later, to discuss when Josh returned with Viktor.

Josh had started to stand but returned to his seat. "Jah, I do. Just one example: He called Abraham to leave his home. Remember? Gott calls people out of the familiar all the time when He wants to teach them something new. He called me away so I could find Him. I believe He'd do the same for you."

Or *did* the same. But what was Gott trying to teach him? Did he really need to wonder? As many faults as he'd discovered since moving here, he had a lot to learn, for sure.

Not to mention the great adventure of learning to trust and follow Gott when in a foreign land, like Abraham.

He sighed.

Josh leaned forward. "May I pray for you?"

David looked up, startled. Humbled. "Jah, please." Then he hesitated. Should he do a mass dump of everything he needed prayer for? Or just accept the gesture and remain quiet? It wasn't as if he knew Josh well. Just because he was the first friend he'd made here didn't mean he could be trusted.

Then again, it didn't mean he couldn't be, either.

David pulled in a deep breath. "I'm not where I need to be." That statement summed up so many different things.

"Most of us aren't," Josh agreed.

Strange that Josh had picked up on the fact that he was referring to his spiritual state, not his physical location.

Josh shifted. Clasped his hands. Unclasped them, then straightened. Shifted again.

The silence stretched into the awkward stage.

Then his friend bowed his head and folded his hands. "Dear heavenly Father, my friend David needs your help. He's dealing with insecurity, with fear, and with many other issues I don't know, but You do. Put Your loving hand on David. Help him to feel the peace of Your presence. Guide him in every decision he makes, and do it all for Your glory. Amen."

David stared at Josh. He'd never heard a man pray out loud before. The Amish thought it was a prideful thing to do—pharisaical, even. But he rather liked hearing Josh pray.

Maybe Josh was called to be a preacher, too. Or a missionary.

When Rachel went to bed, she tossed and turned, hopelessly restless. Her brain wouldn't shut off, and she was hot, despite the freezing temperatures outside. She got up and opened the window a crack, just to let in some air, but Mary jumped out of bed with a huff and shut it. She liked it warm.

Rachel preferred to be able to breathe.

Sometime after mid-nacht, she carried her pillow and blanket downstairs, opened all the windows, and slept the rest of the nacht on the sofa in the living room.

She awoke to someone slamming the windows shut. "What's the point in having a fire going if you're going to freeze us out?" Sam turned and glared at her.

She sat up. "I was too hot to sleep."

"Thought you were too young to be having hot flashes like Mamm." Sam stomped past her and crouched by the woodstove. He opened the doors with a creak. "Gut. Still have embers."

Rachel stood and gathered her bedding. "Sorry."

"So, what's got you all hot and bothered?" Sam glanced over his shoulder.

Rachel shrugged. "Just a lot on my mind."

"If it's Obadiah, don't worry; I'm sure he has a reasonable excuse for allegedly cheating on you." He studied her a second, then narrowed his eyes. "Whereas you don't have a reasonable excuse for cheating on him."

Shame ate at her. He was right. She had flirted with David, and wrongfully kissed him, without being free of Obadiah. Nein wonder David had wanted to take the high road—leaving her alone—and told her that if she wanted a relationship with him, she had to be completely free. Had to choose between them.

Had to break up with Obadiah.

Well, that was done now. His letter had languished in the mailbox over-nacht, and the mailman would pick it up in mere hours. David's letter would go to the school, delivered via his lunchbox. Still seemed beyond silly to write a man who lived right across the road.

She carried her bedding upstairs and remade her bed, then dressed and prepared for the day before going back downstairs to start breakfast. Sausage and gravy with biscuits sounded gut.

Sam was in the kitchen now, building up the fire there. When finished, he put on his boots, coat, and gloves, slapped his black hat on his head, and walked out the door. A few minutes later, her other brothers trotted through on their way to the barn.

As Rachel reached for the flour canister, Mamm wandered in, filled the kettle with water, and set it on the stove, then started slicing bread for lunch sandwiches.

By the time Daed and the buwe came back inside, the table was set, breakfast prepared, and Mary had run a plate of food over to the school for David.

After the silent prayer, Daed looked up at Rachel. "I'll take you to work this morgen. I have a few visits to make, so I'll need the buggy. Luther will be taking the other one. He's doing a few odd jobs for Widow Fisher today."

Fifteen minutes later, the gelding pawed the fresh dusting of snow as if anxious to get on his way. He snorted when Rachel climbed into the buggy, her lunchbox clutched in her hand. She glanced toward the school as Daed clicked at the horse. A thin line of smoke rose from the chimney. She could see someone... David, probably, walking around.

Why did David—and all his uncertainty—touch her so deeply? Why was he the man who consumed all her thoughts?

She'd never thought about Obadiah this way, not even remotely, and he was the man she'd been planning to marry. Maybe it was because his kisses had never infused her with desire.

Admittedly, desire wasn't everything. She and the man she married would need to have more in common. A lot more. They'd have to be friends first. After all, they would be spending the rest of their lives together, raising kinner, making a home, and doing whatever else marriage entailed.

How would David support a family? By teaching school? He couldn't do that forever. He'd been hired only temporarily, until the regular teacher fully recovered from her injury. And he probably wasn't a farmer, with his leg problems. That was a physically strenuous job.

She probably shouldn't have broken up with Obadiah.

But then again, David had been a much closer friend—albeit by mail—than Obadiah had ever been in person. And now that they had a face-to-face relationship, he still felt very close. Still understood her better than anyone else.

Ugh. Why did life require so many decisions? So many unexpected curves in a road that she'd thought had been straight?

It wasn't fair.

⁓

When the last student exited the schoolhaus the following day, David closed the door behind him, then hurried back to his desk. He reached inside the top drawer for the unstamped envelope he'd discovered in his lunchbox hours earlier but hadn't had time to read yet. Another precious letter to add to his collection. He'd had a hard time waiting, but he'd forced himself to set the letter aside while he'd sat outside with the scholars, watching the little ones as they played on the swings and the older kinner as they engaged in a game of volleyball.

Now he set the letter on the desk, then reached for his mug, which he'd filled with hot water. He added a spoonful of instant koffee from the metal tin—it actually tasted gut, kind of like some of the expensive fancy koffees he'd had on the bus trip from Pennsylvania to Springfield, Missouri, and again on the trip from Springfield north almost to Iowa. "Just a stone's throw away," the driver had said. Someday, when he had access to a buggy, he'd invite Rachel on a picnic lunch and find out how far he'd have to throw that stone to land in Iowa. Maybe he and Rachel could picnic out of state.

He smiled as he swirled the spoon around in the cup, dissolving the koffee granules.

A movement caught his eye, and he glanced out the window. Preacher Samuel and Rachel drove down the road and turned into the Millers' driveway.

His smile widened. He took a sip of his koffee, then reached for the letter.

She'd written him. She must've missed their daily correspondence as much as he had.

He slit the envelope open with his pocketknife and pulled out the single page. Unfolded it.

Dear Obadiah,…

What? David's smile faded as he scanned the note. He reached for the envelope and glanced at it. Definitely addressed to him. Why had Rachel sent it to him instead of Obadiah?

Or maybe she'd copied it, so he'd know what she'd said.

> *There's a man who recently moved to the area, and he fasci-*
> *nates me. I'd like to get to know him.*

His gaze lingered on the two lines near the end. *Fascinate*. That'd been on the vocabulary quiz he'd given the older kinner today. *To draw irresistibly the attention and interest of (someone).*

He *fascinated* her. The notion warmed him almost as much as the delicious koffee.

He glanced out the window again.

Rachel was out by the mailbox, pulling out a big manila envelope and a handful of smaller white ones.

He stood and hobbled over to the door as quickly as he could. Without the crutches, despite her mamm's orders. And flung the door open.

She approached across the schoolyard. A shy smile appeared as their eyes met. He stepped aside so she could kum in.

"Danki." He shut the door behind her.

Rachel put the mail on a scholar's desk, then took off her coat and draped it over a chair. "You're welkum. For...?"

"For sending me a copy of the letter you wrote to Obadiah. It's a really sweet note, but—"

"What?" She swayed, the color draining from her face, leaving it as pale as the overcast sky. "Nein, that can't be so. I sent it to him. Let me see it."

"It's on my desk."

Rachel shed her mittens as she went, dropping them on another scholar's desk. Her boots left slushy puddles on the wood floor. She snatched up the paper and scanned the contents. Then spun around to face him. "Ach, this is bad. Beyond bad, it's terrible. Actually, it's worse than that. Horrible."

He wouldn't go quite that far. "You put my address on a letter meant for Obadiah. Not that big of a deal, Rachel. Just make out another envelope and send it tomorrow."

"Nein, it's worse than horrible. I sent your letter to Obadiah!"

"You wrote me?"

"Right. *And* sent it to Obadiah."

"You wrote me."

She opened her mouth again and looked at him. Then her lips curved up in a sly grin. "Jah, but it's not so gut. I wrote things that I would never tell him. Things that were reserved for my best friend. You."

David's smile widened as he neared her. He reached out and brushed his fingers over her cheek. She leaned into him, but he pulled back without kissing her. He dropped his hand to his side as he glanced out the window once more.

"Sam home?"

"I don't know. I didn't see him. Daed let me out at the mailbox."

He nodded and stepped away, going around the desk.

She turned, the light in her eyes dying a little. "We can't live our lives in fear of my brother."

"I'm not afraid of him." Well, maybe he was, a little. Mostly of the evil that lurked in Sam's eyes. Of the blatant warning delivered by Preacher Samuel. "But I remembered...." He picked up the envelope and handed it to her.

She looked down at the letter and frowned. "Jah. The high road. You know, what if I change my mind? What if your high road takes you places I'll never go?"

And yet, she was the one with the longing to go places. Or did she mean she shouldn't have broken up with Obadiah?

David sucked in a long breath. He waited until she looked up, then caught her gaze and held it. "Then I don't need to be clouding your mind with kisses."

Her lips turned down. She took the letter and the envelope, then turned away. "I'd best go get dinner on."

He took a couple steps to the side of the desk. "And in regard to the high road, I'll be waiting for you at the other end."

She collected her mittens and flashed a teasing grin over her shoulder. "I'll be waiting for you across the street."

Chapter 17

Nein, Rachel. We're not playing this game anymore. You know I'm the man for you." David's voice held an edge of steel.

Was he drawing a line in the sand?

Rachel's heart pounded. Such audacity. Still, she froze in place. She didn't dare move, afraid she would nod—an admission of his statement—and that would be that. But what about all the unanswered questions? The part of his past that Sam recalled, but David claimed not to? What about his unstable future? They couldn't build a family on nothing but faith. Could they?

She and Obadiah had *plans*. But no best-friendship or foundation of faith.

She balled her mittens in her fists and stared, unmoving, at her coat, waiting on a desk. Willed it to get up, wrap itself around her, and carry her away.

It didn't move, so she'd have to.

"What makes you think it's a game?" She snatched up her coat, slung it over her shoulders, and hurried out the door, slamming it behind her. Let him do what he would with that.

Her eyes burned as she stumbled down the steps into the fresh-fallen snow. Moving toward the road, her shoes found a slippery spot, and her legs went in opposite directions. Her arms flailed, like they had the first time she'd gone ice skating, as she tried to regain her balance.

"Easy there, Rachel."

A hand gripped her upper arm, holding her upright. She looked into Joshua Yoder's blue eyes. Usually, they were dancing, but not now. They weren't even twinkling. He looked serious. Too serious.

"What are you doing here, Joshua Yoder?"

"Call me Josh, danki. I came to visit David." He released her.

"You've been by the last three evenings."

His lips curved upward. "You're keeping watch, ain't so? Not on me, though." Josh nodded toward the school. "Him?"

Rachel shrugged. "I just happened to notice. That's all." So what if she noticed every little thing about David? Scowling, she moved another sliding step. She flailed again, and Josh grabbed her once more.

"Should I see you home?"

"Nein, danki." Then she slid again. And they expected David to kum over for supper, with his bum leg? She'd ask Mamm about having his dinner delivered. By someone else.

Josh supported her for another step. "You should walk in the fresh snow, not where it's packed down and turned to ice, jah? You might get better traction." He released her when she reached a snowy patch.

"I'll be fine. Danki for the help." Obeying his suggestion, she hurried through the deeper snow, then looked back. "Want to stay for supper? It's a long walk home in the snow. David will be coming." *Maybe.* She kicked at the white powdery stuff.

"Nein. Besides, it's not bad. I've walked in worse. I'll watch until you get home. See you later, jah?"

She nodded and continued on her way. When she reached the porch, she glanced back and waved. He returned the gesture, then turned and headed toward the school. Where she'd left the family's mail. Including the big package she'd gotten from someone in Montana.

Why had Josh dodged her comment about his frequent visits at David's?

It didn't seem so strange when she recalled the Josh Yoder she'd known before he'd left home. Usually up to nein gut. What was he getting David involved in?

⁓

David tossed another log on the fire before heading to his bedroom to get his Bible. Might as well get some studying in before it was time to go to the Millers' for dinner. As he lifted the Bible from the shelf, he glanced outside. The snow was falling more heavily now, and the two inches, more or less, that had been on the icy ground when Rachel had kum was supposed to increase to almost six by nacht. Or so one of the older students had told him. David hadn't asked where he'd gotten the information, but watching the snow fall now, he didn't doubt it.

It was early in the season for an ice storm, let alone snow. But both had arrived. He frowned, remembering the Pennsylvania winters. Would they get much ice or snow here? Many blizzards? Or would it be more like Seymour, where the worst he'd experienced had been a random ice storm that had brought down the Englischers' power lines and left them helpless in their electric houses.

They could take a lesson or two from the Amish. In more ways than one.

Then again, maybe the Amish could learn a lesson or two from the Englisch. This German/Englisch Bible was easier to read and understand than the one written in German, though he'd be in trouble if anyone found him reading it. The traditional view was that Gott's Word was sacred and thus was to be read solely from the German.

Sam probably knew, if he'd looked at it before throwing it across the classroom. David smoothed his hand over the permanently bent cover as he returned to his desk. It felt gut to get around without crutches. He'd use them when he went for dinner, so Rachel's mamm wouldn't scold him.

There was a knock on the door, and then it opened. Josh peeked in, as he had the nacht before. "Getting bad out there." He stomped his feet before coming inside, then took off his hat and hung it on a peg on the wall.

David nodded. "Jah. What are you doing out?"

"Viktor's home. He and his grossdaedi want to meet with us. Tomorrow nacht, after dinner?"

"His grossdaedi?" Who else would commit to attend the Bible study before they formally organized? Maybe the better question was,

How long would it be until they were discovered and forced to kneel and confess to being prideful or having too much biblical learning?

As if desiring to learn more about Gott were a bad thing.

"His name is Reuben. He's one of us."

One of us. One of those who'd stayed within the confines of the Amish but still confessed the saving grace of Jesus—not the merits of one's works.

David pulled in a breath and nodded.

"Heard that you're a craftsman of sorts. What do you do?" Josh sat on the front desk.

"Basket weaving and tying flies for trout fishing." David frowned. He wouldn't ask where Josh had heard about his skills. Word traveled fast from one community to the next, and it was likely someone in Seymour had told someone from here. Had the person included the part about his irrational fear of riding in open buggies? Or the inevitability of his becoming fat and lazy?

He cringed. He shouldn't allow himself to think the worst.

Josh studied him a moment. "You missed the auction this month, but there's a Christmas festival coming up at the end of November. I'm making birdhouses to sell. Maybe if you have enough baskets or flies made, we could share a booth. Rachel or her mamm will be selling quilts, and Gret—" He shifted. "Some women will be selling jams or baked goods."

David smiled. "Sounds like a plan. I'll be sure to have some products prepared." He'd have to ask Rachel to order the materials he'd need so that he could work in the evenings.

"I'd better head on home, but I wanted you to know." Josh grinned. "You'll probably need to go to the Millers' haus before too long. Rachel mentioned you were coming over."

David glanced at the windup clock on his desk. "Jah. I probably should." Within the hour, anyway. He laid the Bible on the desk.

Josh immediately picked it up. "You won't be carrying this on church Sundays."

"Nein." He reached over and tapped his all-German copy, which lay on the corner of his desk for the daily Bible readings and lessons. Not that Josh necessarily noticed. He was still thumbing through the dual-language Bible.

"I have an all-Englisch one," Josh confessed. "Keep it hidden in my room, so I won't offend my parents." He handed back the Bible and swiped his hand over his jaw. "Anyway, I better go. Do you want me to see you safely across the road? It's getting slick out there." His gaze darted to the crutches, leaning against the wall.

David shook his head. Josh was a friend, but even so, he didn't want the embarrassment of not being "man enough" to do it on his own. *I know pride goes before destruction, but, Lord Gott, please keep me upright.* "Danki, anyway."

Josh nodded, then pulled his gloves out of his pockets and tugged them on. "See you tomorrow." He grabbed his hat from the peg on the wall, opened the door, and stepped outside.

Wind whistled around the building. David walked to the window and peered out. He could barely see across the street, with the thickly falling snow being whipped about. At the Millers' haus, smoke rose from the chimney. Excitement coursed through him at the thought of seeing Rachel again so soon. Hopefully, whatever it was that had prompted her to stalk out of the schoolhaus earlier was a minor frustration she'd since gotten over.

Why did she act as if their relationship was a game? He was serious. Maybe she wasn't. Maybe she was interested in the flirting alone. Liked having men devoted to her when she didn't care for them. Liked using them. *Lord, please, help me. Give me wisdom…and the fortitude to stick to the high road.*

He bypassed the desk, where his Bible waited, and returned to his room. He dug deep inside his bag and unearthed the supplies needed to tie flies. He'd wait until he could get around better to go into the woods and collect what he'd need for basket weaving. He could also make walking sticks—it'd be easy to find suitable branches once the snow stopped.

Or perhaps he could send the scholars out to scavenge for them, as soon as the weather cleared.

If the school board discovered that he'd planned the outing for the purpose of personal gain, he'd be reprimanded, for sure. Unless he taught them to weave baskets. Or somehow turned the excursion into a science lesson.

David sighed, realizing he would need to venture out on his own—once his ankle healed. He sat on the edge of the bed and started assembling flies. He'd done it so often, it'd become a mindless activity. While he worked, he spent time praying for each of the students. William Miller flashed through his thoughts. He hadn't been in school today, and now he weighed heavily on David's mind. He prayed for him, in particular, and lifted other scholars der Herr put on his heart.

The sound of male voices and thumping boots outside his window interrupted his prayer time. A horse whinnied.

David set aside his craft supplies and stood. Beneath his window was a farm wagon piled full of wood. Bishop.... David frowned. He couldn't remember the man's name. The bishop and one of his sons tossed the split logs in the general direction of the neatly stacked pile he and Sam had made earlier that week.

But the dual-language Bible was on the desk. He decided to go get it, in case the men came inside.

He supposed he should be thankful that the bishop had remembered him.

Either that, or the man was making sure the woodpile was well-stocked for the return of the regular teacher.

A chill worked through David.

Yet another thing to pray about.

If they asked him to leave, where would he go?

⌒

Rachel added that week's collection of leftover vegetables to the kettle and gave them a quick stir. The stew would be hot by the

time the men came in from the barn. She dumped the potato peel-
ings into the slop bucket to feed to the hogs later, then washed her
hands before checking the biscuits. They had just begun to turn a
nice golden brown. She shut the oven door and turned to survey the
room. Mary had already set the table, except for David's plate, which
waited on a tray. Mamm had said that one of the buwe could take it
over later.

Maybe Luther would deliver the meal. He was due home from
his job any moment. That would teach David for teasing her as he
had. She imagined the banter she'd miss.

Maybe she would take the meal over, after all.

Footsteps—accompanied by a series of taps—sounded across
the porch. She peered out the window and saw David pass by. He'd
made it across the street! Her heart fluttered as she hurried to open
the door.

"Danki." He came inside and stopped on the rag rug in front of
the door. After handing her the crutches, then shrugged out of his
coat and turned to hang it on a hook. He hung his black hat on top
of it.

"We had planned to send someone over with your supper so you
wouldn't have to go out in the storm." It wasn't necessary for him to
know that she would've been the one to kum over.

David frowned. "I'm not helpless. I can get around."

"Jah, but, your leg…your ankle."

His gaze caught hers. His eyes were dark, unfathomable. She
stared into their depths. "I'm fine, Rachel."

"Jah, you are fine." Her face heated at the bold implication.

David's eyes widened. He glanced down at her lips and made
a slight move toward her, then jerked back. Straightened. His gaze
returned to hers, but an expression akin to regret lurked in the
shadows.

He bent over and began untying the laces of his tennis shoes.
His socks probably were soaked, since the snow was more than ankle
deep.

"Don't you have any boots?"

He put the shoes in the plastic tray, then straightened. "Jah, but I guess they're still in Seymour. I asked a friend to send them to me once I got an address. Nein mailbox at the school, you know."

"You could give him mine."

"I impose on your hospitality enough."

"It's nein problem. I'd be happy to deliver them." She turned back toward the stove but allowed herself to walk so close to him that her skirts and arm brushed against him. His breath hitched sharply. She grinned and added a little sway as she crossed the room, just in case he was watching.

She cringed inwardly at her behavior, but she wanted to keep his interest. Even though she was still frustrated with him.

"I saw Bethany Weiss—the bishop's dochter—and her mamm at the grocery store this morgen, before it got bad out. We talked about you." She'd hated that Bethany had mentioned David. She thought of him as being hers, and she didn't want Bethany intruding. "She said she'd remind her daed to bring some firewood by the school." She swirled the wooden spoon through the stew.

"Danki. I wondered why…. The bishop was still there unloading wood when I left." His voice held a note of concern. He glanced outside.

"Did you talk to him?" She turned to look at him.

"Nein." He didn't meet her gaze. "I didn't. How is the real teacher doing?"

She heard a hint of worry in his voice. "Dory feels better, but she doesn't think she's ready to return to teaching. Some of the bigger buwe are difficult to handle, and she's left-handed, so she can't yet grade papers or write assignments on the board. She'll be out awhile yet. Bethany said it'd probably be about four more weeks."

David nodded, a look of relief replacing his show of concern. He moved closer. "Smells gut in here."

She smiled. He would be living across the street for at least another month. "Danki. It's just stew and biscuits." She set the spoon aside and peered in the oven, then grabbed a pot holder. "Speaking of the bigger buwe, you aren't having problems, are you?"

"Ach, nein. I have some concerns about William Miller…he gets angry occasionally. Depressed, sometimes. He always obeys, but sometimes, he's not…well, I don't know. One time he took a knife and stuck it through a girl's kapp string, basically pinning her to his desk. And he wasn't in school today. I can't put my finger on anything specific, but I'm concerned about him."

"William's my cousin. Greta's brother. You met her this week, remember?"

"Jah." David glanced away. "He's your cousin? I knew he had the same last name…."

"Onkel Andy was injured in a farming accident recently. William is the oldest bu. The bishop says he's to stay in school until he's fourteen. His birthday is a few months off, but Onkel Andy needs him now. Daed sent a couple of my brothers over to help, but Onkel Andy told them to go back home. I don't know why. I asked Greta, but she never answered, really."

"I've known a few Amish men who are too proud to ask for help."

"Such as yourself?" Rachel turned to face him.

He shrugged. "I have help. Your brothers keep the wood box full and the fire going; your daed and brothers added handrails to the steps and put shelves in my room; you do my laundry, and—"

"But it bothers you. Accepting help."

He moved a little nearer. Close enough to reach out and touch, if she dared.

"Jah, it bothers me." He lifted a finger and trailed it over her cheek.

She leaned into his light touch.

"I don't like appearing weak to you."

She fought the urge to wrap her arms around his waist and press her cheek against his shoulder. "Weak, David? You are the strongest person I know."

His finger came to a stop at the corner of her lips.

Her breathing was shallow. Her heart hoped he'd get the hint.

His breath feathered over her, warm and peppermint scented. His head started to lower.

Feet pounded across the wooden planks of the porch. The doorknob creaked.

He moved away, his hand falling to his side. "Not so strong."

Her lips tingled with want, with need.

Whoever had entered didn't matter to her. She kept her eyes on David as he hobbled across the room to the sink.

The door shut.

Rachel glanced over her shoulder, then did a double take. The bishop?

"We need to have a little chat, bu."

Chapter 18

David finished scrubbing his hands and arms before turning to see who had kum inside and interrupted the kiss he'd been on the verge of giving Rachel. Probably a gut thing, since he didn't want to cloud her mind with passion. He reached for a towel, then swiveled around to face...the bishop.

He still couldn't remember the man's name.

The bishop hung his coat on a hook.

Wait a minute. By "bu," the bishop was referring to him? Had he discovered his dual-language Bible? Or maybe his fly fishing supplies? Worry pooled in his chest.

"Bishop Joe, what a surprise." Rachel grabbed a mug. "Care for a cup of koffee? Daed's in the barn, but I'm sure he'll be here in a minute, if you care to wait. Or you can go out there, if you want." She filled the mug with steaming water from the kettle, then added a teaspoon of instant koffee and carried it to the table. "Do you take cream?" Again, she didn't wait for an answer but retrieved a small pitcher and set it next to the mug.

Bishop Joe glowered at David, ignoring both Rachel and the koffee.

What had he done? Was this about Sam and the false claims? The drugs? Had word already gotten out about the Bible study? Or had he messed up as a teacher somehow? Had the kinner complained about the wrinkled papers and stained schoolwork he'd handed back to them? It was hard to prepare for an attack when it came from an unknown direction.

He pulled in a shaky breath, straightened his spine, and firmed his shoulders. Whatever it was, he could explain. Maybe. He hoped.

Rachel filled a plate with cookies and set it on the table, next to the koffee mug. "Please, have a seat." Her voice was too chipper for the concern that filled her green eyes.

"I never gave you permission to get a dog." The bishop whipped his hat off his head and clutched it in both hands.

Okay, that had kum out of nowhere. "A dog?"

"Four-legged creature. Long tail. Sheds. Barks."

David shook his head and snapped his mouth shut. He decided not to match the bishop's sarcasm. "Uh…I don't have a dog." He stood still, not sure whether he should move closer or back away.

The bishop scowled.

Maybe it wasn't a gut idea to contradict him, either. But, really. A dog?

Not that he wouldn't mind having a dog. But he never would've even considered asking permission to keep a pet of any kind at school. He was only the temporary teacher. For all intents and purposes, homeless. Hardly in any condition to take care of anything—other than himself. Not that he did that very well.

"Don't lie to me, bu. I've seen it. Border collie. Female. I told her to go home, and she did—right up the school steps. Those are smart dogs. She knows where 'home' is."

"I think it's a stray." Rachel pulled out a chair for the bishop, doing everything short of pushing the man into it. "That dog's been hanging around our farm, too. The kinner feed it scraps from their lunches."

How would Rachel know that? The only days she'd had off since his arrival had been Thursday and Sunday. And unless she'd peered out the window during the lunch break on Thursday….

David shrugged. "If it's a stray, it'll move on eventually. Maybe one of the kinner will take it home." His lips quirked. "But in the meantime, may she have permission to hang out at the school?" He didn't mean to provoke the bishop but wanted to show that he could do things the correct way and ask permission.

Bishop Joe narrowed his eyes. And worked his mouth, but nothing came out.

Maybe he shouldn't have said what he had. The man had nein sense of humor.

The bishop turned to face Rachel. "This bu bothering you?"

Rachel's jaw dropped for a moment. Then she shook her head. "Nein. More likely I'm bothering him."

David frowned and looked at the floor. That was truer than she knew. But probably in a different way from how she'd meant it.

The bishop returned his attention to him. Gave him a stare that said, "I'm keeping my eyes on you." Then he sat in the chair and picked up a cookie. "The stray dog can stay with the stray bu until they both find gut homes." He chortled, as if he'd made a joke.

Rachel winced.

David bit his tongue to keep from responding. But really, what could he say?

He was a stray.

~

Rachel made another cup of koffee for Bishop Joe after he drained the first. Then she moved back to the stove and set the pot of stew on the warming burner. "Would you like to join us for dinner, Bishop Joe? Daed and the buwe will be in any minute now."

"Nein, danki. My sohn is finishing up stacking the wood." He resumed staring at David.

"Appreciate it." David lingered by the sink, the hand towel still in his grasp, as if he wasn't quite sure what to do after he'd hung it up.

He probably wouldn't have that problem if the bishop left. They'd be flirting. Make that, *she'd* be flirting, trying to find a way back into his arms.

A dangerous place to be when her brothers and daed would kum in at any moment. And with her sisters and mamm right upstairs, finishing a quilt. Anyone could walk in without warning.

Just as Bishop Joe had.

"I'll head back over to the school and see how my bu is doing," the bishop finally said. But he didn't get up. He just sat there, calmly eating another shortbread cookie. Sipping koffee. And keeping an eye on David. It made Rachel nervous, too. She wasn't sure how to act in her own home. She spun around and stirred the stew, just to give herself something to do.

Footsteps clomped across the porch, and the door opened. Daed stepped inside. He hesitated by the door, his gaze taking in the bishop, David, and finally Rachel. He winked at her, then looked back at Bishop Joe. "What gives us the pleasure of your visit?"

"The stray," he muttered.

"The stray." Daed frowned, his gaze returning to Rachel. "I wouldn't mind a cup of koffee." He shrugged off his coat and hung it up. "Perhaps you'd like to join us, David."

A muscle jumped in David's jaw. He draped the towel over the rack and limped to the table. He pulled out a chair—Rachel's—and sat.

"Would you care for some koffee?" Daed motioned for Rachel to get another mug, and then he kicked off his boots, set them in the tray, and headed for the sink. After he washed up, he went back to the table.

David didn't answer the question. His lips were pressed together, the muscle in his jaw still quivering. Rachel set a full mug in front of him and squeezed his shoulder. It was tense. Hard. He flinched at her touch.

She started to work her fingers in a massaging motion, but Bishop Joe's watchful—and critical—eye fixed on her. She dropped her hand from David's shoulder and hurried back to the oven, pulled out the biscuits, and dumped them into a towel-lined basket. She tucked another towel around it to keep them warm. Hopefully, the bishop wouldn't stay much longer. Especially since he'd said he wouldn't join them for dinner. But now the meal would be lukewarm. So much for impressing David with her cooking skills.

"The stray," Daed said again as he lowered himself into the chair next to Bishop Joe. "I'm not sure I understand."

The bishop grunted, pointing with his head. "Him."

Daed frowned, his gaze going to David. "The stray." This time, his voice sounded less questioning. More thoughtful. "His name is David."

David's expression softened a little.

"Is there anoth—a problem with David I need to keep my eye on?" Daed took a sip of his koffee.

Another problem? Rachel glanced at Bishop Joe to see if he'd noticed.

"The dog. I'll let you handle it." Bishop Joe finished his cookie and lumbered to his feet. "I need to head on home. My frau is probably wondering what's keeping me." He pulled on his coat and slammed the door behind him.

Rachel used a mop to wipe up the melted snow his boots had left to vent her frustration and stay busy. "His frau is probably hoping that whatever is keeping him will keep him longer."

"Now, Rachel, that's unkind." Daed's voice was stern, despite the grin that tugged at his lips. He looked at David. "The dog?"

David lifted a shoulder. "He says there's a stray Border collie at the school. Thought it was mine. I've never seen it."

Daed smiled. "Ah. Rosie. Jah, she's been hanging around here for a while now. A few weeks. Mostly in the barn or back in the pasture with the cows. She was probably lured to the school by the kinner. Mary named her, but…." He shrugged. "We've so many strays around here, I doubt she'd miss one. Especially if Rosie chooses to move across the street. And I won't have a problem if you let her into the school."

David blinked. "What are you saying?"

"I'm giving you permission to have a pet, if Rosie chooses to stay at the school. But she stays outside when the scholars are there. You can let her in, if you want, when you're alone."

"But the bishop—"

"I'll talk to him. And, not to gossip, but he's usually not so rude. Curt, jah, but not rude. He's had a rough summer and fall, and this is the anniversary of his oldest sohn's death." Daed started to reach for a cookie but pulled his hand back without taking one. "Dinner about ready?"

Rachel nodded and smiled at Daed, then opened the door and rang the dinner bell. Immediately, a stampede started from upstairs. Moments later, the door burst open, and most of her brothers stomped in.

Only Sam was missing. And maybe whatever kept him would keep him longer.

~

David bowed his head for his after-dinner prayer, then looked up. "The stew was delicious. Danki. May I be excused?" It bothered him that Sam had kum in for dinner so much later than the others. Especially since the school was unlocked. He didn't trust Sam. David looked at Preacher Samuel. "Did you ever get a key for the school?"

Preacher Samuel glanced toward Sam. "Ach, nein. I forgot. I'll have Rachel do it when she goes to work tomorrow." He took a final bite, then pushed his bowl away. "Jah, you may be excused."

"I won't forget the key." Rachel grinned. "Since I fixed supper, Mary and Jenny take care of the dishes. I'll walk back you back to the school."

"I can find my way." He didn't want Rachel to see any damage that might've been done in his absence. He glanced at Sam, who spooned stew into his mouth, apparently oblivious to the conversation.

"I know," Rachel said, "but I'll be at the store tomorrow, and I might as well stop over to make a list of anything you might need."

David shrugged. He didn't need much. "Maybe a tube of toothpaste. A bottle of shampoo." To replace what Sam had destroyed. He avoided looking at him.

Preacher Samuel grunted. He glanced at Sam and raised his eyebrow. "We have extra upstairs. Jenny, run upstairs and get some, please."

Sam looked away.

"More koffee, probably." Rachel grinned at David and reached for her coat. "And maybe a few snack items. Not too many, though, or you might invite mice in for the winter."

So, she intended to accompany him, anyway. He blew out a puff of air and tried not to look at Sam, but he couldn't help it. Surely, if he'd trashed the place again, or had done something equally heinous, he would try to deter his sister from going over and seeing it. And still he didn't say a word. His only reaction was a look of mild concern, which might have stemmed from his realization that David and Rachel would be alone. Together. In a locked building.

David's blood heated.

Jah, the school would be locked. Because if he gave in to his desires and kissed her senseless, he didn't want to be interrupted by a fireplace poker knocking him unconscious.

His head suddenly hurt. But with Sam monitoring his every move, he wasn't about to rub it. Instead, he reached for his shoes. "It might still be slick out there." One last effort to get her to change her mind.

She shrugged and reached for her black bonnet. "I need to pick up our mail. I left it at the school."

Now Sam glared.

Mary hurried to the cookie jar and started filling a sandwich bag. "We didn't have dessert yet, so you can take yours with you."

"Danki, Mary." David forced a smile.

Jenny returned to the room with a bottle of shampoo and a tube of toothpaste, which she loaded in another bag, then handed it to Rachel.

David nodded. "Danki, Jenny. Preacher Samuel."

Once he had bundled up and put his shoes back on, Rachel held the door for him, and he headed outside, carefully maneuvering the crutches down the steps. When he reached the ground, he glanced across the road at the school. On the top step was a black-and-white form that stood and made a little whimper as they approached. Must be the Border collie Bishop Joe had accused him of harboring.

The dog beat its tail against the top step as they drew nearer.

He looked at Rachel. "Rosie?"

"Jah. That's what Mary named her."

"Welkum, Rosie." He balanced a crutch under his arm and held his hand out for the dog to sniff.

Her tail thumping harder, Rosie sniffed, then offered a lick. David pulled back with a chuckle. "Nice dog."

"Jah, she is. If she stays here, she'll be gut company." Rachel scratched Rosie behind the ears.

"But I'll be in trouble with the bishop."

Rachel shrugged. "You already are, ain't so? Though I can't believe he called you a stray. That was just plain mean."

"It's the truth, though." David opened the school door. Nothing seemed out of place. He stepped aside to allow Rachel to go first. Then he patted Rosie. "Stay." She didn't try to follow them inside.

Rachel gasped.

David stumbled inside and glanced around. Then he followed Rachel's horrified gaze.

On the whiteboard was a message, written in a masculine scrawl with red marker.

"Thou shalt surely die." —Genesis 2:17

Chapter 19

Rachel stomped across the floor and swiped the eraser across the hateful words written in handwriting she immediately recognized as Sam's, leaving the whiteboard clean. If only the memory of the message could be erased as easily.

How dare her own brother threaten the life of the man she was coming to love? She expelled a breath, firmed her shoulders, and spun around to look at David. The pain in his eyes made her cringe. And now she was about to destroy any sense of peace he might have.

"It won't do any gut, you know, for me to copy a key to the school. Daed keeps his hanging on the hook by the door. Anyone could grab it and kum over here."

David pressed his lips together. He held her gaze for a long moment before he swallowed. "There's nein point to locking it, then, ain't so?"

She frowned and shook her head. "Unless we change the locks, and I'm not sure the board— But wait a minute. Rosie doesn't like Sam. Daed basically gave the dog to you, without saying as much. You'll definitely want her inside at nacht. I'll talk to Daed about the locks."

David turned back toward the door. "I need to talk with Sam. He has to tell me what I did. Who I killed."

"You killed someone?" Rachel heard the tightness in her voice.

David shook his head. "I don't know. I don't think so. But your daed said that Sam...well, something about an eye for an eye, a tooth for a tooth, and a life for a life." Staring at the floor, he shook his head. "Never mind. I have nein proof he did this." He shrugged off his coat and hung it on a hook, adding his black hat on top.

"We both know he did."

"Jah, but we can't prove it. I'll talk to him sometime, but I'm not going to confront him without proof."

David could be noble if he wanted to, but Rachel wanted answers.

And besides, where would they get the proof? She'd already erased the writing on the board, so she couldn't show Daed. He would have recognized Sam's handwriting, for sure. He should know that Sam was up to some sort of mischief.

And with that in mind....

She waited until David turned around, then caught his gaze and held it. "You probably weren't aware that Joshua Yoder is a known troublemaker. He used to party harder than anyone, including Sam. Are you sure you want to hang out with him? You might get a reputation as being one of the bad buwe."

David tensed for a moment, then seemed to relax. "I think Josh is on the up-and-up."

"And what makes you think that? I know him. We grew up together. And he...well, he used to court Greta. And...I don't want to gossip, but—"

"Then don't."

"People died, David. And two of the buwe involved disappeared. Joshua being one of them."

David shrugged. He approached the desk, his crutches thumping across the floor. "He's changed."

"How can you say that? You didn't know him before."

He hesitated a moment. "But I know him now."

"You just think you do. But I think he's planning something."

David opened his mouth. He worked it for a second, then shut it and shook his head.

"Well?" She planted her fists on her hips. "What is he up to?"

~

"Aren't you the curious one?" David passed Rachel on his way around the desk. He leaned the crutches against the wall beside the bookcase. "What if I won't tell you?" He didn't mean to tease, but he wasn't sure he should leak the plans for the men's Bible study. Josh knew whom they could trust. He knew who the believers were. David didn't. And he'd gotten the impression Josh wanted only a select few to kum.

Rachel muttered something in reply, but he didn't catch it. He glanced across the street at the Millers' haus. A man—probably Sam—stood on the porch, staring at the school. An uncomfortable tenseness grew in David's chest. He shut his eyes. *Lord, I'm in over my head here. I don't understand Sam, I don't know how to deal with him, and, to be completely honest, I'm scared.*

How could Gott have asked him to leave the comforts of home for all the drama, stress, and uncertainty he faced now? And had faced, even in Seymour? Yet he couldn't retreat to Pennsylvania and expect normalcy. Nein. He was in this alone. And he would probably lose his life because of the apparent vendetta Sam had against him.

Dark waters of despair closed over him. The man on the porch headed toward the Millers' barn.

David rested his fingers on the windowsill and leaned his forehead against the glass. *Lord, help.*

Gott must have some reason for putting him through this. He knew he needed to place his life completely in His hands. "If der Herr wants me here, even though He is absent, then so be it."

"Even though He is absent?" Rachel came to stand beside him. "How can you say that?"

"Sorry." He hadn't meant for her to hear. The words had been intended for himself only, but thinking them hadn't been enough. He'd needed to hear them. Gott *had* led him here, ain't so?

Don't shut Me out, sohn.

Rachel's hand rested on his forearm. "Don't shut me out."

Those very words had played through his mind a microsecond before she'd said them. A message from Gott? *Lord, help my unbelief.*

David uncurled his fingers from the sill and pushed away. He hobbled back to his room and reached for the bottle of pain pills waiting on the shelf. Not that he needed one right now, but he needed to see if they'd been tampered with. He unscrewed the lid and looked inside. They appeared to be what they were supposed to be. But just to be sure, he shook out several onto his palm.

"What are you doing?" Rachel stood in the doorway.

"Just checking." He dumped the pills back inside the bottle and returned it to the shelf.

"You're scaring me. What's going on?"

David shook his head and raised his arms toward the sky in a show of frustration. "I don't know, Rachel. But somehow I landed right in the middle of it."

Just then, he recalled what Pastor Samuel had said about its being the anniversary of the death of Bishop Joe's sohn.

His knees buckled. He fell beside his cot and bowed his head.

Wasn't it around this time of the year that he'd stared into the unseeing eyes of the bu in the car with the Missouri tags?

After a moment's hesitation, Rachel knelt beside David. Apparently, he was praying—but for what? For whom? Sam? Or for himself? Sam's seeming hatred of David didn't make sense. He had nein reason to dislike him. Unless he did know David from somewhere. But then, it didn't make sense that David wasn't aware of it.

She bowed her head, too, but she didn't know what to pray for, other than the obvious.

"Two years ago, when I was still living in Pennsylvania, I went to a bonfire." His voice was quiet. Hushed. "It was a huge party, hosted by some Swartzentruber Amish."

"Ach, David." They had the wildest parties. Surely, he would've known that.

He shook his head. "Amish had kum from all over. Different districts, different states. There was plenty of alcohol and drugs— a deadly combination. Everyone participated...even me. But I didn't like what the drugs did to me, the way they made me feel. So I gave them away to someone else."

Rachel raised her head and stared at David. His head was still bowed. His past wasn't anything like she'd imagined it. He'd been a partier like Josh? But…he wasn't the same now. Somehow, sometime, he must've changed.

"The combination of whatever I took, mixed with the alcohol, made me see demons in the fire. I was terrified and became convinced I was going to die and go straight to hell. It scared the alcohol right out of me, and I fell on my knees and prayed, begging Gott to forgive my sins, to forgive me for…I don't remember what else. And then I gave my life to Gott. Knelt for baptism in the Amish church, but that came later.

"That nacht, as everyone was leaving, there was a terrible accident. Everyone rushed to the scene, including me. A car with Missouri plates was wrapped around a tree. There were two buwe inside. One had already died. I didn't recognize them, but one might've been the bu I'd given the drugs to. I can't be sure. Everything is a blur. Was a blur."

Rachel gasped, and she grasped David's elbow as she remembered the late-nacht knock on the door when someone had kum to inform them about the accident. The angry threats Sam had voiced against the nameless, faceless man who had caused his injuries and killed Ezra. The prayers she had sent heavenward on behalf of Sam, pleading for his recovery. Her mind whirled. Had it really been David?

"The other bu…he yelled a lot. What he said, I don't remember exactly. Threats I didn't—don't—understand. Cries for help. A combination of both. He was pinned in the car. People came to cut him out." David straightened and turned to look at her. "That is all I can think of. It's the only reason I can kum up with for why Sam might hate me. But it doesn't make sense."

"It makes perfect sense," Rachel whispered. "Sam's car accident happened in Pennsylvania. The same accident that killed Bishop Joe's sohn."

Chapter 20

David froze at Rachel's revelation. "That means I am somewhat responsible for the death of Bishop Joe's sohn. And Sam wants me to pay for it."

"You need to tell Daed." Her voice sounded choked with tears. Filled with worry.

He hated hurting her. "I did. At least, I told him most of it when he questioned me regarding Sam's accusations about drug use. That was all I could think of. It was the only time I've ever willingly taken illegal drugs. And I gave the rest away."

"Ach, David." Her fingers moved from his elbow and began rubbing his shirt sleeve. The touch felt nice...too nice. And they were alone, in his bedroom.

That wasn't gut.

He started to push himself up from the floor, but he couldn't get traction—couldn't position himself correctly with her so close beside him. He quit trying and stayed on his knees. He didn't want to appear completely weak and helpless in front of her.

"You need to go, Rachel."

"Jah, I will, but—"

"At least move into the other room. And shut the door on your way out. Danki."

"Okay...." She got to her feet and stared at him.

He avoided her gaze. "Please. I have my pride, and it's not going to be pretty watching me try to get up." It hurt to say that much.

"Do you need help?"

"Nein. I can do it. Just go."

Rachel frowned and shook her head before walking out and shutting the door behind her.

Hopefully, she wouldn't open it again in the middle of his struggles. But he could do this. He could.

He shifted on his knees so he could grab the wooden chair and managed to get his gut leg under him, supporting himself enough to stand.

Why did he always play the fool around her?

He'd thought that his sprained ankle was getting better, but now it throbbed. He adjusted his weight, wishing for his crutches, but he'd left them in the other room. He swallowed a pain pill without water.

Then he opened the door and entered the main part of the school. He scanned the room, noticing the clear plastic bag of the Millers' mail hanging on the doorknob. Rachel's coat remained on the nearby hook. Rosie was curled up next to the stove, sleeping. Rachel must have let her in.

She looked over from where she stood by a window. "Sam left. I saw his car drive out just a few minutes ago."

That was gut. Meant he wouldn't be lurking in the shadows, watching for one inappropriate move on his—or her—part.

David met her gaze, but he couldn't quite find a smile. As long as Obadiah was in the picture….

"I broke up with him, remember?" She'd apparently read his mind. Either that or he'd spoken his thoughts out loud.

"You accidentally sent his letter to me, ain't so? That means you aren't broken up yet."

She sighed. "I figured we could talk."

"In the dark?" Not that it was totally dark. Dim, jah. He made it as far as his desk, then lit the flashlight lantern he had sitting there. He leaned against the desk, letting it support most of his weight.

In the light, he saw her blush. She waved his question away. "You never did answer me. What is Joshua planning?"

Considering the current situation, with the discovery that he was likely the one responsible for the accident that had injured Sam and killed the bishop's sohn, keeping Josh's plans a secret no longer seemed so important. And given Rachel's worries about Josh's partying past, he figured it might not hurt to reassure her.

David rubbed the sudden pounding in his forehead, hoping the pain pill would kick in fast. For the sake of both his ankle and his head.

"Josh said he might join the church next time the classes are offered. In the meantime, he has in mind a...an accountability group, of sorts. A Bible study, too." That should alleviate her concerns. "He has a few people lined up to participate. Someone named Viktor, Viktor's grossdaedi...and myself."

Rachel stared at him, slack-jawed.

He replayed his words in his mind, hoping he hadn't revealed too much. None of it had been overly shocking, as far as he could tell. Spiritual accountability and Bible study...maybe she had read more into it than he'd said.

"Viktor married my cousin Esther."

Of course, he had. Seemed everyone he'd met thus far was related to everyone else around here.

"Is Esther coming?" Rachel pressed. "Because if she is, I'd like to."

"Ah. Josh didn't mention Esther, so I don't know. I think it's supposed to be a men's group, but let me find out for sure. I'll let you know."

She came over to the desk and sat next to him. "I'm resending the letter to Obadiah tomorrow."

Her hint was obvious. Desire burned. But....

He straightened, stepping away from the desk, and resisted the urge to turn into her arms, to gather her close, to kiss her senseless.

Under the current situation, how could he?

"Let me know when he responds." He'd said the same thing the day before, but everything had changed since then.

Now, he had to figure out how to confess to the bishop the part he might have played in the death of his sohn.

～

When David walked behind the desk and settled in his chair, Rachel slid off and followed him around, then sat again, facing him. He propped his leg up and leaned forward, his long fingers kneading his ankle. Then he untied his shoe, took it off, and set it on the floor beside him. He pulled off his sock and unwrapped the long ACE bandage. His ankle was red and still a little swollen.

"Does it hurt?" *Stupid question.*

He massaged his ankle gently. "Not as bad as before, but worse than earlier today. I probably overdid it."

"Mamm said you should keep using the crutches, even if you feel like you don't need them."

"I know." He shrugged it off. "I need to talk to your daed about this stuff. Probably with Sam present."

"You said you joined the church afterward." She leaned forward, watching his fingers move. "Your sins were forgiven and forgotten, ain't so?"

David looked up. "Jah, as far as Pennsylvania is concerned. But this is a whole different place, different people, and I've just discovered that I might have unintentionally hurt more than a few. I need to confess my wrongdoing to them."

"You might lose your position in the school. Then what?" She held her breath. What if he was forced to leave? Tears burned her eyes.

He sighed. "I don't know. Gott will take care of me." His brow furrowed, and he looked away. "He will." He said it firmly, as if he needed to convince himself.

"What did you do at home, in Pennsylvania? Or in Seymour? In a letter, you said you wove baskets for sale. Did that support you?"

"I tied flies for fishing, too. And, jah, it did. But at home, I also farmed and hired out for a greenhaus. I told you my parents sold the land, right?"

"Jah. So now what? How will you support a family? What are your plans?" She wanted answers, but would she push him too far?

Maybe she should hold on to that letter she'd written to Obadiah.

David shut his eyes briefly. When he opened them, a muscle jumped in his jaw. "I don't know yet." His tone was quiet. His dark gaze caught hers. "But since I'm not courting anyone, it isn't a concern yet. When it is time to consider it, we'll see where I am, and how der Herr leads me."

Rachel looked away, her heart aching. Quick tears stung her eyes. She blinked them back. He wasn't courting anyone? What about her? Was it all in her head?

Must be. It was merely wishful thinking.

Then again, he'd been pretty clear that he believed she was still attached to Obadiah and therefore not free to be courted. But once she sent the letter and received a response from Obadiah....

Her face burned with shame. She'd basically thrown herself at him. She needed to stop acting like a silly, infatuated schoolgirl and let him do the chasing if he was interested. Starting now.

She slid off the desk and stepped around him. "I'd better get home. I'll tell Daed you want to talk to him."

"Danki," he said quietly. "Rachel, if I were courting someone, you'd be my first choice."

Her mood brightened immediately. She smiled.

"But right now, everything is way too unsettled."

⌒

After dinner the next nacht, David looked up from his paperwork as a pickup rumbled into the school driveway. Beside him, Rosie flapped her tail against the floor. A few minutes later, a door slammed shut. He stood and peered out the window. A blue truck was parked to the right of the building.

Anxiety swirled in David's stomach. What would Bishop Joe say about an Englischer's pickup truck parked in front of the school, considering the way he'd reacted to a stray dog hanging around?

He was halfway across the room when someone knocked. A second later, the door opened.

Josh peeked in, and Rosie greeted him, nose sniffing, tail wagging. He bent down to pet her. "Hallo. I caught a ride with Viktor and Reuben. Viktor is helping his grossdaedi out of the truck."

"I didn't realize Viktor was Englisch." He couldn't be Amish, or even Mennonite, with a blue truck.

Josh hesitated. Another door slammed outside. "He's not. Well, he's not quite sure what he is yet. He's straddling the fence. He did tell Bishop Joe he'd consider joining the church, but baptism classes don't start until next year...." He shrugged, then turned and opened the door even more. An older man stepped into the room, holding his back, followed by a dark-haired man in jeans. Reuben and Viktor.

David hobbled forward. "I'm David Lapp. You must be Reuben and Viktor. Nice to meet you both."

Viktor grunted, shifting his weight uncomfortably. He muttered something David didn't understand as he glanced around. Then he took off his jacket and hung it on a hook.

"Welkum to the area, David." Reuben gave a slight nod. "The school hasn't changed a bit since Viktor was a bu." He eased out of his coat and handed it to his gross-sohn.

After Josh discarded his outerwear, he made his way to the front of the room and snagged a peppermint from the jar. "Want one?" He offered the jar to the other men.

"Danki." Viktor took one, but Reuben declined.

Josh returned the jar to the desk. "As you know, we're planning a men's prayer meeting and Bible study. I figured to-nacht, we'd start by getting to know each other. It might help Vik's comfort level, since he's more reserved." He grinned at his friend. "And it'll help David get to know all of us. Since David is called to be a preacher, we'll let him practice on us with a Bible study." He winked at David.

Hopefully, he'd live up to the hype and not disappoint them.

Rosie turned three circles and curled up on the floor at David's feet.

After the introductions, Josh pulled out a chair and sat. "So, David, is there anything pressing on your mind that you want to discuss to-nacht?"

David's gaze went to the white board. To the words, now invisible, that had haunted him the previous nacht. Then to the verse that Gott had directed him to when he'd thumbed through the Bible after Rachel left.

"Jah. I've been struggling with fear lately. Someone has a vendetta against me. I'm actually in fear for my life." David frowned and looked down at the ground, hoping he hadn't just given out too much information. Hoping that none of the men there would gossip. "When I was reading the Bible last nacht, der Herr directed me to Nehemiah four, verses fourteen and fifteen." He reached for his Bible and opened it to the page where he'd stuck a bookmark. "It says, *'And I looked, and rose up, and said unto the nobles, and to the rulers, and to the rest of the people, Be not ye afraid of them: remember the Lord, which is great and terrible, and fight for your brethren, your sons, and your daughters, your wives, and your houses. And it came to pass, when our enemies heard that it was known unto us, and God had brought their counsel to nought, that we returned all of us to the wall, every one unto his work.'"*

David scanned the faces of the three other men. They all appeared interested, so he continued. "As I read this passage, I noticed that Nehemiah and the other Israelites faced discouragement and fear because the surrounding nations wanted them to fail. And yet Nehemiah had committed to building a wall that would protect Gott's people. A crucial tactic the enemy uses to discourage and defeat the children of Gott is 'divide and conquer.' The enemy works most efficiently when we are divided and confused. He brings one set of troubles to me, another set to Joshua, and yet another set to Viktor or Reuben; and pretty soon, we are all so busy trying to figure out our own problems that we forget about other people and their burdens. Nehemiah saw the same thing happening as they tried to rebuild the wall."

Josh reached for another peppermint candy. He unwrapped it, put the candy in his mouth, and set the empty wrapper on the desk.

David picked up the cup of koffee he'd made earlier and took a sip. "And I realized that since I've been called to teach His Word, I need to remind others what is at stake and what they are fighting for. I am called to mobilize an army to glorify Gott. And—"

Heavy footsteps sounded thudded on the outside stairs, then stopped. David looked up as the door squeaked open. Rosie lifted her head and thumped her tail.

And Preacher Samuel entered.

Chapter 21

Rachel was a dummchen, plain and simple. She still couldn't believe she'd sent the wrong letter to Obadiah. She sealed the letter she'd meant to send him in the first place and double-checked the address before carrying it to the mailbox.

She was on her way back inside when Daed strode past her. "I'm going to the school for a few minutes," he said without slowing.

Rachel hesitantly returned to the haus. If only she could go over there with him. Maybe she shouldn't have mentioned anything to him about the Bible study. Would David get in trouble as a result? She sat on the porch and hugged herself as she stared at the building across the road. Viktor's truck was parked out front—another thing that worried her. Viktor refused to sell his truck. Refused to give up his job on the river. And still dressed in Englisch clothes.

Daed disappeared inside the school.

Through the lit windows of the school, she saw David leaning against the desk, holding a book, with the three men sitting in a semicircle facing him. They appeared to be listening attentively. But when Daed entered, the three turned and looked toward the door.

Rachel couldn't take the suspense. Dread overtook her.

Daed pulled up a chair and joined the other men in the semicircle. He was *participating*?

Headlights lit the driveway as a car pulled in. Sam's. He drove the beat-up vehicle behind the barn and parked. A car door slammed.

About a minute later, Sam stepped up on the porch. "You need to stop mooning over him." He gestured toward the school before sitting next to her.

"Jah, but…." She gave her brother a sideways glance. What kind of mood was he in? He didn't seem angry. "I wrote Obadiah and asked for a break."

Sam pressed his lips together and looked away. "If you aren't going to be faithful, that's probably best."

Her defenses flared. He accused *her* of being unfaithful? "*He* wasn't being faithful in the first place."

"Maybe so, but you can do better than *him*." He nodded toward the school. "You can't trust him. Besides, he's handicapped. What gut is he, Rachel? He can't work. How would he support a family?"

Jah, she knew. Hadn't she entertained those very questions?

"He could get a job in a cabinetry shop, or in a greenhaus or garden center," Rachel ventured.

Sam glanced away.

Darkness settled in Rachel's soul. "If you don't kill him first."

Sam gave her a sharp look.

"Don't tell me you didn't write that death threat on the whiteboard. I recognized your handwriting." They'd skirted around the issue long enough. She crossed her arms over her chest and stared him down.

He shrugged. "He deserves death threats after what he did."

"And a fireplace poker to the skull? And swapped-out pills? He doesn't even remember, Sam. He told me about the accident in Pennsylvania…said it might've been the one you were involved in. But he isn't sure."

"He was there. He gave Ezra the drugs. I'll never forgive him." Sam's eyes flashed with unprecedented anger as he aimed a glare across the street.

"*Jah*, but he didn't force Ezra to take the drugs. He didn't make him get in the car and drive. Those decisions were Ezra's, not David's. Someone else gave David the drugs. He didn't like what they did to him." Was Sam even listening to her? Would he back off?

He clenched his fists. "Then he should've destroyed them."

"He admits that." Rachel pulled her coat more tightly closed and looked at the schoolhaus. What were the men talking about? Her curiosity was making her crazy. "But he also says he was a stupid teenager then. He confessed in front of his church in Pennsylvania,

Sam. And he joined the church. That means his sins are forgiven. Shouldn't that be true here as well as there?"

"Nice. He has you fighting his battles for him." Sam rose to his feet. "In theory, what you say might be true. But in reality, it's a different story. He hasn't confessed to us. And we're the ones he hurt." His lips curled.

"Would you forgive him if he did?" *And stop threatening to kill him?*

The door slammed shut behind him.

~

David's breath hitched when Preacher Samuel entered the school, pulled up a chair, and settled next to Reuben. He glanced at Reuben's Bible, then looked to David. "What did I miss?"

A look of alarm flashed across Josh's face, and Viktor's expression registered some unidentifiable emotion that disappeared before David could identify it. Only Reuben appeared unruffled.

David didn't know how to respond. He'd closed his German/ Englisch Bible with his index finger marking his place.

"Rachel said you were having men's meeting," Preacher Samuel said. "If I'd known Reuben was involved, I wouldn't have worried so much."

David wouldn't lie to Rachel's daed. If he got in trouble, then so be it. It wouldn't be the first time in this community. He just didn't want his new friends to be penalized. "It is for accountability, but it's more of a prayer meeting and Bible study, Preacher Samuel," he answered.

Josh coughed. David avoided his gaze, but in his peripheral vision, he caught Josh subtly shaking his head.

"That so? What are you studying? Mind starting over so I can listen in?"

Reuben gave a slight nod. Josh choked, then coughed again, violently, as if he'd swallowed a piece of peppermint candy whole. He got up, hurried to the bathroom, and shut the door.

Soon, the coughing quieted some, and Josh returned to the group. David looked back at Preacher Samuel. "Jah, I can do that." Strangely enough, a sense of peace filled him.

After quickly rehashing what they'd covered so far, he said, "I am called to mobilize an army to glorify Gott. And—"

"Army?" Preacher Samuel's eyebrows shot up. "To glorify Gott?"

David made eye contact with the preacher. "Figuratively. I'm called to His service." He braced himself for the inevitable comment.

Rachel's daed grunted. "Preachers are called by lot, not individually or personally." He held David's gaze.

David pinched his lips together and glanced at the Bible in his hand. "Forgive me, but I disagree. Gott *did* call me, individually and personally." It was no surprise that his belief was frowned upon. It went against everything the Amish were taught.

Preacher Samuel shook his head. "I guess we'll have to agree to disagree. However, as long as Reuben sits in, I don't think it'll hurt any of you buwe to discover more of Gott…and maybe to consider kneeling for believer's baptism." Preacher Samuel's gaze speared Viktor, then Josh, and finally David.

David squirmed slightly, resisting the urge to inform him that he'd already knelt for baptism in the Amish church. For then he'd have to acknowledge even more beliefs and rules he'd struggled to accept and obey.

Nobody else answered the preacher, though Reuben did give another nod of his head.

"I might join you buwe again." Preacher Samuel stood. "For now, have a gut nacht." With that, he walked out, shutting the door behind him.

The silence stretched for ages. David glanced out the window and watched Preacher Samuel cross the road to his haus.

"So, who told?" Josh finally asked, looking around at the others.

"I told Rachel." David closed his Bible and placed it on the desk. "But I suppose he gave us his okay…." Sort of.

Reuben smiled. "Sounded like it to me. David, you did a fine job. I think Gott does have His call on your life. It just might not be within the Amish faith."

He'd already considered that. And the shunning that would result if he pursued that course. The thought broke his heart, because though he'd already moved across the country, far away from his family, he still loved them. Wanted to associate with them and be allowed to visit. And there was Rachel. Even though she'd made her attraction to him more than clear, and he'd probably expressed his infatuation just as plainly, she would be lost to him.

Granted, she wasn't yet his, anyway.

Viktor stood, frowning. "I've already discovered that Gott doesn't fit inside either box that the Amish or Englisch try to shove Him in. He's much bigger. Far more amazing. And even though I told Bishop Joe I would consider kneeling, I may not. I'm not much for following rules I don't believe in." He glanced at his grossdaedi.

"Gott doesn't fit in a box, for sure," Josh agreed.

"Are you ready to go?" Reuben slowly pulled himself up from his chair. "David, I'll see you next week. Danki for talking with us to-nacht."

"Wait a minute. I hadn't quite finished." David pulled in a breath as the others watched him expectantly. Reuben paused in the midst of pulling on his coat. "Because der Herr is watching over us, we don't have to fear the dangers around us. He knows about them, and He will never allow any harm to befall us that He hasn't authorized."

Reuben gazed steadily at David. "Very gut point, sohn. Something we all need to remember, ain't so?"

Jah. If only he could take that truth to heart and believe it totally and completely, without the fear of man—particularly Sam. Or the bishop.

❧

Rachel jumped to her feet as Daed approached the haus. He came up the porch stairs, his forehead furrowed, his lips pursed in a slight frown.

"Daed?"

He blinked, then met her gaze. "You're still out here. What were you dropping in the mailbox earlier?"

"Um...a letter to Obadiah."

Daed stumbled. He reached for a post to steady himself.

"Are you hurt?"

Daed shook his head. "Is that wise?"

What? Rachel frowned. "I don't understand."

"You've made your attraction to David Lapp very clear. Your mamm and I have noticed you as gut as throwing yourself at him. Is it therefore wise to encourage Obadiah?"

Rachel's cheeks burned. Her parents must have noticed her sneaking glances at him during meals and her frequent trips to the school. "I am breaking up with Obadiah. And I'm sorry if you've thought I've been acting inappropriately with David. I didn't mean to."

Daed pulled on his beard. "Sometimes, when it's right, you just have to take action, appropriate or not. Your mamm did. She set her kapp for me, and I never knew what hit me. I'm sure David's reacting the same way."

Did Daed really think she and David were meant for each other? She couldn't keep from smiling. "What were they doing over there?"

Daed glanced over his shoulder. Viktor and his grossdaedi came out of the building and made their way to the truck. Daed looked back at her. "It's a Bible study, for sure. Nein accountability, as far as I could tell. But maybe it's too early for that." He hesitated a moment. "I think I'll go again."

"To a Bible study?" Rachel's voice shook. Bishop Joe would likely send David packing unless he had his lessons reviewed and given the OK. "They're studying approved passages, ain't so?"

"Jah, but...." Daed shook his head. "This bu is not going to stop there. When he gains his confidence, he's...." His chest rose and fell with a heavy sigh.

Nein. David would get himself into trouble.

"I want Sam...." Daed frowned. "Where is he?"

"Sam?" Rachel looked over her shoulder at the screen door. "He went inside."

"I'll find him." Weariness filled Daed's eyes. "Don't go over there, Rachel."

"To the school?" Rachel was confused. Hadn't Daed sanctioned their relationship?

"Jah. From now on, someone else should deliver the meals he takes there." Daed started for the door.

Rachel's lips tightened. "So, you're forbidding me to see him, unless he comes here for dinner?"

Daed stopped and turned around. "Nein. But you need to give the bu a chance to decide what he wants. And to catch up if he chooses. It's his decision, Rachel. You don't want to make it too easy on him. The way you're going, you'll get a reputation like...well...." Another heavy sigh. "Lily."

Rachel gasped, hurt tearing through her. *Lily?* Pregnant by an unknown man who refused to marry her and who called her a tramp, Lily had found only Henry—a man who'd been forced to kneel and confess his violent anger and abuse—to take on her shame as her ehemann. Rachel didn't know whom she felt sorrier for. Either way, it wasn't a gut situation. Not at all. And Daed thought she'd get *that* kind of reputation? *Ouch.*

"There's something to be said for playing hard to get." Daed quirked an eyebrow and stepped inside. A moment later, he stuck his head back out. "But not too hard. We don't want him giving up hope, ain't so? I don't mean that you should pretend you aren't interested. But you don't need to openly chase him."

And that meant Daed *did* approve of David.

Still seated on the top step, Rachel stared across the street at the school. How did a girl play hard to get?

Chapter 22

The snow and cold ended as quickly as they'd kum, with temperatures soon soaring into the fifties. After the freeze, it felt almost balmy on Friday. Thanks to the winter warm-up, mud was the word of the day—both the literal substance and as the topic of a creative writing assignment for the scholars. They were to compose a short story or a poem that featured the stuff.

At the end of the day, David swished a damp mop over the classroom floor, cleaning up all the dirt and dried leaves that the students had tracked in. Did the female teacher usually scrub the floor during lunch break, while the scholars played outside? Or did she clean only when school was over, as he did? Maybe she was smart and kept the kinner inside when the ground was damp.

The floor finally clean, he opened the front door and dumped the pail of formerly sudsy, lemon-scented water. He paused in the open doorway and gazed at the haus across the street for what seemed an eternity, hoping...hoping....

Rosie rushed past him and into the school, tracking fresh mud. David sighed as he passed the mop over the trail of wet brown paw prints.

A week had gone by without a single glimpse of Rachel. Mary had told him that until the weather cleared, he should stay at the school; someone would bring his meals over. The instruction hadn't meant much to him at the time. Rachel *had* been doing that. But now, Rachel never came. Luther did. And he never stayed. Without a word, he would unload the contents of the silver tray on the desk and then hurry back home, leaving David alone to battle that wonderful disease known as cabin fever.

He missed Rachel. Missed the teasing, the conversations, the energy that seemed to flow between them. She made him crazy, but he didn't want to live without her.

At least he had the Bible study that evening to look forward to. And he'd almost forgotten—earlier that day, he'd received word from Mary that he could kum to their haus for dinner, if he wanted to. He couldn't keep from smiling. The invitation almost seemed like a lifeline. Especially with the opportunity to see Rachel.

When the paw prints were wiped up and the cleaning supplies put away, David straightened the rows of desks and cleaned the whiteboard. He glanced at the windup clock. Would he appear too desperate if he walked over to the Millers' right now? Probably so, especially if he went to the kitchen door. But maybe not so much if he went to the barn and offered his help. He could do something, especially since his ankle was mostly healed.

Perhaps he should stop first at the phone shanty and call his parents. He'd destroyed the initial letter he'd started to them and had yet to write another. When their letters to him in Seymour were returned, stamped "Addressee unknown," they would be alarmed.

He also needed to order the supplies for fly ties and basket weaving he'd run out of. He grabbed a pad of paper and quickly wrote out a list of what he needed, then stuck it in an envelope with a check from his Pennsylvania account and addressed it to a local crafting supply company. He'd never bothered to open a new account in Missouri.

David headed outside and across the road to the mailbox. It felt wunderbaar to walk without crutches, without his ankle wrapped. He used a cane, but only for support on the uneven surface of the dirt road.

He glanced up at the sky and saw nothing but dark clouds. Something was blowing in. Another snowstorm? Ice? Thunder rumbled. A rainstorm? Missouri had odd weather. Ice one week, rain the next.

He put the letter in the mailbox and raised the flag, then went inside the phone shanty, picked up the receiver, and dialed home. Or what used to be home. A fresh wave of bitterness washed over him. If he'd only known....

The phone rang once.

David blew out a breath of air. Jah, if he'd known, he might've done things differently. He wouldn't have met Rachel, but....

Two rings.

Wait. Wishing to have known, to have done things differently, implied he didn't believe he was where Gott wanted him. That he'd followed his own paths. *Lord Gott, please make it clear that You want me here. Or tell me where You want me, if not here.* Peace filled him.

Three rings.

"Hello?"

David didn't recognize the voice. It didn't sound like his brother-in-law. Or like Daed. "This is David Lapp. Is my daed around? Daniel Lapp?"

After a long hesitation, the man on the other end stammered, "Oh, no. He can't come to the phone. He's...well...I shouldn't.... I could take a message."

Okay, that sounded confusing. Alarming. But the voice sounded more Englisch than Amish. It didn't have the German accent David was used to. Still, he was tempted to ask what words should've filled the blanks the man had left. "Just tell him I called, I'm fine, and I'll write soon. I moved, so any letters Mamm might send to me in Seymour will probably be returned."

"Got it. I'll have someone call, if you give me your number."

David read the phone number off the paper that was taped to the phone, thanked the man, and hung up. He was disappointed that Daed hadn't been home. Surely, he lived in the dawdi-haus. The man had said that Daed couldn't kum to the phone. What did that mean, exactly?

David tamped down the fear that rose in his chest. He would write soon. And he'd definitely call again later.

Overhead, thunder rumbled. David glanced out the window. Lightning flashed across the sky.

He exited the phone shanty and saw that the Millers' barn doors stood wide open. Male voices drifted out from the interior. He headed for the building, figuring he could push a broom around or shovel out

Think about it. Isn't it frustrating to speak to someone, wanting to be understood, only to have them change the intent of what you are saying? Doesn't such behavior tend to stifle honest communication? In the shared-meaning process, the listener's response should be devoid of counsel, admonition, criticism, or commentary; it should be a simple and accurate report of what he or she heard.

When the listener finishes reporting back, he or she says, "Is that what you said?" This statement in turn leads to step 3 . . .

Step 3: The speaker acknowledges the listener's accuracy.

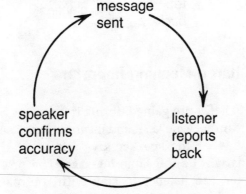

At this point, the speaker has two courses of action. If he is satisfied that the listener has heard him accurately, he can respond by saying, "Yes, that's what I said." Or, if he feels that the listener has misunderstood, omitted, or distorted his message, he can clarify what the listener missed and request another response by again asking, "What did you hear me say?"

The shared-meaning process could be as simple as the three steps I've outlined above, or it could go on with more speaker-listener exchange until the shared-meaning process is complete. Any additional steps are basically a continuation of steps 1–3, carried out until each person is satisfied that a shared meaning has been achieved:

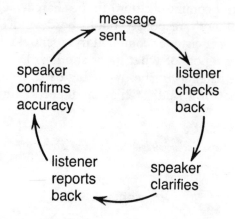

Why Is Shared Meaning Important?

Several benefits are gained during the process of reaching a shared meaning. One, a shared meaning increases the likelihood that what the speaker says and what the listener understands will be the same message. The process forces both speaker and listener to stay with the dialogue long enough to achieve an accurate perception. Step by step, mutual understanding is achieved.

Working to achieve a shared meaning also increases two people's awareness of one another's perspective on a given issue. It challenges the listener to become intently involved in what the speaker is saying. A person who knows he is working toward a shared meaning realizes that he is accountable to respond to what his partner says. He has to demonstrate, "I've been listening," and so listens more carefully.

If two people will accept the discipline of the process, it can greatly benefit both speaking and listening skills. Typical conversations have little or no monitoring process to check on the accuracy of communication. The shared-meaning process is a self-imposed discipline to monitor how well and how accurately two people communicate. Both speaker and listener are accountable to contribute their skills to the process.

Reaching a shared meaning is most important when the *message* is especially important. Its greatest value comes when it is used with issues that are considered vital to a relationship—I value issues which have practical applications. The persons involved in each situation will have to decide what concerns are especially significant to them. In an employee-employer relationship, a crucial concern might be mutual understanding of company procedures or working relationships. In a marital setting, shared meaning might relate to financial matters, in-law relationships, rearing children, and so on.

There is another situation in which the shared-meaning process is especially valuable—a situation in which there is danger of a misunderstanding or when one partner is fearful that his or her message will be heard incorrectly. Think back on situations with your partner when you have felt misunderstood, or times when he or she said, "You've got it all wrong; that's not what I said!" Perhaps you might want to list issues that the two of you have struggled with in the past; these may represent concerns that would profit from the shared-meaning process.

The shared-meaning process has great potential for aiding partners to come to common understandings. It can leave individuals feeling happy because they are understood. The positive benefits it offers makes the discipline it requires worthwhile. Consider it for your important relationships.

Putting Shared Meaning into Practice

This concept is probably new to many readers. The exercises that follow will help you gain a better feeling for the shared meaning process. Work through each step with a partner.

---

1. List several issues you would like to discuss with someone, and the specific persons with whom you would like to discuss these issues. The issues should be those over which you want to reach a shared meaning.

   Person   *Issue*

   _____   _____
   _____   _____
   _____   _____
   _____   _____

   Do the persons involved understand the shared-meaning concept? If not, how could you acquaint them with it?

2. Schedule time with the persons you have listed above. Remember to plan time when both of you are rested, relaxed, and undistracted. Work through the shared-meaning process.

3. Evaluate the outcome of your discussion:
   a. Did you follow the three-step process?
   b. Did you stay on the issue?
   c. Did you avoid accusations, ridicule, name-calling?
   d. Did you understand your partner's communication?
   e. Did your partner understand you?

stalls. He could even milk cows or feed the other animals. Maybe, if he started making himself useful, Preacher Samuel would let him borrow a horse and buggy, and he could make the necessary visit to the bishop and start confessing his sins to this district. Followed by a trip to town for some supplies.

A cherished verse from 1 John flashed through his mind. *"If we confess our sins, he is faithful and just to forgive us our sins, and to cleanse us from all unrighteousness."*

So comforting to know Gott was faithful. Too bad man wasn't. David set his jaw as he entered the dark interior of the barn. He took a moment to orient himself. The voices came from the back. He wrinkled his nose as the dust and strong animal smells assailed his senses. Then he followed the sounds to a flimsy wooden door. He opened it and looked down six concrete stairs into the cow barn. There was nein railing, but he could do it.

In the cow barn, Luther was filling the troughs with water. Preacher Samuel sat on a stool with his head resting against the flank of a cow. He looked up at David and raised his eyebrows. "Starting to go stir-crazy, David?"

"Maybe." *Definitely.* "Is there another pail? I can help milk."

"Stool's hanging on the wall." The preacher nodded toward the clean pail sitting beside him. "What's on your mind?"

Would it be better to blurt out his problems or to talk about the weather first? More thunder rumbled, as if trying to sway his decision.

"Church will be here Sunday, if you'd like to join us." Preacher Samuel spoke first.

Two days from now. David grinned. He'd missed the fellowship, the long songs from the Ausbund, and even the messages. Of course, he'd be an outsider, but he worshipped the same Gott. "Danki." He leaned his cane against the wall and lifted down the stool.

Rachel's daed grinned back at him. "Glad to see you're healing."

"Jah, as long as I can keep from stepping in holes." Or getting hit by trucks. But that was a different story. And one he didn't care to repeat.

David set the stool beside a cow, reached for the pail, and then sat and started to position himself. Then it hit him: How would he get up again? He'd have nothing to use to support himself.

Except for a bovine that might or might not feel like being helpful.

He shut his eyes. Jah, he really was a dummchen.

❧

Rachel pressed "play" on the answering machine in the phone shanty.

"Rachel, this is Obadiah. I'll call you Friday afternoon at four." He sounded the same, his voice a soft tenor. She smiled, but it quickly morphed into a frown. What would he have to say for himself? And... wait. This was Friday. He'd call today? Soon, actually. It was almost four.

Should she be upset that he'd made an effort to call her only after she'd sent him the second letter? The letter she'd intended for David but had mailed to Obadiah had probably arrived there a day or two ahead of the breakup letter. He'd probably read it, taken some time to think, and then called to leave a message requesting that they schedule a phone conversation. Planned, to the day. Hour. Minute. The way Obadiah liked it.

The way she liked it, too, if she were honest. Plans were gut. Far more certain than leaving it up to whim. Fancy. Faith.

Attraction.

The type of knee-buckling, breathless attraction she felt around David. David, who trusted all things to Gott with blind faith.

Wasn't there a verse in the Bible about a man planning his way but Gott directing his steps?

A twinge of guilt worked through her. She resisted looking out the window of the shanty. She didn't want to see the school or David. Not now, when, at least in her mind, she was cheating on him.

Nein, right now, she had a phone date with Obadiah. Unexpected on her end, but this would determine where she'd go from here.

Whether she would be Obadiah's girl or David's. Too bad she hadn't found out about the scheduled phone call earlier.

Though, if Daed knew she had a phone date with Obadiah, he'd reiterate what he'd said earlier about leading him on when she had strong feelings for David. She deleted Obadiah's message as a streak of lightning flashed across the sky. Seconds later, a clap of thunder sounded overhead.

She sighed. She had to consider her future, too, didn't she? Obadiah would be a gut provider. And they'd known each other a long time—almost forever. What if David was nothing more than a diversion?

If he was, it was a diversion she was falling in love with. A diversion she dreamed of kissing. A diversion she wanted to spend the rest of her life with.

She blinked away the moisture that suddenly filled her eyes. Was it wrong to hope that Obadiah wanted to break up?

Obadiah must have timed the call so that she would have to rush to the haus afterward to finish supper preparations. A flash of irritation matched the lightning outside. Of course, if things went the way she wanted, they wouldn't have much to say. *"Jah, Rachel. You're right. We're through. I love someone else."* Someone whose name started with Ab-. Abigail, probably.

At the sound of a horse's hooves pounding down the road, she whirled around. A buggy pulled up beside the shanty, and the horse tossed its head with a snort. Rachel looked at the driver, and her breath caught. Obadiah. He'd kum, just like David had had said he would.

And that meant…. Her heart shattered. That meant he didn't want to break up. That meant she had to make the right choice—Obadiah. She wouldn't be wrapped in David's strong arms, kissed thoroughly by his irresistible lips, for a long time. Never again, actually.

She stared at Obadiah, speechless.

His lips, thinner than David's, stretched into a smile. He held out his hand, an invitation to join him in the buggy. "Glad you waited. I haven't seen you in ever so long. Kum. Mamm is expecting us."

Rachel glanced toward the haus. Mamm was probably focused 100 percent on her current quilting project. She wouldn't think of dinner until one of the menfolk reminded her or her stomach growled loudly enough to get her attention.

And David…. Despite her earlier resolution, Rachel glanced toward the school. Briefly. Not long enough to search for David. He'd been invited for supper, and she'd looked forward to seeing him.

She turned back to Obadiah. He waited, his hand steady. "Kum on, Rachel. It's been ages since we were together."

"But…." She glanced at the school once more.

"Rachel. Please. You owe it to me to hear the truth."

The truth. Did that mean he might want to break up, after all?

There was a flash of sky-to-ground lightning, followed immediately by a loud boom that made Rachel jump. Maybe it'd be safer in the buggy. She didn't know where the lightning had struck, but it'd been close. She took Obadiah's hand, clambered up into the buggy, and settled beside him.

Grinning, he flicked the reins, and the horse set off at a canter.

What about supper? Rachel glanced at the kitchen window. She could see Mary, still working on biscuit dough. When her sister glanced up, Rachel waved to let Mary know she was leaving. Hopefully, she would tell Mamm that she'd gone, so Mamm would realize she needed to start supper.

Everything would be okay.

❧

The streams of milk sputtering into the bucket ceased as David released the teats and leaned back from the cow. Her udder was mostly spent, judging by the way it had softened as he'd worked. He moved the bucket out of the way and scooted back with a glance at Preacher Samuel.

David needed to speak now...or wait until after dinner. Now would be better. That way, he could face Rachel with a clear conscience. More thunder rumbled overhead. It sounded like a full-fledged storm, but he didn't hear any rain pouring down.

"Uh, Preacher Samuel?" he spoke over the din. "I need to talk to you and...and Sam...about...some things."

The preacher rose, bent to pick up the stool, then turned his steady gaze on David. "I figured so."

He didn't look condemning but rather compassionate. Understanding.

Possibly even forgiving.

Gott, please, let it be so. With Sam, too.

The preacher turned away. "I'm going to carry this bucket up to the haus. Then I'll find Sam, and we'll talk. Be right back."

David turned his attention to the black cat that had suddenly appeared, weaving between the cow's legs. It looked up at David with a plaintive meow.

Outside the cow barn, Preacher Samuel said something, and Sam answered, his voice low. Maybe grumbling.

Please, Gott....

Sam's voice sounded more distant now, and creaking boards sounded outside the door. Preacher Samuel came back in. "Sam's taking the milk to the kitchen. Looks like you're finished. Will you need help getting up?"

David wished he could say nein. He tried to bury his pride deep inside. He'd need a gut dose of humility to get through this remorse. This shame. Emotions he hadn't felt this strongly since two years ago.

Now, it was done. Over. Forgiven.

Except with the people here.

He looked up with a nod. "Jah, danki."

Sam burst through the door, his eyes wide, his chest heaving.

"Fire!"

Chapter 23

More lightning flashed across the sky as Obadiah slowed the buggy and pulled to the side of the road to let a minivan pass. Rachel sent him a sidelong glance. He'd yet to say anything since driving away from her haus, and they'd passed three or four farms. Maybe he needed to think.

She, for one, was content to sit in silence and let her thoughts wander...to David. How would he react to finding her gone? After a week, did he miss seeing her as much as she did him? Enough that he'd start to seek her out so that she wouldn't have to resume chasing him?

That would make Daed happy, ain't so?

"So, you're 'fascinated' with another man?" Obadiah's voice intruded on her thoughts. "Unique way of saying you miss me, Rachel. You knew I planned to kum home for Christmas. That's only two and a half months away. Does this 'other man' even exist?" A slight smirk appeared on his face.

Anger rose within her. She tried to tamp it down. "He's just as real as the girl you started taking home from singings."

Obadiah glanced sideways at her. "Abigail? She's my boss's dochter. He asked me to look out for her and give her a ride home if nobody else offered. Completely innocent, Rachel. You're the girl I plan to marry."

So, he *hadn't* kum here to break up. He'd kum to salvage the relationship. "I'm sorry." But that meant she'd still be promised to Obadiah and doomed to merely daydream of David. Would she forever wonder what'd it be like to marry the one who made her heart sing? Even when she was old and gray?

Would that be fair to Obadiah? To David? To herself? To her future kinner?

She pulled in a shuddery breath. "As I said, he does exist."

Obadiah blinked. "Who?"

"The man who fascinates me. He's here, originally from Pennsylvania."

His eyes skimmed over her, then refocused on the road as another streak of lightning lit the sky. Thunder rumbled nearby. "You sure, Rach? Breaking up isn't so easily undone."

He'd found her weak spot. She wasn't sure. She looked away. "I…I don't know."

"Then we have this time to reconnect, ain't so? Take some time to get to know each other again before you decide to call it quits?"

She supposed that was only fair.

"Jah, we should. I do have feelings for you, Obadiah." Just not the crazy, over-the-top, fluttery ones she had for David.

He smiled. "And I care for you, Rachel."

"Feelings." "Care for." Was it wrong to notice that neither of them had used the word "love"?

Somewhere behind them, an emergency bell started clanging.

Rachel glanced over her shoulder. Unease flickered through her. "Should we go back?"

Obadiah hesitated only briefly. "Nein. Mamm and Daed are waiting. Besides, we don't know where the fire is. They'll have plenty of help."

That was true. Every man within hearing distance—whether Amish or Englisch—would drop everything and run to help.

Except for Obadiah. He flicked the reins again, and they were off.

Why was he unwilling to help? Just because of his parents? Maybe he was merely tired after the long bus trip from Ohio to northern Missouri.

~

Sam turned and ran in the direction he'd kum from. Luther and Preacher Samuel scrambled up the stairs and out of the room as the emergency bell clanged.

David was left forgotten. Alone. Well, except for the cows and the cat.

Somehow he managed to bolt to his feet. Probably from fear and adrenaline. What was on fire? Was it the school?

It would figure, with everything that'd been happening around here. But would Sam really have resorted to burning David's residence? Probably not unless David was inside, asleep. Not when he was across the street, in the milk barn, and would survive.

Lord, forgive me for such bitter thoughts.

He stumbled up the stairs, down the narrow hallway leading to the main part of the barn, and out the big doors.

Black smoke billowed from the haus. Flames were shooting up from one part of the roof.

Ach, nein. *Rachel....*

His cane forgotten somewhere in the barn, David forced himself to run, despite the pain, toward the haus. Past the bucket of milk Sam had abandoned.

Sam, Luther, and Preacher Samuel had all run inside the haus. The littlest girl—even though she was one of his scholars, he couldn't think of her name—stood outside by the pump, crying.

David's feet faltered as he ran past her. "Stay there." She was safe. The others...*Rachel....*

Inside the kitchen, flames devoured the wall behind the stove. Mary stood there, wide-eyed, her hand slapped over her mouth and nose. Preacher Samuel disappeared upstairs while Sam and Luther fought the fire with wet towels.

Rachel wasn't anywhere in sight. Though she might be upstairs. David started for the steps, then remembered the preacher had gone that way. He pivoted, ran for the sink, and started wetting more rags. Filling kettles and pots with water.

The ceiling burst into flames. Sam yelled something and dashed upstairs, too. Luther still battled the wall of fire, which expanded with every second. David went to help him fight the flames.

A pickup truck tore into the yard.

David gave Mary a shove toward the door. "Go outside. Stay with your sister."

With a wail, she scampered out the door.

Viktor appeared in the doorway. "Get out! Find buckets. I called nine-one-one."

Luther hurried to obey.

David bolted for the stairs.

Preacher Samuel pushed past him, his arms full of quilts. "Get out. Unsafe."

"But what about Rachel?"

"She's not down there?" Alarm flashed across her daed's face.

"Nein."

"Hurry."

David lumbered up the stairs and burst into the first room he came to. Rachel's Mamm was there, piling more quilts in her arms. "Get the rest," she told him.

"Where's Rachel?" Quilts didn't matter.

She hesitated. "I thought she was in charge of dinner. Maybe she's in the garden." She turned and rushed out the door to the stairs.

Rachel hadn't been in the garden.

David scurried to the next bedroom. Empty. Then the third. Sam was loading boxes in his arms.

"Where's Rachel?" David shouted.

"I don't know. Hopefully outside. Here, take these." Sam pushed a stack of boxes toward him.

Thick smoke poured into the room, bringing with it unbearable heat. "Kum on," David insisted. "Your belongings don't matter."

"Take them," Sam growled.

David did. The weight of them surprised him. "Kum. Now."

Sam grabbed a couple more boxes and ran for the door. David followed right behind him.

Flames filled the doorway, blocking their exit.

David kicked the door shut and pivoted. "Open the window."

Sam stood there. Frozen.

Right. He'd do it himself. He set down the pile of heavy boxes to free his arms, then shoved the window upward. He hefted the boxes and shoved them out the window. Then reached for Sam's load and dropped them out, too. Pushed Sam forward. "Go!"

Sam climbed out the window, then hesitated for an endless moment, dangling there. He breathed heavily as he stared at the ground.

"Jump!" David's throat was raw. It was getting harder to breathe as black smoke filled the haus.

After what seemed like an eternity, Sam released the ledge and dropped. He landed on his feet but stumbled forward and fell to his knees. Someone David didn't recognize helped him up and led him away.

David leaned out, breathing in precious gulps of air. "Rachel down there?"

"Jump!" another stranger shouted up to him.

"Rachel?"

The man shook his head.

David spun away from the window and ran for the door.

⌒

Obadiah reached for Rachel's hand as he drove her home. She allowed him to hold it, but she couldn't help comparing it with David's touch. Nein shivers. Nothing. It was like holding her brother's hand.

If only she'd refused to go along with him. She'd missed a chance to see David for the awkwardness of spending time with Obadiah and his parents. She hadn't wanted to hang out with them after dinner and had begged Obadiah to take her home.

As they neared the haus, she noticed a plume of black smoke ascending in the cloudy sky. The unmistakable odor of burnt wood assailed her senses.

She'd thought the fire would be long out by now.

She wrinkled her nose, then covered her mouth with her hand. Home came into view—or what used to be home.

She straightened, jerking away from Obadiah, and stared open-mouthed at her haus. Flames flickered in the windows. Out the chimney. As she watched, the roof collapsed.

"Whoa." Obadiah pulled the reins to stop his horse. "Wow."

With a sharp jerk of her head, Rachel jumped off the buggy and raced through the throng of other buggies, pickups, fire engines, police cars, and ambulances parked in the yard. As she ran, one of the ambulances turned on its flashing lights and pulled into the road, sending out a scattering of mud from its tires. The driver didn't turn on the siren, probably so as not to startle the horses.

Her family stood by the water pump. Her gaze skimmed over them. Daed, Mamm, her sisters, her brothers...except for Sam and Luther. She looked toward the ambulances. Another one drove off, lights flashing.

She didn't see David. But he had to be somewhere in the crowd.

"What happened?" she called as she approached.

"Where were you?" Daed's voice was sterner than she'd ever heard it.

"Obadiah— I went to dinner at his parents'— But what happened?"

"Don't you think you should've told someone?"

"Mary saw me." Rachel looked at her sister. "I waved."

Mary shook her head, mute. Tears flowed down her cheeks.

Rachel looked back at Daed. "What happened?" she asked once more.

"Lightning, probably." Obadiah came up behind her. "I never thought it'd be your haus."

"Possibly compounded by a kitchen fire." Daed glanced at Mary, then looked back at Rachel. "The fire department will investigate."

Her chest hurt. "Sam and Luther?"

Daed looked after the ambulances. "Luther will be okay. Smoke inhalation, minor burns. Sam had severe smoke inhalation. But David...." He frowned.

Rachel's heart stalled.

"Daed? What happened to David?" She couldn't keep the keening wail out of her voice.

"He got Sam out, then he went looking for you. Wouldn't stop." Daed shook his head, sadly. Tears trickled down his ash-stained face. "The firefighters got him out, but he'd already been overcome by smoke. He…he may not survive."

Rachel sucked in a painful breath and fell to her knees. She buried her face in her arms and sobbed. Wailed. Shook uncontrollably.

Ach, Gott, what have I done?

Chapter 24

David hurt. Everywhere. He fought his way through a thick, dark cloud. Each breath was a struggle.

His swollen throat burned. He was strapped down to...something. He couldn't move, as hard as he tried, fighting for freedom, fighting for life, fighting for—

Something settled over his nose and mouth. A cool rush of oxygen started making its way to his lungs.

A gentle hand rested on his. Soft words he couldn't understand floated over him, calming him.

And then a sharp prick on his wrist.

He flailed.

More soft words.

A door slammed. An engine started.

He stopped struggling and allowed himself to relax.

The pain subsided as comforting blackness closed over him.

❦

A hand gripped Rachel's shoulder. "Hey, Rach. Calm down." Obadiah patted her. "Kum on, get up."

She struggled to control her sobs. But she couldn't.

She heard Daed say something. Obadiah answered him. He continued his annoying patting, as though she were a dog. The bishop's voice merged with the others.

She sucked in a breath and mustered her courage. She couldn't allow herself to make a scene in front of the bishop. He'd remind her that life would go on, despite her sorrow and guilt. It was time—past time—to pull herself together and face whatever happened.

Her fault...all her fault. If she'd been home....

Well, she couldn't control the lightning. That was up to Gott. But if she'd been home, David would be okay. Not teetering on the line between life and death for the second time in a year.

She stood but kept her head bowed. Nobody reached out for her. She walked, unhindered, away from her family, away from Obadiah and the bishop, and hid in a dark corner of the barn. It wasn't far enough. She wanted to let loose, to scream at Gott, to cry out all her pain and agony.

None of that would be allowed.

She needed to be alone.

Nein, she needed someone to pull her near, to tell her that it would all be okay. That David would live. That Gott had forgiven her. That she was worthy of mercy, grace, and love.

If only she might be found worthy somehow. *Gott, forgive me. I'm so sorry for playing games with David. For misleading Obadiah. For running off with him, away from my family....*

So many bad decisions.

Hot tears burned her eyes and flowed unhampered down her cheeks.

"Rachel?" Daed came into the barn.

Rachel huddled into as small a space as she could, but hiding from Daed pricked her conscience, especially on top of everything else. She slowly straightened and made her way out of the shadows. "Jah." Her voice broke.

Daed frowned. "I'm sending your brothers and sisters home with some of your aenties and onkels, until I find a place we can all be together. But I thought you might want to ride with your mamm and me to the hospital."

"Jah, I would." She wiped her fist across her eyes. "Daed, what are we going to do? We don't have a home anymore." It came out as a wail. Her letters from David...gone. Her library of books...gone. Her postcards from Esther and her other pen pals...gone. But that was nothing compared to losing David. "And David! Ach, Daed...." Her voice broke again, and she crumpled against the wall.

Daed pulled in a breath. "I know. I know." He gave her an awkward hug. "They put him on oxygen in the ambulance. He wasn't breathing...."

Her body racked with sobs.

Daed sighed. "I probably shouldn't have told you that." He shook his head. "Don't worry. Gott knows. He cares. And David is in His hands."

Rachel sniffed, starting to collect herself. "I can't marry Obadiah."

Daed rubbed her upper back for a moment, then he pulled away. "I think we all realize that, Rachel. Even Obadiah. You made that plain. I will pray for David. For his healing."

"Danki, Daed."

"Kum now. And don't worry about a home. Gott will provide that, too. Besides, the bishop indicated some help might be forthcoming from the church."

That'd be a blessing. The Amish did barn raisings all the time, but would they do a haus raising? She'd never heard of there being one. She had heard, however, of people who lived for years in unfinished cellars, in shacks, or even in their barns while they saved money to build or buy a haus.

Daed raised a shoulder. "Also heard of property for sale not too far from here. It has a small haus. Might be okay until we get something bigger built. I'm going to check it out tomorrow. Besides, someone in the family might be in need of a starter farm in the not-too-distant future."

Someone like Sam, probably, since he was dating a girl.

Rachel followed Daed out of the barn and over to the huge four-door diesel pickup of one of their Englisch neighbors. She blinked at the sight of the huge step she'd need to take to get inside. The Englisch man lifted a stepstool from the pickup bed and positioned it on the ground. Mamm climbed into the backseat, and Rachel followed her. Daed got in the front seat. Some buggies remained, but Obadiah's was gone. He must've left.

As they drove down the endless stretch of highway from Jamesport to Chillicothe, Rachel made several attempts at prayer, but Gott seemed so far away. As if He couldn't bear to have her draw nigh to Him. As if her prayers rose no higher than the roof of the pickup truck.

Her mind kept struggling to process that David was on the verge of death because he'd gone looking for her...all because she'd left without telling anyone. A cold chill worked through her when she realized that he'd essentially done what she'd wanted: she'd wanted to play hard to get and thereby prod him into action, so that he'd start chasing her. And he had. He'd chased her all over the haus, looking for her, in a fire.

If David died, she'd never forgive herself.

"Daed, did Obadiah say we're through?" If Gott answered her prayers and kept David alive, she needed to make absolutely sure it was over with Obadiah.

Daed turned to look at her, a frown on his face. Wordlessly chiding her for her rudeness in speaking their language around an Englisch man.

She got the message, loud and clear. She stayed quiet and made another attempt at prayer, hoping that, despite the perceived barrier between her and der Herr, He might hear her and answer, after all.

When they reached the hospital, the driver let them out in front of the emergency room entrance. Rachel scurried inside, followed by Daed and Mamm. They went straight to the information desk.

"I'm Samuel Miller," her daed began. "I had some boys...family... brought in from a haus fire. Sam Miller, Luther Miller, and David Lapp."

The woman behind the desk tapped some keys on her computer. "If you'll take a seat over there, someone will be out to talk with you shortly." Another woman wrote something on a pad of paper and walked out from behind the counter, then disappeared through a door.

Rachel followed Daed and Mamm into the far corner of the waiting room, the side farthest from the TV. On the screen, a man sat behind a big brown desk, reporting the nightly news. Across the bottom of the screen was a stream of words that said something about

Dow Jones, with a string of numbers that meant nothing to her. She sat next to Daed, folded her hands in her lap, and bowed her head.

So far, they were the only Amish there. That would change as soon as news of the injuries got out to the community. Then people would flock to the hospital to wait with the family.

In the meantime, she could pray.

Would pray.

If only Gott would hear her prayers and give her another chance, she'd never play games again.

⟞

An obnoxious beeping sound filled the air around David. Where was he, anyway?

His entire body felt like lead, dragged down. Heavy.

He tried to speak, but it hurt his throat, his lungs. He tried again. Some sort of raspy croak emerged that couldn't possibly be his voice. And the attempt made the rawness worse. Something unnatural pressed against his inflamed tissues.

Someone poked at him. A finger forced his eyelids open. A flashlight blinded him. A male voice muttered something he couldn't understand.

Something cold pressed against his chest. It stayed in one place for a moment, then moved to a different spot. There was a tight pressure around his upper arm.

Was he in a hospital?

It would make sense, considering the pain he was in. Except this time, it wasn't in his leg.

Memories assailed him. Thick black smoke. Flames. Oppressive heat.

He jerked, fighting against the dark cloud that threatened to suffocate him.

Rachel! He tried to yell her name, multiple times. But with the rawness of his throat, all he could manage were weird grunting sounds.

He had to find Rachel. Make sure she was safe.

The male voice said something again, sharply, and then the pain-free blackness overtook him once more.

Chapter 25

A doctor from the emergency room, accompanied by a nurse, came out and approached Rachel and her parents. Daed stood to his feet. The doctor frowned at him. "You lost your home as a result of the fire?" He turned to the nurse. "I planned to release the younger one, but with no home to go to...." He shook his head.

"I can send him to my brother's house." Daed fingered his suspenders the way he did when he was worried. And Rachel knew why. With Daed's brother injured, the family struggling, it would only cause more problems to send Luther there.

The doctor looked up, his expression grave. "We'll keep him one more night for observation, just in case he shows some breathing problems that haven't surfaced yet. A nurse will bring you to your sons as soon as they're settled in a room."

"What about David Lapp?" Daed asked. "Any word on his condition?"

The doctor frowned again. "He's your son, as well?"

Daed shook his head. "No, but he may become my son-in-law someday."

Heat filled Rachel's cheeks.

The doctor's gaze skimmed over her. "Be that as it may, due to patient privacy laws, I can't give out any of his medical information without his permission. I'm sorry." He started to turn away, then hesitated and asked Rachel, "What is your name?"

"Rachel." She glanced at Daed for a moment, then looked back at the doctor. Why did he want to know her name?

He consulted his folder. "Give us a few minutes. I'll have someone come get you so you can visit briefly. It might do him some good."

"Dank—thank you."

"So, he's alive, but critical?" Daed asked.

The doctor nodded. A smile flickered on his face as he turned away without further comment.

Rachel watched him go. If only she could follow him down that endless corridor, find David, and know firsthand how he was doing. Apologize to him for the injuries he'd sustained while trying to save her. And tell him that she and Obadiah had officially broken up.

Or had they?

Daed never did actually say one way or another.

"Daed. About Obadiah…?"

Daed frowned. "He wishes you the best, and if you change your mind, you know where to find him."

It was really over? Relief washed over her. "I won't change my mind. David wouldn't be here, fighting for his life, if Obadiah hadn't kum by and made me go with him to his parents' haus. Or if he'd waited around to see what was on fire! Nein, he had to—"

"Rachel, he didn't force you into the buggy," Daed said stiffly. "You made the decision to go without telling anyone. How much trouble would it have caused to step inside and tell Mary? Or to kum into the barn to tell me? You cannot blame Obadiah. Besides, David fought the fire alongside your brothers. He made the choice to go upstairs when the fire got out of control. But, just so you know, I would've gone back in to look for you, too."

"I'm glad you didn't." Her guilt over causing David to require hospitalization, to make him fight for his life yet again, was enough. She couldn't imagine bearing the weight of the blame if the same things had happened to Daed.

"Viktor Petersheim stopped me as the firefighters arrived. They said they'd find anyone who might be still inside."

Rachel nodded. "Was Sam looking for me, too? Is that why he went upstairs?" She'd need to apologize to him, as well.

Daed hesitated. "I don't think so, Rachel. I don't know what his reasons were."

The door to the emergency room opened. Joshua Yoder strode in. He hesitated a moment, then came over to them. "Preacher Samuel. Any word?"

Daed narrowed his eyes. He glanced at the entry, then returned his gaze to Joshua. "Did you kum alone?"

Red crawled up Joshua's cheeks. "Viktor drove me, though I borrow his pickup from time to time, since my driver's license is still valid. But the bishop has already called a driver and arranged for a van to bring the others. It'll just be a matter of time before they arrive."

"Still driving. Borrowing Viktor's pickup." Daed's expression grew stern.

Joshua smiled sheepishly. "I shouldn't, I know. Sorry. Any word yet?"

Daed shook his head. "Officially, nein. Unofficially, he's alive and in critical condition."

Rachel choked back another sob.

Joshua released a sigh and bowed his head for a moment. "The phone in the shanty rang soon after you left. David's mamm called. His sister and brother-in-law were killed in a buggy accident. His father is in the hospital. They think he had a heart attack. They want him to kum home."

At least, that was what Rachel had thought she heard. But with the TV blaring and the loud conversation of another group of people nearby, plus her shaky emotional state, she wasn't sure.

She must've heard wrong. Gott wouldn't allow so many bad things to happen to one person. Not all at once.

❧

"Do you know where you are?"

"Hospital." David's voice sounded like a raspy whisper.

"Can you tell me your name and your date of birth?"

David blinked at the male nurse who'd introduced himself minutes before, but his name had sunk, unregistered, into an ocean of pain. The man leaned over the bedside table and wrote something on a clipboard. Then he lifted David's wrist, the one with the hospital ID bracelet, and angled so he could read it. David nodded toward the bracelet and raised an eyebrow. Easier than trying to talk.

The man met his stare. "I need you to tell me."

Can't you read? He bit back the sarcastic comment and instead recited the information, still in a raspy whisper. As the nurse scribbled something in the file, he croaked, "Rachel…did they find her?"

The nurse set down his pen and looked at David. "She should be on her way back here to see you. I sent a volunteer to go get her. But you'll have to stay at the hospital for a few days. You have carbon monoxide poisoning, so we need to monitor you. We've got you on antibiotics so you won't develop pneumonia, and you'll also be receiving oxygen therapy."

Intense relief filled him. He sagged against the bed. Then he shook his head. "I can't…stay. I have to…teach school. I'm new. Less than a…a month…."

The nurse raised his eyebrows and wrote down something else. The black blood pressure cuff around his upper arm started to squeeze. He hadn't realized they were automatic these days.

"They can get a substitute." The nurse turned away. "I'll bring in some ice chips to soothe your throat. Do you like popsicles? Cherry? Or would you prefer grape?"

David didn't particularly care. "Grape." He closed his eyes for a moment, then opened them again, fixing his gaze on the doorway. Someone had gone to get Rachel, and he didn't want to miss seeing her. Where had she been during the fire?

It felt as if hours had passed by the time the volunteer, dressed in yellow scrubs, stopped outside his room and ushered in Rachel, dressed in her long, plain green dress and black apron.

Hot tears blurred his vision. She really was safe.

He reached for her.

With a cry, she flung herself into his arms.

⌣

David winced, and Rachel became conscious of the tubing that protruded from his arm, leading to an IV bag hanging from a metal pole beside his bed. He'd also suffered from burns. He wore a white and blue short-sleeved hospital gown, and from the waist down, he was covered by a thin white blanket.

His arms didn't appear badly burned. For a second, she allowed herself the luxury of resting her head against his shoulder and studying the muscular arm across from her. Enjoying his strength as he held her close.

As much as she longed to crawl into the bed and lie beside him, she forced herself to pull away. She slowly straightened, giving him every opportunity to hold on to her. To stop her from going. He didn't.

There was the matter of impropriety, if someone were to kum into the room. Especially Daed. After his lecture about throwing herself at David, it wouldn't be gut to get caught bundling with him in the hospital bed.

And there was the matter of his painful injuries, all the result of her stupidity.

"You are...safe." His voice was hoarse, as if he suffered from a severe sore throat.

"Jah. I...." She took a deep breath. "I wasn't there. Obadiah was supposed to call...."

David drew back as an emotion she couldn't quite identify crossed his face.

"But he didn't call; he came instead, in a buggy, and I went with him to his parents' haus for dinner." She hung her head. She hadn't been forced to go, as Daed had said. And as a result, she'd caused David pain, first physical, now emotional.

He lowered his eyes and shook his head.

She sucked in a longer, deeper breath. "We broke up. He wished me the best. We're free to—" How could she add "court"? Asking would be up to him.

David's gaze returned to her, but he didn't smile. Instead, he studied her, as if trying to assess how truthful she was being. "I still... can't court...you."

Why not? But she couldn't question him. Hurt and anger shot through her. She wanted to stomp her feet in a childish display. But temper tantrums had never worked for her as a child. Nein reason to believe they would prove effective now.

Tears stung her eyes. She blinked them back. She'd counted on hearing a declaration of love. At the very least, a request that she be his girl.

But maybe he was being wise. Giving her time to heal from her breakup with Obadiah so she wouldn't kum to him on the rebound. Not that she was.

And besides, he would soon be released from the hospital and likely sent back to Pennsylvania to tend to things there. She wasn't sure exactly what would happen. She knew only the brief information Joshua had shared, and she wasn't even sure she'd heard that right.

But if she had, then his sister and brother-in-law were dead, and his daed had been hospitalized for a probable heart attack.

If it were true, Daed needed to be the one to tell David. Not her. It was too terrible for words and would only cause him unnecessary pain and worry.

What would this do to them? Contrary to the popular saying, in her experience, absence didn't make the heart grow fonder; it was "out of sight, out of mind."

He would be devastated by this terrible loss. She swallowed hard. "How do you feel?"

David's gaze skittered away, then back. "Been...better."

She interlaced her fingers with his, careful of where the IV entered his hand. "Are you in pain? You were burned, ain't so?"

"Mostly first degree...some second. They're concerned about my lungs. Pneumonia." He glanced at the IV line and sighed. "Hurts to talk." Now he was whispering.

Maybe they could kiss instead.

But if he still wouldn't court her, he wouldn't want to kiss. Besides, that might be painful for him, too.

Ach, she was so selfish. Shame ate at her. "I'm so sorry for not being there. I prayed God would save you."

She glanced at David and thought she saw the sheen of tears glittering in his dark chocolate eyes.

Shuffling sounds came from the doorway. A female nurse entered. "Mr. Lapp? We're going to move you to a room now." The woman glanced at Rachel. "You'll need to go back to the waiting room. We're taking your husband to the ICU. Someone will call you when he's settled."

"Not my...wife."

Did he have to say that? Rachel started to pull away.

"My...girl."

Chapter 26

David picked up a magazine that one of the aides had brought in, and glanced at the cover—a photo of a skimpily clothed woman. The title read, *Sports Illustrated—Swimsuit Edition*. His cheeks flamed, and he dropped the magazine on the table next to the water pitcher. The cover still faced up. He shoved the table further away.

Two days had passed with nein visitors. The male nurse had explained to him that they allowed only family members and members of the clergy into the ICU. But he hadn't been in ICU long—a little more than a day—when he was moved to a regular room. He considered calling the phone shanty at home and leaving a message, but he didn't know the hospital number. Plus, acute boredom hardly constituted a gut reason to call.

The interminable hours were broken up only by nursing staff and doctors making their rounds. He was grateful for the Bible he'd found in the bedside table—it kept him from going crazy. Granted, he would have preferred his dual-language one, with all his personal notes. This Bible was stiff, as if it were new or rarely used. Still, the Word of Gott filled the void as he read page after page of Psalms.

He doubted anyone else would kum to see him. After all, Preacher Samuel was busy trying to find a new haus, on top of trying to keep up with his regular farm work. And Bishop Joe probably wouldn't think of visiting the "stray." David hadn't met any of the other preachers.

He blew out a frustrated breath as the nurse's assistant attached some kind of clip to his fingertip to check for who knew what. She looked up at him. "Want to watch TV?" Her voice was chirpy.

"No, thank you."

"You sure? It'll help pass time."

He didn't answer. At least, not verbally. But the silent glare he aimed at her apparently got the message across.

With a smile, she concentrated on checking his pulse. "You're Amish, right? You'll probably get some visitors soon."

In a normal situation, she would have been right. The whole community would eventually show up. But in his case? He could count on one hand the people he knew here.

If only Rachel would kum see him again. But she might have picked up extra hours at the store to help save up money for a new haus. The memory of her almost tumbling into the bed with him on her only visit still kept him warm at nacht.

Footsteps sounded outside his door, and Bishop Joe entered the room, holding his black hat in his right hand. The nurse's assistant surveyed him with raised eyebrows, then gathered her supplies and scurried from the room. The bishop's stern expression seemed to have that effect on people.

Including David. A surge of apprehension worked through him. Was the bishop going to fire him because he would be unable to teach for at least a few days? Since the fire had happened on a Friday, he'd been out of commission for Saturday and Sunday only—nein school days.

The bishop scanned the room, his gaze alighting with displeasure on the TV, even though it was turned off, then on the issue of *Sports Illustrated*. David's face burned. He should have asked the nurse's assistant to remove the magazine before the bishop saw it and started making incorrect assumptions about David's character.

Bishop Joe's frown deepened as he turned his eyes on David. "You doing okay, bu?"

David swallowed, his hand closing around the edge of the open Bible in his lap. His throat still hurt, but not as badly as it had when he'd first awakened in the emergency room. At least he could talk, though his voice still sounded husky. Probably like a sick bullfrog. The doctor had said that his vocal cords were inflamed. He wanted a glass of water, but reaching for the pitcher would only draw more attention to the scantily clad woman on the magazine cover. "Jah, I'm fine." He sat up straighter in bed.

"Preacher Samuel made a down payment on a farm for one of his kinner." The bishop shrugged. "Sam, probably. I gave the family permission to stay in the schoolhaus until they can take possession of the home, which will be soon. Preacher Samuel is planning a work frolic to start rebuilding his home."

"Gut." David was glad they had a place to stay. He imagined Rachel sleeping in his cot...on his blankets. His heart rate increased. Best not to think of that.

"Rachel moved your things into their barn. Your dog is staying there, too." The bishop paused. "I appreciated your teaching for a few weeks. Danki."

It wasn't his dog, but he wouldn't argue. Especially since Rosie appeared to have adopted him. "Danki. I can resume teaching as soon as I'm released, if you still need me." He didn't know where he'd go, otherwise. The doctor had said he'd be released in a day or two. He'd be willing to sleep in the Millers' barn if they were still staying at the school.

"We'll see. If you kum back."

If? The bishop's statement left him feeling uncertain and confused. But David merely nodded, not knowing what else to do. Too bad teaching wouldn't be a sure thing. If they hired him as the permanent teacher, he could court Rachel.

Now he might have to look for other employment. Meanwhile, with all this mandatory free time at the hospital, he could be weaving baskets or tying flies. He flexed his fingers. But first, he had things he needed to say. *Danki, Gott, for giving me the chance to talk with the bishop alone, without an audience. Give me courage....*

That reminded him of a verse he read just minutes before, in Psalm 56: *"What time I am afraid, I will trust in thee."*

"Bishop Joe, I need to talk to you. Your sohn...." How could he confess that he might've been the one to give Ezra the drugs in the back field on that awful night? He wasn't totally certain about anything. There was no guarantee that the party he'd attended, and the one after which Sam and the bishop's sohn had gotten in an accident, had been one and the same. Besides, it'd been years ago. Who could be sure of details after so much time had passed?

David pulled in a breath. "Sam Miller says...well, he thinks...."

"You knew my sohn?" The bishop studied him, a desperate look in his eyes.

David didn't want to hurt him. *Lord Gott, I need strength to get through this confession.* "Nein, not really. But we might've met. And I might've been partly responsible for his death." He rubbed his sweaty hands over the nubby hospital blanket.

The bishop moved closer, towering over the bed. "You *might have* met him? You *might have* been partly responsible? Explain yourself, bu." The stern look reappeared, accompanied by a piercing gaze.

David looked down. Sweat beaded on his brow. His vision blurred. There was nein easy way to say this. "I don't know for sure, but I might've been at the party your sohn attended the nacht he died. Someone gave me some drugs, and I tried them, but I didn't like what they did to me. So, being young and foolish, I handed them off to a stranger." He forced the words out. "Sam says he remembers me. I don't remember him. But Sam says it was your sohn I gave the drugs to. And for that...I am truly sorry." His voice broke.

The bishop remained silent, so he pressed on.

"I kneeled and confessed in front of my home church. I prayed to Gott for forgiveness, too." Something that had meant far more to him than apologizing to the church at large.

Bishop Joe released a heavy sigh. "Then your sins were forgiven, bu. Besides, there's nein way of proving it was you."

The tears in his eyes escaped, just as they had when he'd fallen on his face before Gott. Forgiveness...a wunderbaar thing. David wiped his eyes with the blanket and studied the pattern of the fabric.

"For what it's worth, I forgive you, too." The bishop patted David's arm. "Hope the situation at home will be all right. Must be hard to be hospitalized at a time like this, so far away, with your daed and all."

David frowned and looked up. "What?"

"Preacher Samuel told me. You probably missed the funeral, but I'm sure your mamm will be glad when you're home."

Funeral? Daed? David threw back the covers and dived out of bed, ripping the IV needle from his hand. Blood started spilling out.

He'd just survived one of the worst days of his life, and now the horror had started all over again.

"My clothes...I need my clothes." He stumbled to the closet.

⁓

Rachel carried a plateful of cookies to the large table at the Petersheims' and set it in the middle. Her friend Esther followed with a large tray of teacups and a teapot.

Mamm dropped into a chair with a sigh. "I know I said this before, but it sure is nice of you to let us stay here. The school was shelter, but it wasn't very comfortable."

Viktor's grossmammi, Anna, patted Mamm's hand. "It's the least we can do, dear. After all, your family did the same for us for a few days, after we lost our home."

Rachel sat in the empty chair next to Mamm while Esther unloaded the tray, serving the men first. Sam slouched at one end of the table, next to Daed, blatantly ignoring Viktor, despite his family's kindness in taking them in. Luther, seated on his other side, reached for a cookie. The rest of the family had been farmed out: Mary and Jenny were staying with their favorite girl cousins, Eli and Andy with their best friends' families.

Esther handed Rachel a teacup. "These were a wedding present from Viktor." She glanced at her new ehemann and blushed. "Aren't they beautiful?"

Rachel nodded. "I love them. So pretty." She carefully sipped the hot liquid.

Buggy wheels crunched over the gravel in the driveway in front of the haus. Viktor looked up from his cup of koffee. "It's the bishop."

Esther peered out the window, then pivoted. "I'll get another koffee mug."

Viktor rose and strode to the door.

A second later, the bishop entered the haus. He stood there a moment, surveying the group. His gaze flittered over Rachel to the others, then moved back to her. An emotion she couldn't identify flickered across his face. "I thought you'd be at the school."

"We offered them a place to stay." Viktor closed the door and headed back to the table. He pulled out a chair. "Sit a spell, if you're able."

"Don't mind if I do." The portly man reached for a cookie. "I just got back from accompanying the stray bu to the bus station."

"What?" Rachel's teacup wobbled in her hand as anger ignited within her. David was not a stray.

Her ire was quickly replaced by hurt. Why had David gone without saying gut-bye? When would she see him again?

"How could you let him do that?" Daed set down his teacup with a clatter that made Esther wince as she set a mug of koffee in front of the bishop. "He was hardly in a condition to be released from the hospital."

"How could I stop him? The very second I expressed my condolences about his father, the bu ripped the IV needle from his hand, jumped out of bed, and got dressed. It was a sight to behold."

"Wait. What about his father?" Daed leaned forward.

"You told me he died."

"Nein. It was his sister and brother-in-law who died. His father is in the hospital, recovering from what they think was a heart attack. But he's still alive, as far as I know."

Grief washed through Rachel. Her heart ached for David, the way he'd learned the bad news—and the wrong version of it. Daed had decided not to tell him until he was out of intensive care, but it seemed he'd waited too long. Her hand trembled, causing tea to slosh out of her teacup. Esther reached for the cup, and Rachel gladly relinquished it. She didn't want to break her cousin's precious wedding gift.

Sam straightened his posture, interest lighting his eyes.

The bishop waved his hand dismissively. "Someone died. The bu told the nurses, in nein uncertain terms, that he was checking himself out. That he had to go home. He did allow a nurse to bandage his hand, because it was bleeding quite badly."

Picturing David lying in his hospital bed, Rachel couldn't imagine he was in gut enough shape to travel anywhere. Tears pooled in the corners of her eyes.

"He didn't even want to take the time to collect his belongings," the bishop said with a shake of his head. "'Since we're already in town,' he told the driver, 'just take me straight to the bus station.'" He shook his head again. "That bu has some kind of courage."

"He thinks he's called to be a preacher," Daed said.

Ach, why would Daed say that to the bishop? Was he trying to get David in trouble?

Both Viktor and his grossdaedi suddenly seemed fascinated with their tea, as if trying to avoid getting involved in the conversation. Or maybe it was because they shouldn't participate, since it was between preachers.

Sam made a quiet sneer and aimed his gaze at the table.

The bishop reached for another cookie. "He apologized to me for my sohn. Took me by surprise. He's not even responsible for the choices Ezra made, and yet he apologized. Not often one sees that. I wouldn't be surprised to someday have that bu draw the lot to become a preacher. Not at all. "

Sam looked up, his pale face registering shock.

Daed picked up his teacup again. Took a sip. Then set it down, gently this time. "I think he might leave the church."

Rachel gasped. "Daed, nein."

Daed ignored her. Esther reached for her hand.

The bishop frowned. "Did he say that?"

"Nein, but David has been studying the Bible on his own. I looked at some of his notes over the past few days. I've been using his

Bible, since mine was lost in the fire. He's smart and has a lot of Bible knowledge. He's not going to be satisfied—"

Sam bolted to his feet and headed for the door.

Daed looked after him. "Going somewhere, sohn?"

Sam didn't pause. The door slammed behind him.

⁓

The trip to Pennsylvania took forever, with long stopovers in St. Louis, Chicago, and Cleveland, but the bus eventually pulled into the Lancaster station. David took out his wallet to look for the number of the driver to call for a ride home. Or what used to be home. His eyes burned. Hard to believe Daed was gone. Mamm and Daed had wanted to travel. They'd planned on going to Pinecraft, Florida, this winter. Mamm had said they'd rented a small haus there. Maybe the money could be refunded, for he couldn't imagine Mamm would go alone.

He couldn't find the phone number in his wallet. At least he had a little money to buy food and water. The contents of his billfold had been shifted through, probably when he was taken to the emergency room—someone would have searched for his ID card for identification purposes. He hadn't been asked for any information when he'd awakened.

David found a vacant bench against the wall, sat down, and started methodically sorting through everything, putting it back into order. The movements stung the parts of his hand that had been burned.

"David."

The voice was familiar, but David couldn't place it as belonging here, in Pennsylvania. Besides, he hadn't told anyone he was coming. He looked up. Blinked. And looked again.

"Sam? What are you doing here?"

Rachel's brother sat down beside him. "Thought you might need a ride home."

David scratched his neck. If he'd known Sam would drop every-thing and kum in his beat-up car, getting there even before the bus, he would've just asked him for a ride. Or maybe not, considering their relationship. Or the lack thereof. "So, you drove from Jamesport to Lancaster to give me a ride when I could have called a driver for it?" He started returning his wallet's contents to the proper compart-ments. A scrap of paper caught his attention, and he pulled it out. The elusive phone number. He slipped it back where it belonged.

Sam fidgeted. "Well, that, and we're overdue for a talk."

David looked up and met his gaze. "Jah, we are." This was hardly the time or the place, but at least he'd have the matter settled before he faced Mamm. "I'm sorry for any part I may have played in the death of your friend—"

"Nein. I mean, danki. But that's not it. I need to apologize to you. I hated you. Threatened you. Attacked you. And you were… well, not exactly innocent of the charges, but…." Sam released a long breath. "You rescued me from the fire. Took the time to throw my books—my future—out the window before you made me jump. You risked your life to look for my sister. And then you apologized to Bishop Joe. He'd grieved hard, but he forgave you. It impressed him that you would take responsibility, when it was Ezra's bad decisions that ultimately caused his death." Sam scuffed his tennis shoes over the filthy floor.

How would Sam know all this? David shook his head. He must have missed something due to his travel-fogged mind.

"It impressed me when the bishop mentioned it to my family, and I wanted to apologize to you. I thought about what to say, how to do it, the whole long drive here. I'd want someone to speak of me the way Bishop Joe spoke of you. Not as someone who hurt other people. There's nein easy way…." Sam pulled in a shuddery breath. "I just have to say it. I'm sorry, too, for misjudging you. Would you forgive me?"

David studied Sam's expression, looking for genuine remorse. And there it was. Sorrow over his actions. Regret. Remembering the great relief he had felt at being forgiven, he stood and shoved his wallet back into his pocket, then turned to face Sam as he, too, rose to his feet. "Consider yourself forgiven." He awkwardly pulled him into a hug.

Sam returned the gesture just as awkwardly, then stepped back.

"Where are you staying?" David asked him. "I'd invite you to stay at my sister's haus with me, but…. Well, I suppose we could share a room. Deborah shouldn't mind too much."

Sam looked away for a moment. "There's been another misunderstanding." His gaze returned to David. "Your sister…and her ehemann…they're the ones who…passed on. Your daed is fine. He had a heart attack, but he survived. Your mamm said he had triple bypass surgery."

David shut his eyes, relief warring with fresh pain. He'd mourned Daed the whole bus trip, across four states, only to find that it was Deborah and Adam he should have been grieving. Mamm had been so excited about having her first of many grosskinner…. He cleared his throat, blinking back tears. Those could kum later.

"So, um, how'd you know when to meet me? And when did you talk to my mamm?"

"I knew when you left, and I checked the schedule. Your parents let me stay with them the past two nights while we waited for you to arrive, since you and I are…friends." He looked down and shuffled his feet again. "I will probably head back home early in the morgen. Just wanted to say what I needed to say, since I didn't know when or if you'll be returning to Missouri."

David didn't know when, either.

It wasn't a question of *if*. He would return. Even if it was just for a visit.

Especially after he'd claimed Rachel as his girl.

But she probably wouldn't go for another long-term, long-distance relationship.

Would she?

Chapter 27

Rachel filled the dishpan with hot water after adding a squirt of soap, then carefully lowered the supper plates into the suds. Beside her, Esther grabbed a dish towel. "We've hardly had a chance to talk the whole time you've been here," she lamented, "and now you're fixing to leave for your new home."

"*Temporary* new home. It's such a blessing the previous owners are letting us move in now. Not that we have much to move. After I got off work at the store, Daed had me stuffing mattresses with hay all afternoon." Rachel lifted and lowered her sore shoulders. "He jokes that it's as if he and Mamm are starting over as a newly married couple—except with a whole family ready-made." She rolled her eyes.

A car engine rumbled outside, the tires scattering gravel. Probably just someone turning around in the driveway.

Esther grinned. "Since I moved into an established home, I didn't have those start-up problems."

Rachel smiled back. "I'll be glad to share. The fun part is going to garage sales, looking for dishes and other household items." She'd also found a new postcard she planned send to David...if he wrote her first. *Wish you were here....*

"I've wanted to talk to you about David. He must be pretty special to you, for you to have reacted the way you did when Bishop Joe mentioned that he'd left."

Rachel dipped her head and concentrated on washing the plates. "He was my pen pal. From Seymour. I told you about him."

"Jah, a long time ago. You didn't tell me that the David teaching school when I returned from Florida was the same David. *Your David.*"

The relationship was still so new. So unsettled. So uncertain. Rachel didn't want to talk about it. Not even with Esther.

She handed each clean dish to Esther to rinse and wipe dry. After a long silence, Esther looked up. "I understand. I didn't want to talk about my relationship with Viktor when it was brand-new and up in the air."

Rachel forced a smile that hardly stayed in place long enough to be a flicker. "I know. And…he's in Pennsylvania, over a thousand miles away. I'm not sure when I'll ever see him. Or if I ever will."

Esther blinked.

"Ach, so dramatic." Sam's voice drifted in from the kitchen doorway.

Rachel whipped her head around and stared at him. "*Me*, dramatic? You're the one who vanished without warning. We haven't seen you for days. Mamm and Daed have been having whispered conversations of concern for their 'wayward sohn.' Where have you been?"

"Pennsylvania."

"Be serious." He was so heartless to tease her about a subject that hurt her. It probably thrilled him that David had gone so far way.

Sam shrugged. "Where's Daed?"

"Fine. Don't tell me." Rachel glared at him. "Daed's probably taking Mamm's quilts and the other stuff we saved from the haus to the new farm."

"Then I guess I'll go home and get started on chores." Sam pulled a long envelope out of his pocket and dropped it on the table, then stalked out the door.

Rachel dropped the silverware into the water and started scrubbing each piece. "I don't know why he can't be truthful. Pennsylvania? In the middle of the week? Not like he'd be going for a party."

Outside, Sam's car engine roared to life, and he tore out of the driveway.

Esther put away the stack of plates. Out of the corner of her eye, Rachel saw her stop by the table and pick up the envelope Sam had left. Then she set it back down. "It's addressed to you."

"Really?" Rachel reached for a dish towel and wiped her hands as she hurried over. She looked at the handwriting. "It's from David!" She dropped the towel on the table, snatched up the letter, ripped open the envelope, and yanked out the note.

Dear Rachel,

I'm sorry for leaving without saying gut-bye. I have no excuse, other than that I was in—am in—a horrible spot. I told the nurse you were my girl, and that was presumptuous of me, since we hadn't agreed on it together. Especially since I had no idea what would happen in my life, how I would support a frau, or anything. I still don't know. All I know is, what God wills, He'll work out.

Daed is recovering from triple bypass surgery. He's gaining strength back every day, and they are talking about releasing him from the hospital soon. I'm not sure what's happening with the farm. It might've reverted back to Mamm and Daed, since it was a private sale and it wasn't paid for. When I saw Daed earlier this evening, he asked if I could handle a farm after my accident. I told him I could. But there is the matter of you.

She sank down in a chair. David might consider staying in Lancaster and farming?

The man who owns the farm next to ours is Joshua Esh. He signed up for the same man swap in Seymour that I did. But, unlike me, he didn't plan to stay. He thought it'd be a gut way to see another part of the country. And it was. But he also found a girl there, and she relocated to Pennsylvania with him. They went back to Missouri last winter so she could see her family.

I know it's a lot to ask—your moving so far away from your family. I know how close you are to them, as well as to your cousins. But I also know your desire to travel.

She would like to see Pennsylvania. Especially since he was there.

Pray with me, Rachel. Pray that Gott will lead us in what He wants us to do regarding our relationship. Pray for clear guidance in future plans. Pray for Daed's healing and for our family's grief as we struggle to accept the loss of my sister and her ehemann.

And maybe, if we see our way clear, you'd be willing to kum to Pennsylvania to visit me. Or would welcome a visit from me.

Ich liebe dich.

Rachel caught her breath. *Ach, David. Ich liebe dich, too.* If only they could be together, whispering those three sweet words. Making plans. Stealing kisses.

She turned her attention back to the letter.

Even though I have done so, I have nein right to say that to you. Yet. Maybe never.

My address is below, if you want to write.

Sam said he'd deliver this letter for me so you'd get it faster.

So, Sam hadn't lied? He'd really gone to Pennsylvania to see David? Why?

With his pen, David had scratched out multiple closings, but she could still make them out: "Love." "Yours always." He hadn't replaced them with a "Sincerely." Or "Warmly." It thrilled her to know how he'd wanted to close the letter—and relieved her that he hadn't chosen a bland substitute.

He loved her. Rachel wiped away a tear, then refolded the letter and started to slip it back inside the envelope. Then she noticed the postcards enclosed. She pulled them out. There was a photo of the St. Louis Arch. A Ferris wheel against the Chicago skyline. And another of downtown Cleveland, along the lakefront. She smiled. She hadn't mourned the loss of her hundreds of postcards anywhere near as much as she'd mourned David's absence, but it was sweet of him to restart her collection this way. She returned everything to the envelope before sliding it into her pocket.

"Ach, Esther...." She looked around, but the kitchen was empty. At some point, her cousin had discreetly exited to give her privacy. So thoughtful.

Rachel slipped her shoes on and hurried out of the haus. She had to find Sam.

There was so much she needed to know.

～

David slumped in the chair next to Daed's hospital bed. He'd spent the last six days recovering from surgery, and the doctor had said that if all continued to go well, he might be released tomorrow. But it would take a full eight weeks before he'd be allowed to return to work, since Daed was a farmer and did heavy labor.

David didn't want to appear unsympathetic, but being here in Pennsylvania, running the farm, hadn't been part of his long-range plans. Especially not with his lungs still raw from smoke inhalation, and with a bum leg and a sore ankle. But it surprised him how well he'd been able to keep up with the work, even if his injuries slowed his pace.

But then, he hadn't really formed any specific long-range plans. He had a calling from Gott to preach, and he'd followed a pipe dream to Jamesport to pursue Rachel, believing it to be Gott's will. But all that seemed so pointless now. He'd gone full circle and ended up right where he'd started.

Daed's fingers twitched, but he appeared to be asleep. David bowed his head and closed his eyes. In an effort to clear his mind, he breathed deeply, releasing much of the stress and tension he'd felt in the four days he'd been home. Focusing on Gott. And not himself.

He'd given himself far too much attention lately, feeling sorry for himself. Everything had hit at once, building and building, until the physical and emotional pain had seemed insurmountable. *Lord Gott....* The lyrics of a contemporary Christian song he'd heard on the Christian radio station Sam had played in his car came to mind.

Sam had said it was the only station he could pick up at that moment, whatever the reason.

And there his mind went, wandering again. Why did that always happen when he tried to pray?

Lord Gott, tell me once again who I am—what I am—to You. Tell me, lest I forget who I am. I belong to You.

Daed reached over and rested his hand on David's bent head. "Thanks for praying, Sohn." His voice was low. Weak. Frail.

David had been selfish, praying for his needs and not Daed's.

He remained still before Gott, with Daed's hand on his head, and shifted his prayer focus to Daed, for healing. To Mamm, for strength to handle all the changes ahead. To the Samuel Miller family, for their current situation. To Sam.

And to Rachel.

Tears burned his eyes.

"Ich liebe dich, Sohn."

Gott, danki for reminding me that family is important.

He raised his head and met Daed's gaze. "Ich liebe dich, too, Daed."

⌒

Rachel hurried along the dirt road from the Petersheims' haus and her home. It was only about three-quarters of a mile—not far at all. Still, she hoped one of her neighbors would kum along in a buggy and offer her a ride.

She couldn't imagine why Sam had gone to Pennsylvania to see David. And after she'd called him a liar, she might have to eat humble pie before she managed to convince him to tell her anything. Frustrating male.

The smell of smoke and charred wood lingered as Rachel neared the blackened remains of their haus. Daed seemed upbeat about this opportunity to start over, but how much of it was forced? Rachel couldn't see any of this as being a gut thing. Not the hay-stuffed mattresses, not the mismatched secondhand plates and cutlery, not the hand-me-down dresses and kapps from relatives. Of course, she was grateful to have clothes to wear, even if they were the dresses nobody wanted anymore. Too worn. Or a color they'd tired of. Or too small.

She tugged at the waist of the dress she'd put on that morgen. While it didn't fit quite right, at least it wasn't too tight. Maybe Daed would replace their treadle sewing machine soon. If not, she could hand-sew some new dresses. Or Mamm could, since she loved the task so much.

"Hallo, Rachel."

She looked up. Joshua stood outside the phone shanty. "Don't you have a life away from the phone?" she asked him.

Red flooded his cheeks. "It would appear not." With a shrug, he glanced toward the burned shell of her haus. "Your daed make any plans yet?"

Rachel frowned. "The men are talking, but I don't think anything has been settled yet. Except Daed bought that tiny two-bedroom haus that used to belong to the…well, to your aentie and onkel before they put their farm up for sale to move to Montana. But you knew that."

"Actually, I didn't. I knew they were thinking of selling but hadn't heard the sale had gone through. That'll be a tight squeeze for your family. Guess he's thinking about a starter farm for Sam?"

Rachel lifted her shoulder. "Speaking of Sam, I'm looking for him. Have you seen him recently?"

Joshua shook his head. "He didn't kum by here. I've been talking on the phone for the past forty-five minutes or so."

Rachel stared at him a moment, then shook her head.

He frowned. "How's David?"

"He checked himself out of the hospital. Went home to Pennsylvania." She started to turn away.

"I figured he would. I'd do the same, in his shoes."

Rachel pivoted on her heel. "That reminds me. Daed said something that indicated David might be leaving the Amish. What is going on? What kind of 'Bible study' were you having, anyway? Is it because

4. Extra practice: Role-play the following situations using the shared-meaning process. Take turns being the sender and receiver.

   a. Your partner has not been keeping the bank book balanced.

   b. You and your partner differ on child-rearing practices. Each holds out for his or her own way.

   c. You have been left at home too many nights by your partner. You feel very lonely and neglected.

   d. Your parents are coming for a visit. They are very critical of you and your spouse.

   e. Your relationship with your partner has been very unsatisfying.

   f. You and your partner plan to purchase a new automobile. You each have certain preferences.

   g. You are starting a new job. You feel nervous and unsure of your job skills.

SIX

SPEAKING SO
OTHERS WILL LISTEN

My FRIEND MERI once said, "If we took seriously the principle that people do not listen effectively, we would change the way we teach." Some of us may not realize that most people have poor listening habits. But even those of us who do often continue to speak as though our listeners heard clearly everything we said. We continue with our long, abstract lectures and give no opportunities for questions or feedback. We talk about issues that influence our relationships without inviting the listener to check out what he has heard.

Poor Listening Habits

What do we know about how people listen? What are some typical habits that cause people to be poor listeners? One fact we know is that a listener tends to be fickle. The focus of his or her attention is liable to change suddenly and unpredictably. One moment he may be following our conversation, the next he will be thinking about the exciting basketball game he watched last night. The listener's attention is unstable, apt to flee from our grasp at any second.

If we do not know how to gain and hold his or her interest, it will most likely depart.

We also know that a person's listenability is usually influenced by his or her opinion of the speaker. Imagine yourself ready to attend a lecture on your favorite subject by your favorite speaker. He has not traveled in your vicinity for several years. You tell a work associate of your anticipation, and she says, "I heard him last month in Dallas. He's not the same since he's aged. His mind is not as sharp as it was. He doesn't have those colorful illustrations that are so effective. You'll be disappointed." What are you probably feeling at that moment? How will your friend's comments influence you as you listen to the speaker? Aren't you likely to be on the lookout for all those failings of which you had been warned?

We also know that listeners build listening barriers that hinder their receptivity—in chapter 2 we talked about a number of the obstacles that block the communication process. Physical, social, emotional, and spiritual barriers can keep a listener from hearing clearly what the speaker wants to share. A speaker may have information that the listener desperately needs, yet listening obstacles may prevent the listener from hearing. We need to know how we can remove some of these barriers or convince a listener that he or she needs to tear them down.

Finally, we know that listeners develop poor listening habits. In this case, poor listening is not a barrier that is deliberately constructed; rather, it's a *pattern* of relating we allow to develop that short-circuits communication. Trying to listen to a child while reading the newspaper may be one person's bad listening habit; another person may listen to a favorite radio station throughout the day and be distracted from listening to other people.

Since these hindrances stand in the way of accurate, effective communication, what are we to do? Can a speaker do anything to cope with such problems? Are there strategies we can employ to gain and maintain a listener's attention and interest?

Five Ways to Gain a Listener's Attention

I can answer an enthusiastic "yes" to the preceding questions. Speakers can practice specific skills which will increase their chances of being heard. These skills apply whether a speaker is facing a large audience, a small group, or one other person. The following tips can help any speaker gain a hearing:

1) *Begin with your appearance.* When we speak, our appearance should complement what we want to say. Let me illustrate. Art Jackson is invited to speak at a gathering of professional people. He is excited about the opportunity. Yet, he defeats his goal, for his appearance does not encourage respect from his listeners. His clothing is "loud" and poorly matched. His tie is loosened from his shirt. He does not appear to be an organized, knowledgeable person, and therefore he tends to "turn off' his listeners' attention.

A speaker who dresses in an appropriate manner creates a favorable impression and gains a hearing more easily. I am not suggesting expensive clothing or elaborate dress. Clothing should complement the person wearing it, creating a warm, relaxed picture in the listener's mind. Appearance should encourage respect and confidence on the part of the listener.

This issue is relevant in home situations. When teenagers are frequently among others who dress neatly and attractively, then come home to see Dad slouched in the chair in a dirty undershirt, they will find it more difficult to listen to him with respect.

2) *Use "hooks" to capture attention.* With a little creative

thought a speaker can entice other people to listen.

Winnie related to me an incident that illustrates this point. She recently attended a reentry program for nurses who desire to update nursing skills. At the conclusion of the course the director of personnel at the host hospital was asked to explain employee benefits at the hospital. She began her presentation by sharing a recent newspaper article which outlined the jobs and benefits available to nurses in the 1880s. Winnie commented, "It was an excellent way to get us interested in a potentially dry subject." The personnel director used an effective "hook" to capture the attention of her audience.

Attention-gaining hooks come in many forms. A topic of current interest, a human interest article or story, a thought-provoking question, an eye-catching visual, a humorous exercise—all may be effective attention-getters. Two key characteristics of a good hook are ability to involve the listener and appropriateness to the subject matter that follows.

Hooks are just as appropriate in one-to-one conversations as in public-speaking situations. An effective speaker will choose an approach which will capture undivided attention. Sitting in a position that encourages eye contact and direct confrontation also invites attention. A good speaker will sit directly across from his listener, so the listener can look into his face.

3) *Speak authoritatively and energetically.* Adequate preparation can do much to gain a listener's respect. When we speak, we would do well to ask ourselves ahead of time, "Am I prepared to gain a hearing? Do I have information gathered which is clear and informative? Could I do some basic research which would tell my listener I have something worth hearing?"

The manner in which we speak is equally important for keeping an audience's attention. We can ask ourselves, "Do

I manifest enthusiasm, excitement, or 'gusto' for my concern? Can others sense that it is important to me? Is my voice level appropriate—loud enough to be heard, but not so loud as to drive my listener away?"

Think of individuals you enjoy listening to. Jot down on a sheet of paper what voice characteristics and body gestures they use that express their enthusiasm for their subject. Which of these would enrich you as a speaker?

4) *Speak to the listener's interests and needs.* Consider this basic principle of communication: people enjoy listening to information relating to them, their interests, and their needs. Whenever we aim our words at personal interests and needs, people begin to listen.

We often communicate better when we introduce the communication with the benefits we are prepared to offer the listener—if we have any. Imagine yourself sitting down with your eight-year-old daughter. You want to help her learn to care for her bedroom, to keep it orderly. How could you approach the topic in a positive way that would help her feel that something good would come from the conversation?

Consider evaluating television commercials for one week. How do they speak to the viewers' interests and needs? What could we learn from their approach about gaining a hearing?

5) *Defuse negative emotions.* People listen poorly when they are struggling with intense emotions, especially negative emotions. For example, the individual who is wrestling with feelings of anger will hear less of what we are saying and will filter all of it through his fear filter. The person who feels very defensive will be busy checking his emotional walls and gates for any holes. He will be planning what he should say in response to protect himself. He will not listen receptively, positively, or constructively.

We ask, "How do I defuse their emotions? Don't they

own their own emotions?" It is true that individuals are responsible for their own emotions. However, we can do much to create a climate that helps or hinders a listener. I have found two principles which I use consistently. First, I state my intentions in advance. For example, I may say, "Jean, I need to talk to you about a problem that involves you and me. My intention is to find a solution helpful to both of us, not to embarrass you or put you down." Notice what I'm seeking to communicate. I want Jean to know that I feel positive toward her and that I am not trying to exploit, blame, or humiliate her. I have found this approach very helpful in reducing negative feelings in the listener.

The second principle I use to defuse negative emotions is to avoid "you" statements in situations where strong feelings are involved. "You" statements are statements which begin with "you" or imply a judgment of the listener, and which are accusing, advising, ridiculing, threatening, or demanding. The following are examples:

You never think of anybody but yourself.
[you] Get in the house right now.
Your reports are always late.
If you studied more you wouldn't get failing grades.

I find it helpful to use "I" statements in place of "you" statements. "I" statements focus attention on the feelings the speaker is experiencing, or the concern he or she has. They take the focus off the listener; consequently, he or she is less likely to feel threatened and respond hastily or negatively. The following "I" statements could be used in place of the above "you" statements:

I feel lonely being home by myself every night.
I have supper ready. It's time to come in.

I feel more relaxed when reports are in by five o'clock. Then I have time to record them before I leave.
I'm worried about your failing grades.

The five ways I've outlined to gain the listener's ear will help us know we are more likely to be heard. They can help motivate the listener to become involved in what we say. They can increase listenability. For many speakers, these ideas may be new and will require diligence in learning the skills. The benefits, however, are worth the effort.

Holding Listener Interest

Gaining attention is the first step in the process of speaking so others will listen; holding that attention as we communicate our message is the second. Both are essential to the total communication process. These five ideas for holding the interest of a listener have proved helpful to me as a communicator. I use them with my family and friends, as well as in my public-speaking ministry.

1) *Eliminate distractions.* Listeners can be distracted very easily; therefore, a wise speaker removes as many competing influences as possible from the environment. The speaker who has an important message plans in advance to remove as many disturbances as possible.

Distractions can be grouped into visual and auditory types. What will the listener *see* that will distract? Is the television on? Are people walking in and out of the room? Is something moving? What is present that the listener may be tempted to read? Such visual distractions may be removed or may require that a better location be chosen.

Sounds may also be distracting—a radio, stereo, or television; street noise; and adjoining conversation. Any distracting noise threatens message receptivity; if the message is important the speaker must consciously reduce the likelihood of outside influences interfering with it.

2) *Involve the listener actively.* Unfortunately, most public speakers consistently violate this basic principle. Communication is an active two-way process; the more a listener is involved, the more his or her interest will be maintained. Communication is improved when the speaker thinks in terms of talking *with* the listener rather than talking *at* him.

I recall an extremely frustrating afternoon I spent in the company of a person who talked *at* me the entire time. Although only four of us were present, this one person would talk for long periods of time. The experience was very taxing and unprofitable for us as listeners; it was a real temptation not to listen at all!

To involve listeners in a speaking situation, three practices are helpful. First, using thought-provoking questions forces the listener to participate actively in the communication process. Questions are basic to listener involvement; wise questions can stimulate a listener to think. Even when verbal response is not possible, such as during a speech before a large group, questions keep an audience involved by stimulating the *spirit of inquiry.*

A second way to involve listeners is to *visualize* whenever possible. Whether it takes the form of a simple drawing used in a one-on-one conversation or an overhead projector used before a large audience, visualizing a message keeps a listener's attention by involving his eyes as well as his ears.

The third way to increase a listener's involvement in a message is to provide a worksheet on which the listener can record information that the speaker is giving. Some ministers provide a sermon note sheet for the congregation to use as they preach. Some committee leaders provide agenda sheets with room for participants to record impor-

of your meetings that Daed said what he did?" Then again, Daed had spoken highly of David's scriptural knowledge and Bible study notes....

Joshua hesitated. "It was just what we said—a Bible study, Rach. And your daed is probably right. I think Viktor will be deciding against kneeling for baptism, too. But I can't say for sure on either one of them. Shouldn't speculate, really."

"But why? Anyone who leaves the Amish will be eternally lost. Why would anyone risk that?" Tears burned her eyes. If David left....

Joshua touched her elbow. "Walk with me awhile, Rachel." He nodded toward the barn, probably intending to head into the fields beyond.

He started walking, and she fell into step beside him. "I recently read a quote that stayed with me. I don't remember it verbatim, but it went something like this: 'You can have a relationship with Gott only on His conditions. You can take it or leave it, but you can't change the rules.' I hate to say this, but the Amish Ordnung isn't necessarily Gott's conditions."

"What?" Rachel stared at him. "I can't believe you'd say such a thing. The Ordnung was handed down over the years, and you know the preachers decide—"

"Do you hear yourself, Rachel? The *preachers* decide. But Gott doesn't change. And He says, in Ephesians, that it's by grace that we are saved, through faith. It's the gift of God, not by works, so that none of us can boast. He doesn't say we are saved by joining the Amish church and following the Ordnung or doing gut works."

A strange lump formed in Rachel's throat, threatening her breathing. She recognized the truth in his words, but they challenged the very foundation of her daily life. She shook her head, tears welling. "You— You're— Nein." She gulped. "Are you saying...David believes as you do?"

"Jah. David believes, and he knows he's saved."

"He can't know." He couldn't. Nobody knew for sure he was saved until he got to heaven. One could only hope to be gut enough. "Nein...." If only she could know for sure.

"Rachel, the Bible says in John that whoever believes in the Son has eternal life, but whoever rejects the Son will not see life, because Gott's wrath remains on him. And in First John, it says 'Gott has given us eternal life and this life is in His Son. He who has the Son has life; he who doesn't have the Son of God doesn't have life. I write these things to you that you may know that you have eternal life.' Did you catch that? That you may *know*."

Rachel opened her mouth, but nein words would kum. She would be shunned if she embraced these thoughts. She shook her head. "I'll talk to Daed about it."

A look of sadness crossed Joshua's face, but he nodded. "I hope you will. I'll give you a list of the verses, Rachel. You and your daed can look them up together. Then, if you have any questions, ask David or me."

The phone rang.

Joshua stopped walking. "Promise me, Rachel."

She nodded.

He grinned. "Excuse me." He spun around and jogged toward the phone shanty.

Rachel saw Sam's car approaching the driveway. She waited until he had parked, and then she hurried over to his open window. "What, you left before I did, and I beat you here?"

Her brother shrugged. "I had some things to do, okay?"

Rachel took a deep breath. "I read the letter you brought from David. You really did go out there. I'm sorry I didn't believe you."

Sam's gaze snapped to meet hers. He opened the car door, forcing her to step backward. He got out. Slammed it shut.

"Why didn't you tell us you were going out there?"

He smirked. "Because you would've wanted to kum along, ain't so? Both Daed and Bishop Joe would've had something to say about that."

"How is he?"

Sam shrugged. "He survived the trip. Was happy to see me. He gave me a hug." The smirk grew. He turned and strode off.

David had hugged Sam? Not likely. Why couldn't Sam be truthful?

"Next time, you'll take me with you, ain't so?"

He raised his hand but didn't answer.

From the phone shanty came a whoop. Joshua darted out and ran down the road.

Chapter 28

David helped Daed up the porch stairs and into the kitchen of the dawdi-haus. None of them had entered the haus where Adam and Deborah had lived before the buggy accident that had claimed their lives. Everyone felt the impact of the loss, but nobody knew what to do or say, other than the most mundane of things—while inside they died of grief.

Daed breathed heavily, sweat beading on his forehead, despite the coolness of the day. He slumped into a kitchen chair and looked toward Mamm. "Koffee?"

Mamm glanced at David. "Is he allowed to drink koffee after a heart bypass?" She turned away to peruse the list posted on the refrigerator.

David shrugged. "The doctor didn't mention it specifically, but he did say to limit caffeine. If it isn't on the list of stuff to avoid, one cup might be okay."

Daed smiled weakly and reached for the stack of mail Mamm had dropped on the table. He thumbed through it. "Why do they keep sending us advertisements for these satellite dishes and other TV services? We get at least one a week. And pest elimination services? What do they consider pests, anyway? Ach, David." He held out a white envelope. "You got a letter. Feminine handwriting. You have a girl back in…." He peered at the return address. "Jamesport? Thought you were in Seymour."

David sat in the chair next to Daed and reached for the letter. The handwriting was Rachel's. He battled the urge to open it. Gut thing Sam had really delivered his note. "Jah. I mentioned her when you were in the hospital, Daed. She lives in Jamesport. I recently moved north to get to know her better. Her name is Rachel."

Mamm looked at Daed. "Ach, remember that nice young man who came to visit you before David got home? Sam Miller. He said he lived across the street from the school where David was teaching, and that David almost died saving his sister. That's Rachel's brother."

Sam had gone to the hospital to meet Daed? Really? David took a moment to process that piece of information. "Rachel and I aren't courting, exactly. But someday, maybe…."

"Why aren't you?" Daed chuckled. "I mean, why haven't you?"

David shrugged again. "A variety of reasons. I don't have a home. I don't have a horse or buggy. I didn't have anything other than a temporary job. And, up until recently, another man was courting her." Not to mention, Rachel's brother hated him.

But that may have changed. At least they'd exchanged apologies, even if they'd treated each other with uncomfortable wariness the evening before Sam had left. Neither had known quite how to behave. David certainly hadn't been comfortable enough to ask Sam why he carried a tablet computer in the trunk of his car. Though Sam must have known he'd seen it, since he'd moved it to the side to make space for David's bag of hospital junk.

"If you were there now, would you court her?"

David swallowed a sudden lump in his throat. "Nothing would change. I love her. I want to marry her. But without a horse and buggy, I can't take her home from singings. Without a job or a home, I can't support a frau. And the bishop there calls me a 'stray.' Which, to be honest, is what I am—a stray bu, surviving on handouts." He couldn't keep the touch of bitterness from his voice, even as he inwardly chided himself for it. Gott *had* provided for every single one of his needs.

Just not his wants.

Though, to be fair, he had kissed Rachel, for a few too-brief moments. And der Herr had given him some new friends who shared his faith.

He blew out a frustrated breath.

"How do you feel about a long-distance courtship?" Daed reached for the mug of koffee Mamm had carried to the table. "Just a tiny dash of cream?" he pleaded.

Mamm glanced at David.

Weird that Mamm seemed to want him to make all the decisions. Or was she so stunned with grief that she needed help thinking? "Is it on the list?" David asked her.

Mamm checked the sheet, then shook her head.

"So...a little, jah?" Daed asked. Begged, really.

David nodded as he swirled the koffee in his own mug.

"So, about long-distance courtship?" Daed prompted him as Mamm dribbled a bit of cream into his koffee. "You have a home. You have a job. You have a horse and buggy, not that those will do you any gut if she's there and you're here."

David fingered the unopened envelope. Hope rose within him. He couldn't wait to go up to his room and read the letter. "I'll have to see if she's willing."

~

Rachel spread a cloth over the small square card table they'd set up in the kitchen of their temporary haus. Her brothers and sisters were all back with the family, so Mamm had said that the menfolk would eat first. Just like on church Sundays, when the bishop, the preachers, and the other men went before the women and kinner. At least she was used to it.

As Mamm carried two platefuls of food the table, Rachel headed to the counter to finish serving. She poked at the casserole, a mixture of wild rice, broccoli, mushrooms, ham, and chicken, all covered in a gooey cheese sauce. Interesting. She was grateful to whoever had provided this meal for them.

Daed came in and washed his hands, then sat on a bench. They'd found two in the barn, and Sam had repaired them, then cut each in half, making four small seats out of two large ones. They served the purpose, for now.

"Kind of like camping," Daed said with a big smile as he eyed the small table. "Noticed the mattresses on the floor for to-nacht. All we need is a campfire. S'mores, anybody?"

This would be Rachel's third nacht sleeping on the floor. She'd never get used to it. And even the mention of a fire made her cringe. "Daed, please. Don't talk about fires." She didn't know if she'd ever want to attend another bonfire. The flames...losing her family home...David.... Her chest constricted.

Daed gave her a sympathetic look. "Gott works everything together for gut, Rachel, and He'll do the same in our circumstances. Even with the loss of our home. With David's injuries and his return to Pennsylvania. Everything."

"I just don't see how that's possible. What gut could possibly kum from this? You and Mamm are having to start over from scratch, and—"

"Hush. Gott is not responsible for this. He knew about it before it happened, and He could've chosen to prevent it. He didn't, and so we trust He has His reasons. Like I said before, this is an adventure. Try to enjoy it. You have a choice here, dochter: You can choose to trust Gott and His ultimate wisdom in allowing it, or you can continue to mope and moan and groan about everything you lost."

Rachel turned away, stinging from the chastisement.

But that reminded her—it'd been three days since her conversation with Joshua. And she'd promised to ask....

She pivoted. "Daed, about David leaving the Amish—"

"We'll discuss it later." He leveled a stern gaze at her.

Right. Later.

Sighing, she began filling glasses with milk for everyone. Without refrigeration, they had to use it before it soured. She could foresee making cheese, butter, and yogurt in the near future.

Daed would probably scold her for her attitude, but she couldn't resist saying, "Well, whenever *later* gets here, I have some questions."

⌒

David glanced at the postcard he'd thumbtacked to his bedroom wall.

Wish you were here....

Nice to know he was missed. He pulled the letter out of the envelope and sat on the edge of the bed to read it a second time.

Dear David,

I still can't believe you checked yourself out of the hospital and left, just like that. You must be one of the most impulsive people I've ever met.

Not really. It was just that some things—like going home when his family needed him—didn't require much thought.

Daed bought a farm with some livestock, including a horse (and buggy). There's a tiny house on the property. He and Mamm will sleep in the living room, us girls in one bedroom, and the buwe in the other. All of us on mattresses stuffed with hay on the floor. Daed keeps calling it an "adventure." I can't help but feel guilty, though. If I'd been there, and hadn't run off....

Though, as Daed says, I can't control lightning. But then you wouldn't have been hurt searching for me. I don't know if I'll ever forgive myself for that.

Bishop Joe stopped to visit with us on the nacht you left, and he went on and on about how impressed he was with you. He also said he wouldn't be surprised if the lot was eventually drawn for you to become a preacher. Isn't that wunderbaar? I was so happy to hear that. Especially that you'd made a positive impression on the bishop.

I miss you. I know your family needs you right now, but is it shameful of me to wish you were here?

Love,
Rachel

He smiled, running his fingertips lightly over the word *love*. It was the first time she'd ever closed a letter to him with that word.

PS: After talking with Joshua, I have some questions. He suggested I take them up with Daed. I'm concerned about one thing, in particular: Daed said you might leave the Amish. Tell me that's not true.

He could almost hear the fear in her question. How could he answer that?

David rubbed the back of his hand, where his burns were healing well.

He certainly hadn't *planned* on his life going the way it had. A verse from Proverbs flashed through his mind: *"A man's heart deviseth his way: but the* Lord *directeth his steps."*

"Lord, show me plainly the path You want me to take," he prayed.

Chapter 29

Later that evening, after the chores were done, Rachel escaped the overcrowded haus and sat on the top step of the porch, gazing up at the stars. Esther had said she and Viktor used to stargaze together. Did David see the same stars she saw now? Or was the Pennsylvania sky entirely different?

Would he ever kum back? Her heart ached with missing him.

Behind her, the screen door squeaked open, then shut with a soft click. Daed appeared in her peripheral vision and sat beside her. He held a s'more in each hand. Mamm must've given in to his begging.

Rachel grinned, picturing Daed holding the marshmallow over a candle flame to brown it. He liked his marshmallows burnt, so he always caught them on fire and blew them out repeatedly before declaring them done.

"Want one?" He held out one of the gooey treats.

"Sure." Rachel accepted the s'more and took a bite. "Mmmm."

"So, about David leaving the Amish." Daed stretched out his legs. "I didn't say he would. I said he might."

"Joshua said the same thing." The heaviness in her chest grew to fill her whole being.

Daed leaned back against the railing. "I think Joshua may have ulterior motives for returning to the Amish. He claims that Gott found him on the Appalachian Trail."

Rachel turned to stare at him. This was the first she'd heard about that. Had Joshua returned to stir up trouble among the faithful? The bite of s'more turned into a lump in her stomach.

"David openly claims the same thing—that Gott *found* him." Daed shook his head. "Can't help but feel a bit envious. I'd like to think Gott had searched for and found me. But I guess some of us never wandered far from the fold." He released a long, heavy sigh.

"Joshua says that the Amish are wrong—that we can *know* we're saved." Rachel held her breath, waiting for Daed's answer. If only it were true.

Daed bowed his head. "I've had long discussions with Reuben Petersheim about this. He showed me some relevant verses in the Scriptures. Josh discovered Gott on the trail. Viktor and David found Him, too. And, don't think badly of me, Rachel, but they are right. It's just…Bishop Joe doesn't want it discussed. I've been too much of a coward to press the issue. We'll have to pray that he'll someday have a change of heart—of belief."

Rachel blinked. "So, everything we've been taught is *wrong?*" The s'more crumbled in her hand.

Daed shook his head. "Nein, not everything. But the Amish are not the only ones saved. And just because you are Amish doesn't mean you *are* saved. Jesus Christ is the way, the truth, and the life. You aren't bound for heaven just because you kneel for baptism in the Amish church and obey the Ordnung. You have to believe. *'Believe on the Lord Jesus Christ, and thou shalt be saved.'*"

"But I do believe in Jesus. We all do." Daed was wrong. She was certain of it.

Daed nodded. "But Gott's Word says that even Satan and the demons believe in Gott. James two, verse nineteen. You also have to admit you're a sinner, and then confess that Jesus Christ is your Lord and Savior."

Uncertainty washed through her. She was a sinner. The events of the past month had definitely settled that.

She glanced at Daed. He tugged at his beard and stared at the star-studded sky, a muscle ticking in his jaw. His brow was furrowed.

How did she go about confessing Jesus Christ as Lord and Savior? Hadn't she taken care of that by kneeling for baptism and joining the church?

She rested her elbows on her knees and propped her chin on her knuckles. Maybe that was the boldness both David and Joshua possessed—a certainty of their faith. Or maybe it was something else entirely.

⁓

David's daed returned from his daily walk to the mailbox with a rubber-banded stack of envelopes. He sifted through them. "Pay me, pay me, pay me, pay me...ach, David. For you." He grinned and pulled out a postcard. "From *her*."

David couldn't keep from smiling back. He flipped the postcard over to peek at the picture. It was of a Florida beach. Rachel's cousin must've kept her promise to purchase some postcards for her on her honeymoon. Gut thing she hadn't given them to Rachel earlier, or they would've been destroyed along with the rest of her collection in the fire.

> *Dear David,*
>
> *Not much time to write. In a hurry to get to work.*
>
> *I talked to Daed, and he explained some things. But I still have questions.*
>
> *They tore down the burned remains of the haus. Daed said something about scheduling a work frolic to rebuild.*
>
> *How is your daed? How are you?*
>
> *Love,*
> *Rachel*

The trouble with postcards was that they didn't offer a lot of space to write. He had to imagine what she meant by "Daed...explained some things" and "They tore down...the haus." Who was "they"? Her daed and brothers? Other men in the community? At least she'd still signed it "With love."

"David, when I finish the dishes, will you take me into town for a couple errands?" his mamm asked. "We can go while your daed takes his nap."

"I'm not an invalid," Daed grumbled. "Don't need a babysitter."

tant information. In situations like these, the listener pays closer attention in order to write down what is being said.

3) *Use illustrations.* Well-chosen illustrations tend to personalize the message; the listener "sees" it being acted out. If you analyze the messages of your favorite public speakers, you will probably find that they use well-chosen illustrations which allow the listener to see more clearly and vividly the truth or principle being expressed.

Illustrations are valuable in personal conversations as well as in public-speaking situations. Illustrations document our messages and give them credibility; they rescue our comments from being too abstract.

Let's look at an example. A husband says to his wife, "Sweetheart, we need to clean out the pantry closet in the kitchen. I saw bugs on one of the shelves." The wife listens, and the problem is taken care of. Later, the wife tells the husband, "Your saying, 'I saw bugs' helped me know you weren't criticizing me but saw a valid problem."

Here's another example:

MARIE: "Ted, I'm concerned that our children are developing bad relations with each other."

TED: "I don't think there's any problem. They're just kids."

MARIE: "Maybe so, but Jody hit Marty three times today, and twice I had to stop an argument."

In both of these examples, the speakers help the listeners by giving specific illustrations—by documenting what they are saying. In this way, they give their partners a clear idea of what they are trying to communicate.

4) *Maintain suspense.* Recently I attended a seminar. The speaker was very well prepared, obviously knowledgeable on this subject. At the beginning of his presentation, he distributed about four pages of notes, then spent the remainder of the lecture time going through the notes. Later, a friend and I shared our responses to the lecture. Both

of us revealed that we had found it much more difficult to be attentive because we had before us all the information the speaker was going to cover. The element of anticipation or surprise was gone.

This illustrates the fourth means of keeping listener attention—maintain suspense. When information is released progressively instead of all at once, the listener has to keep listening to get the full message. Preachers sometimes violate this principle by giving the major points of their sermons at the beginning. A more effective process would be to give the goal of the message, and then reserve each step toward achieving the goal until its logical place in the presentation.

5) *Show progress.* By this, I mean identifying to the listener the steps the discussion is taking, or describing the way the learning process is unfolding. When I speak or teach, I generally utilize an overhead projector. Frequently people come to me after a lecture or speech and say, "I appreciated your use of the overhead projector. It helped me follow the progression of your talk. I knew I had not missed any of the essential information." The frequency of this response indicates to me that listeners profit from speaker cues which let them know they are receiving the key points. If anyone has missed information, the speaker's review of the most important issues will point out to him what has been missed.

Growing as Speakers

You can speak so others will listen. If you already do, chances are that you are practicing the essential principles that have been outlined in this chapter. If not, perhaps these ideas will enrich your speaking skills and help you evaluate yourself as a speaker. The following questions have been designed to guide you in applying what you have learned.

---

1. Using what has been described in this chapter, develop your own speaker checklist. Jot down the key points that you would look for in an effective speaker.

2. Ask a friend to use this checklist in evaluating your speaking skills. Use the feedback you get from this exercise to find ways that you can become more effective as a speaker.

seven

LISTENING FOR
NONVERBAL COMMUNICATION

Mark entered my office hesitantly. His searching eyes quickly scanned the room. Finally he walked to the sofa and seemed to collapse into its soft cushions. He was fidgety, drumming his fingers on the arm of the sofa. He squirmed around as though he were uncomfortable. When he finally looked at me, I sensed that he was frightened. He took a deep breath and blurted out, "Ahh, I've got a serious problem."

From the moment Mark entered the room he was communicating. Though he did not speak, his every move gave me some indication of his condition. Read back over the preceding paragraph and notice all the ways Mark was speaking. His distress was evident, even before he spoke.

This illustration shows us the importance of nonverbal communication. It indicates how a perceptive person can "listen" to another, even when words are not used. Looking for nonverbal cues that support—or conflict with—a spoken message is an important part of effective listening; paying attention to supportive nonspoken evidence can help us listen more sensitively.

Importance of Nonverbal Communication

What do we mean by nonverbal communication? Why do we use the term?

Nonverbal communication includes every means of communication the speaker employs in addition to the spoken message. Nonverbal communication even includes the *way* we speak, the vocal cues that support our message. It encompasses all our body cues and emotional expressions.

Most of us are used to picking up on nonverbal cues from time to time. We watch another person and say, "How come you're mad?" or "You had a hard day today, didn't you?" or "Donna turns you on, doesn't she?" We observe actions which communicate, many times without being consciously aware that we are attending to nonverbal communication.

But few people fully grasp the importance of nonverbal communication, despite the fact that, according to David Johnson, "in a normal two-person conversation the verbal components carry less than 35 percent of the social meaning of the situation while more than 65 percent is carried by the nonverbal message." [1] Our beginning scene with Mark illustrates this. I had gathered a significant amount of data about this young man *before he spoke.* I could have anticipated that something was troubling him, even if he had never said a word.

Nonverbal cues are not only important to the listener. The speaker, too, profits from knowing how nonverbal actions communicate. David Johnson stresses that "in communicating effectively with other individuals, it may be more important to have a mastery of nonverbal communication than fluency with words." [2] Try this experiment. Imagine that you are very angry with a friend. You are seated across the table from him. Experiment with talking to him using no nonverbal cues. In no way reveal your anger through facial expression, body position, or even voice cues such as word emphasis. If you really were angry you would find this very difficult, unless you had disciplined yourself to disguise nonverbal cues.

Which brings us to a fascinating point. Some individuals become very effective at removing obvious nonverbal cues. They hide actions or feelings which would give away inner emotions. When this happens, the listener is left with fewer clues to understand what the speaker is feeling. He or she has to work from the spoken message alone.

An understanding of nonverbal communication is a valuable aid to adult-child relationships. Since children have a more limited vocabulary, adults need to be sensitive to the total context from which a child speaks. The alert adult knows that the child will use supplementary aids in his communication *and* that the child will be very sensitive to nonverbal expressions from adults. Elizabeth Skoglund observes that "children don't always understand the words we use to explain life to them, but they understand the warmth of touch. Also, children are often unable to express the feelings that are troubling them and therefore need comfort from nonverbal sources." [3] It is fascinating to observe that Jesus laid his hands on the children to express his love and blessing on them (Matt. 19:15).

How Nonverbal Cues Communicate

As we begin to ponder this subject, we quickly see that there are many ways we communicate without words. However, before we examine a number of these ways, a word of caution may be helpful. Already in this chapter I have used the word "cues" to speak of nonverbal communication. This word suggests a hint or intimation, the presence of an underlying attitude or meaning. It is true that nonverbal cues give us inferences, but we should exercise caution not to treat cues as certainty. We should not judge a person's attitude, motive, or meaning according to observed nonverbal expressions; rather, we should treat these expressions as possible clues that can lead us to explore further or seek additional information from the speaker.

Nonverbal communication comes through in at least three basic ways. The first way I will call *body cues*. Body cues include all the ways our bodies support a spoken message or communicate without verbal expression.

We communicate through our body position. If we are weary or discouraged, we might slouch in a chair; if we are anxious, we might sit tensely or move nervously. Sometimes the way we position ourselves in relation to other people communicates our underlying attitudes or concerns. If we become frustrated with a group decision, we may express our withdrawal by sliding our chair back slightly and sitting quietly outside the circle. We express fear, confrontation, or affection by our degree of physical proximity (backing away, "nose to nose," arm around shoulder).

Another important form of body language is facial expressions. Our faces can show that we feel happy, solemn, despondent, excited, and so on. If the corners of our mouth turn up, we generally communicate happiness; if they turn down, the message we give is one of sadness, anger, or similar negative feelings. The phrases "laughing eyes," "chin up," and "starry-eyed" all refer to facial forms of communication.

Body cues also include gestures and nervous habits. Courses in public speaking attempt to teach us how to utilize effective hand motions to complement, support, and stress key points of our message. The uplifted hand communicates worship; the clenched fist, anger or warfare; the open, extended hand, welcome or greeting. Nervous habits include constant hand movement, hair pulling, twitching, nervous eye movements, and general restlessness.

A final body cue is the way we dress. Our clothes say something about us without our saying a word. We may choose "loud" clothes to attract attention or dress sloppily as a reflection of a disorderly life or a spirit of rebellion.

A second basic form of nonverbal communication is *voice cues*. As we speak, we embellish the message by voice volume, tone, and rate of speech. Voice cues greatly influence how people interpret and respond to a message; as Proverbs 15:1 says, "A gentle answer turns away wrath, but a harsh word stirs up anger." The simple sentence, "I love you," can range from positive to negative, depending on the tone and word emphasis. Proverbs also wisely notes, "If a man loudly blesses his neighbor early in the morning, it will be taken as a curse" (27:14).

Another form of voice cue is the speech mannerism. Examine the following chart and decide what each mannerism communicates:

Mannerism	*Communicates*
"I hate to say this, but . . ."	_____ _____ _____
"Thanks, but you really shouldn't have done it."	_____ _____ _____
"It's none of my business, but . . ."	_____ _____

Mannerism	Communicates
"I don't care."	_____
	_____
	_____
"It goes without saying."	_____
	_____
	_____

Most of us use speech mannerisms subconsciously as a means to express meanings, attitudes, or emotions of which we may be unaware. One person I know consistently uses a "yes, but" pattern of speech. When another person makes a comment or expresses an opinion, this person will frequently respond with "Yes, but . . ." and proceed to show why the other person's idea was wrong.

A third important form of nonverbal communication is *emotional cues*. Emotional expressions such as laughter, weeping, giggling, or knit brows reveal inner states and heavily influence how our spoken message is interpreted. Emotional cues cause others to see us as either warm or cool, friendly or hostile.

Characteristics of Nonverbal Communication

Nonverbal communication reveals itself in many forms, but certain characteristics are common to all kinds of nonverbal messages. Understanding these characteristics can help us both as speakers and as listeners.

The first general characteristic of nonverbal communication is that its dominant use is to express or highlight emotions. Feelings seem to be ventilated more easily through nonverbal channels. One possible reason for this is that the emotions can work through the nonverbal routes sub-consciously, whereas the verbal expression is dominated by the conscious mind. What we are reluctant or fearful to admit consciously, we will often release subconsciously. This somehow seems safer, although it is potentially more dangerous.

A second characteristic of the nonverbal is that it is a more ambiguous form of communication than the verbal. This makes it easier to confuse the message received. The listener must be very cautious and tentative in interpreting nonverbal communication. He should feed back his percep-tions and seek confirmation from the speaker rather than assume he knows what the nonverbal expression means.

I want to underscore this point—*nonverbal communication is more difficult to interpret.*

Crying could mean	Happiness or Unhappiness
Silence could mean	Withdrawal and disinterest or Active involvement through careful thought
Laughter could mean	"I'm laughing *at* you" or "I'm laughing *with* you"
Tears could show	Despair or Deep gratitude to God

Feeding back what we observe to the speaker and seeking more information is the most reliable way to clarify nonver-bal data.

Another characteristic of the nonverbal is its limited scope. While the nonverbal can be more powerful, more intense, than the spoken message, it does not have the range of communication. It is much more limited in expressing concepts and ideas.

I am not suggesting that nonverbal communication is less important than verbal; I only want to stress that it has a different function. The nonverbal's primary function is to reinforce or undergird the verbal. It enhances and enriches verbal communication, and it fills speech with greater vitality. Without nonverbal expression, verbal communication would become dull and lifeless. Effective speakers know this, and use nonverbal channels to inspire, motivate, and challenge their listeners.

Four Keys to Listening for the Nonverbal

Skill in listening for nonverbal communication is vital to becoming an effective listener. Often it is the nonverbal cues which help us most in pursuing the underlying meaning of a spoken message. The following four suggestions can promote listening growth by helping us become more adept at reading nonverbal communication.

1) *Become sensitized to nonverbal cues.* Determine not to miss valuable supplemental information as it becomes available. A distinguishing mark of the effective listener is sensitivity to nonverbal communication. We can develop greater awareness of what cues the speaker is giving consciously or subconsciously by reviewing the three basic kinds of cues described in this chapter and disciplining ourselves to look for body language, voice cues, and emotional expressions. At first we may have to plan to observe these signs, but eventually an alertness to nonverbal signals will become a way of life.

As sensitivity to nonverbal cues increases, it is wise to learn to check out our perceptions with the speaker. It is always a good idea to *document what we observe* rather than merely giving an opinion: "For the past five minutes you've been wringing your hands; are you upset?"

2) *Realize that verbal and nonverbal messages should complement each other.* Virginia Satir observes that "a congruent communication is one where two or more messages are sent via different levels but none of these messages seriously contradicts any other." [4] This is an important clue for us as listeners. Do we sense any contradiction between what we are hearing verbally and what is coming across nonverbally? What is the nature of the contradiction?

When verbal and nonverbal do not harmonize, we have what is known as a *mixed message.* Mixed messages put an additional burden on us as listeners; they tell us something is not functioning properly. In such a case, we must feed back the mixed message to the speaker for clarification.

Here's an example. Rita comes into the room, slams the door, and "crashes" on the sofa. Her appearance is gloomy. Her friend Charles asks, "Are you unhappy about something?" but Rita replies, "No."

Rita is sending a mixed message in this instance; her behavior is not consistent with her spoken communication. So Charles says, "Rita, you said you're not unhappy, but you slammed the door and plopped on the sofa, and you look very dejected." As he shares his observation with her, Rita is able to see the discrepancy between her verbal and nonverbal messages and to clarify her communication for Charles.

In listening, it is helpful to think of the various sources of input we're receiving as different channels, then to look for congruence among the various channels, especially between verbal and nonverbal. We can then ask ourselves, "Is the message I'm receiving consistent?" If not, we can clarify the issue by sharing what we observe with the speaker.

3) *Recognize that a listener is more apt to believe the nonverbal than the verbal message.* Nonverbal cues can color a listener's perception of what the speaker is saying. It is harder to cover up the nonverbal. The person who does not want to admit that he is upset cannot avoid being restless, fidgeting with his hands, showing nervous behavior.

When nonverbal behavior is too intense, it can block out or distort verbal communication. The person in distress cannot think clearly and thus is unable to speak clearly. The person struggling with anger speaks from that anger, and anger colors the spoken message.

4) *Realize that the same cue can express a variety of feelings.* For this reason, we should always check out nonverbal cues rather than predetermining what they represent. Family members and work associates frequently "read into" another's actions those ideas, motives, and feelings they believe that person has. This can lead to judgmental attitudes which are destructive to close relationships. One of the root causes of communication breakdown is our tendency to judge an individual's intentions from nonverbal cues we observe. In fact, it is not uncommon to find damaged relationships stemming from misperception of nonverbal cues.

The wise listener determines to withhold judgment on nonverbal cues, choosing rather to feed back his or her observations in a nonthreatening, nonjudgmental form. The speaker can then confirm or clarify those observations. A communication process built on this foundation has high potential to lead to positive relationships.

During one of my writing breaks, I was sharing with Winnie my opening illustration of Mark. She laughed and said, "You should tell about the nonverbal behavior you heard from me this morning. You heard pots and pans banging loudly, matched by my voice, so you came out into

David could empathize. He'd said almost the same thing not so long ago.

Mamm patted Daed's hand. "I know, dear, but I just like to know you're safe." She glanced at David. "Do you think I should ask your aenti Doreen to peek in?"

"I think Daed will be fine." Nein point in smothering him. He'd be more likely to rebel if they did.

David carried the postcard upstairs and pinned it to the wall just beneath the other one.

If only he had time to write Rachel. But he needed to fetch the horse from the pasture—and sometimes the retired racehorse was a bit stubborn about coming when called—and get the buggy hitched up. Maybe he could find a postcard for her in town and write to her to-nacht.

After a bit of cajoling, and with the promise of a sugar cube, David lured Bluegrass out of the pasture. He had just gotten the willful horse hitched to the buggy when Mamm bustled outside carrying a couple of wicker baskets. He hurried to take them from her.

"Be careful with the one that's full of eggs," she cautioned him. "I don't want them all cracked when I get there."

"Selling excess eggs?"

"Jah. Englischers like the brown ones. They assume they're healthier. Never quite figured that one out. The other basket is filled with baked goods. Breads and such. Is your girl a gut cook?"

David chuckled as he gently loaded the baskets in the back of the buggy. "Jah, she's a gut cook. She kind of has to be. She told me in one of her early letters that her mamm is a prize-winning quilter whose designs bring top dollar at the auctions. I know firsthand that she tends to get carried away in her creativity and lose all track of time and place. Rachel basically runs the haushold."

"She'd hate to leave her mamm, then." Mamm sounded sad. She quickly turned away and stepped up into the buggy.

David climbed in after her. "She might. She's always dreamed of traveling, though, so she feeds her desire with postcards she receives, and by purchasing touristy koffee table books. She seems interested in just about any destination. For example, her cousins' ehemann works on a tugboat on the Mississippi River, and she thought his job was the most romantic thing ever."

Mamm pursed her lips. "Doesn't sound romantic to me. I'd rather have my ehemann nearby."

"Jah. I think she would, too. I also think she'd—" He frowned. She'd hate to move so far from home.

He shut his eyes and blew out a noisy breath. He must've wiggled the reins, because Bluegrass pulled the buggy into motion. He straightened, opening his eyes.

"She'd what?"

David shrugged. "Well, we'll just have to see, ain't so?" He guided the horse onto the road.

"Why don't you invite her to visit? Her brother can kum, too. I'd like an opportunity to get to know my future dochter-in-law before the wedding."

David slowed the buggy as a car sped past. "We're hardly at that point in the relationship, Mamm."

Mamm lifted a shoulder and leaned back, smiling. "Ach, you're there, Sohn. You're there."

⌒

"Rachel. Postcard for you." Daed climbed out of the buggy, then turned around and reached for a stack of mail. He sifted through it, separated one item, and held it out to her. The postcard featured a photo of a yellow conversation heart bearing the words "Luv You" against a white background.

Heat flooded Rachel's cheeks. She snatched it from Daed's outstretched hand.

He smirked. "I think this haus might be a gut starter home for you two." He winked as he walked past her into the haus.

Rachel spun around as the door slammed shut behind him. "Really?" But he was gone. She'd have to ask later if he'd been serious.

Had he purchased this farm with the intention of giving it to her and David? She studied the haus and barn with assessing eyes.

Of course, it all would depend on David's asking for her hand. On his returning.

So many variables.

She flipped the card over, anxious to see what he'd written.

Dear Rachel,

> *In town with Mamm. Wanted to get this sent right away.*
> *Daed is doing well. Improving daily. Diet is a challenge.*
> *Feel free to ask any questions you may have. Will do my best to answer.*
> *You think Sam might agree to bring you for a visit? Mamm and Daed want to meet you.*
>
> > *Love you,*
> > *David*

Warmth spread through her. He hadn't crossed out the endearment this time.

But then, he hadn't answered her question about whether he would leave the Amish. Maybe she wouldn't reiterate that one. The truth of the matter was, if he did leave, and if they were a couple, she'd go with him.

But the thought of the inevitable shunning she'd face for "jumping the fence" nearly brought her to tears. Esther and Viktor wouldn't have that problem. They'd never joined the church in the first place. They currently attended the Old Order Amish services, but they also went to a local New Order Amish church on the Sundays in between.

Yet Rachel and Obadiah had knelt for baptism—the first step in their plans to marry. And David had joined, too, while he was living in Pennsylvania.

The screen door opened, and Daed came back outside. He placed a hand on her shoulder. "Tomorrow we'll start discussing the blueprints for a new haus. Might take a few days to finalize, and then we'll start rebuilding. Should be up within the week. I know this is hard for you, Rachel. But, the truth is, it's not so easy starting out unless you move into an established home."

"Or have a well-stocked hope chest that wasn't burned up in a fire," she murmured.

Daed frowned. "You need to learn to make do or go without. And to have a gut attitude about it."

Rachel blinked. Daed thought she was out here sulking? Of course, her bad-tempered words about the hope chest might've given him that idea. "Nein, Daed. I understand. I was just reading David's note and thinking."

"Ah. Thinking about asking Sam to take you there?"

Rachel lowered her eyes. Daed had read what David had written? Of course he had. Probably when he was sorting the mail.

"Jah."

"Don't be surprised if he says nein. And I'd rather you didn't take a bus."

Rachel nodded.

"Maybe you should spend some more time apart in prayer, seeking Gott. It'd be a better use of your energy than moping." He strode out to the barn.

Rachel sighed. Her spirits lifted at the sight of David's Border collie, Rosie, as she ambled up to the porch and nuzzled her. Petting her absently, Rachel said, "You miss him, too, don't you?" It was likelier the dog missed the students, since school had been canceled once again due to the lack of a teacher.

That reminded her.... She bolted to her feet and hurried out to the barn, Rosie at her heels.

"Daed?"

He poked his head out from one of the horse stalls. "Jah?"

"Did you mean what you said about giving this property to David and me?"

Daed studied her. "*If* he comes back and marries you, then jah. But you have to consider his other options, Rachel."

"Danki!" She ran from the barn, Rosie still trailing her. She dashed into the haus, leaving the dog outside, and searched for another postcard. Or a piece of paper.

Anything.

But then she stopped. How could she be so selfish as to ask David to return? He needed to be with his family.

Daed was right. She needed to pray.

She went back out to the porch and sat on the top step. Rosie laid her head in her lap and whimpered, so Rachel smoothed her hand over the dog's head. Then she closed her eyes.

Ach, Lord Gott....

She had so many decisions to pray about. Where to begin?

Something in her spirit moved.

Before I start praying for my own requests, I want to ask to know You, Gott. Personally, like David does. I'm so sorry for my sins. For my bad attitude and immature actions. Please forgive me. I believe Jesus is the Sohn of Gott and Savior of the world....

Something miraculous flooded through her.

Peace. Forgiveness.

She smiled.

Gott....

Chapter 30

Hearing a buggy outside, David stowed the ax in the tool shed and came out of the barn. A man stood on the front porch of the main haus, casually looking around. He was older, with gray hair and a slight limp. He turned, and recognition hit. Deacon James Swartz.

"May I help you?" David nodded toward the dawdi-haus. "Mamm and Daed are still living there." So was he, for that matter. None of them had even set foot in the main farmhaus since David's arrival.

A heaviness descended at the thought of the dreaded chore—going through the belongings of his deceased family members. The conversation he'd need to have with both his parents...and Rachel...and Gott.

The deacon's arrival made him think that all this would need to happen sooner than later. Hopefully, Daed would be up to it, because he was the one who'd need to make the decisions. Or agree to the news—whatever it was—that the church leader had brought.

Deacon James followed David to the dawdi-haus. They entered the kitchen just as Mamm set a steaming casserole dish on the table. He missed the cream pies she used to make for almost every meal, but with Daed's heart problems and the dietary restrictions he was under, maybe it was for the best that she'd stopped.

"Ach, Deacon James." Mamm sounded flustered. Concerned. "Will you join us for dinner?"

David walked to the sink and washed up, trying to ignore the way his muscles tightened with dread.

"Perhaps."

David glanced over his shoulder and saw the older man survey the table. After a moment, he joined David at the sink. "I'll stay. Danki."

Whatever was in the casserole dish must've looked gut. It definitely smelled wunderbaar. David reached for a towel and dried his hands. "Where's Daed?" He hoped the nervous catch in his voice wasn't evident.

Mamm glanced skyward, indicating he was upstairs. "He'll be in directly." Then she retrieved another plate from the cupboard.

"Can I help with anything?" David asked.

"Jah. You can get out the salad. Danki." Mamm pointed to the refrigerator. Not that he needed directions.

David opened the fridge and reached for the clear glass bowl. As he carried it to the table, he studied the contents. Fresh spinach leaves, strawberries, sliced red onions, cherry tomatoes, and feta cheese. Mamm had made the salad several times before, and he'd loved it. Especially the balsamic dressing she made to go with it. Despite his apprehensions surrounding this unexpected visit from Deacon James, his stomach rumbled.

None of the salad ingredients was in season, though. Was this for a special occasion? Frowning, he glanced at the perpetual calendar hanging on the wall. His birthday. How could he have forgotten? Well, with all the sorrow and upheaval he'd experienced of late, it seemed plausible. And Mamm's flustered state might have something to do with the deacon's unexpected intrusion on their celebration.

With that in mind, the celebration would be virtually nonexistent, beyond the special meal. How could they celebrate, with Deborah's recent death and Daed's heart attack?

After setting the salad bowl on the table, David inspected the steaming casserole dish. Pork chops smothered in a white sauce with mushrooms and lots of pepper. Another one of his favorites. And probably a onetime treat, since this recipe wouldn't be on the list of foods approved for Daed. David smiled at Mamm. "Danki," he whispered.

Mamm handed him a couple oven mitts. "Baked potatoes are in the oven."

Just then, Daed shuffled into the room, head bowed.

"How are you feeling, Daniel?" the deacon asked. "We've all been praying for you."

Daed's head snapped up, the color draining from his face, leaving it gray. He eyed their visitor. "Deacon James. What brings you by?"

What had his parents been keeping from him? Had they put certain things aside while dealing with the immediate demands of planning a funeral and undergoing surgery?

Mamm hurried over to assist Daed by pulling out his chair.

Daed dropped into it with a grunt. "I'm feeling fine. Get tired out easily, though."

David opened the oven door. Heat assaulted him as he removed four foil-wrapped potatoes. Smallish ones, so Mamm must've assumed that either he or Daed would have two. Instead, the extra potato would go to their uninvited guest.

The deacon sighed and shifted awkwardly before nodding toward the main haus. "I know the farm was yours, and you sold it to your sohn-in-law, Adam. His family has started to make noises." His mouth twisted, whether in discomfort or disapproval, David couldn't tell. "What can you tell me about the arrangement you made with him?"

Daed exhaled a heavy breath. "Rent-to-own. He made a monthly payment of an amount we agreed upon, with the idea that when the sum of his payments totaled my selling price, the farm would be his."

David's stomach churned. Adam's parents had a reputation of greediness. Would they try to claim the farm and put his mamm and daed out? Surely not.

Yet that would explain his parents' reaction to the deacon's showing up.

Deacon James nodded as mamm set a mug of koffee in front of him. "Then, since he died, it's still yours? I told his parents that I thought it was, but they insisted he had signed a contract."

Daed held the deacon's gaze. "He did. But it was *rent-to-own*, with the stipulation that if he changed his mind or didn't make all the requisite payments, the property would revert back to me and my sohn, David."

The deacon tugged at his beard. "We're looking at a "he said, he said" situation. And I don't want to accuse either one of you of lying, but...."

Daed straightened. "Adam made only eight payments or so. Hardly a drop in the bucket compared to the total cost of the farm. And I know it goes against living by faith, but I was afraid of this happening. Afraid the church would take his family's side." He sucked in a breath. "I have a copy of the agreement upstairs. Do you want to see it?"

"Nein, that isn't necessary. They will still want to kum out here and reclaim their sohn's belongings. His tools. His horse and buggy."

Daed's chest rose and fell. "Of course."

The deacon's mouth settled in a flat line. "I hate to say this, but you might want to have his stuff boxed up and ready to go. They'll likely be by in the morgen."

David pulled in a shuddery breath. How would he manage to handle all the daily farm chores, plus pack up Adam's things? That would mean dealing with the impact of entering his childhood home for the first time since his sister's death, knowing that he would never see her alive again.

Daed glanced at David. "We will trust the gut Lord to protect us."

"In light of the shunning, we won't speak of them again," Deacon James stated.

"Them"—Adam and Deborah? Or Adam's family?

Daed's mouth flexed. Pain filled his eyes, but he nodded.

David swallowed the hard lump in his throat. So, he was referring to Adam and Deborah. What had happened to result in their being shunned right before they died? In this case, it was kind of a double-death. He couldn't imagine the emotional turmoil Mamm was dealing with. He glanced at her as she settled into her seat.

"Looks like we're about to eat," Daed said, his voice gruff. Raw. "If you wouldn't mind leading us in offering thanks...."

Deacon James nodded, then bowed his head for the silent prayer.

David studied the bent heads of the elders around him. How could he even begin to make decisions? Should he ask Rachel to kum here? Or ask his parents to consider completely selling out and moving to Missouri?

The deacon cleared his throat. "Amen."

David quickly bowed his head. *Lord Gott, comfort my family. Give me answers. Soon. Now. Amen.*

Almost a week passed before Adam's family showed up. When they did, Daed went out to the tool shed with the men, while Mamm ushered the women into the farmhaus, leaving David free to do the chores. Mamm and Daed had decided it'd be best to face the separation of belongings with Adam's family, in order to minimize the number of "misplaced" items that might go missing.

As David peeked into the shop, though, greed didn't seem to be an issue. Both families were quiet and subdued, shedding only the occasional tear over a raw memory. David blinked back his own tears. It was hard to believe he would never see his sister again on this side of heaven. He'd never meet his niece or nephew—a fact that had been brought painfully to mind when Adam's mamm asked David to carry out the tiny cradle Adam had fashioned for his unborn boppli. Both mothers had tears flowing down their cheeks as they commented on the tiny boppli quilt that Mamm had made in greens and yellows as she folded it up and packed it away to give to David's future frau someday.

That made him think of Rachel. How many quilts would their future boppli end up with? It seemed to be a popular gift for expectant mamms and daeds, especially among family, with all the aenties and grossmammi wanting to make a cherished heirloom for the newest member of the family.

Adam's mamm provided a one-dish dinner for Mamm to heat and serve, with some homemade powdered-sugar doughnuts for dessert. Temptation for Daed.

As the three of them stood there watching the two overloaded buggies leave the driveway, Mamm sighed. "I hate to say this, but if I *ever* enter that haus again, it'll be too soon. Way too many memories. The deaths of all our kinner...." She startled and glanced at David. "Except for you. I'm just so scared that if we stay, something will happen to you, and we'll be all alone."

"Bad things happen in other places, too, Mamm." Case in point, the buggy accident in Seymour.... He rubbed his leg. The fire in Jamesport.... He flexed his healing hand.

"I know, but I lost eight kinner. Seven of them died in that very haus from various farm accidents or diseases. My only remaining dochter who lived there was shunned and died. My ehemann had a heart attack there and nearly died. The haus is cursed. That's all."

Daed reached for Mamm's hand. "I've actually been giving some thought to selling out, having a farm auction, and moving to Missouri. Getting a fresh start. Maybe David could see if there might be a farm for sale there, if he's agreeable to the idea."

David rubbed his jaw and looked around. Even though he'd been away for two years, this still felt like home. But with Mamm's strong feelings....

Daed smiled. "You'll be closer to your girl."

And that was the icing on the cake. David grinned, a lightness flooding his being.

Mamm pulled free and started for the haus. "I'll start dinner warming. We can discuss this more over the meal."

"I'll put this farm up for sale. We can auction off the livestock and any items we don't want to take with us," Daed said.

David smiled. Nein need for a dinner discussion. It seemed Daed had already decided.

He couldn't wait to tell Rachel that his parents were moving to Missouri. This time, he wouldn't be homeless. He wouldn't be jobless. And he'd be able to court her.

He couldn't wait.

"Could you contact the bishop in the Jamesport area?" his daed asked. "Get the feelers out for a farm for sale there?"

David nodded. "Jah, I'll contact someone. But not Bishop Joe. I'll ask Preacher Samuel. He seems more on top of things than the bishop, anyway."

Daed hesitated. "Are you sure you're fine with this? Or do you want to live here?"

David shrugged. "I'm fine with it. I'll miss this place—I grew up here, after all—but it's not home anymore. And I intended to settle somewhere else, anyway."

"Jah. Seymour. Still not sure how you ended up in Jamesport."

David chuckled.

"Of course." Daed grinned. "You did tell me. *A girl.* Always a girl."

David leaned against the barn door. "But not just any girl. *My* girl."

Chapter 31

The haus was coming along quickly. Daed had even built an all-season room big enough to leave quilting racks set up all the time, along with a cutting table and a sewing machine, whenever they purchased replacements. Mamm surely would enjoy this room for her sewing. All the windows in the big room were wunderbaar. Rachel looked around. It'd be great to read in—if she could do it without getting roped into a project of Mamm's as assistant seamstress.

She dipped her brush into the bucket of off-white paint and glided it over the edge of the wall where the roller couldn't reach. This room would be a favorite, for sure. Hidden behind the haus, it would be free from the prying eyes of those passing by. Someday, she'd like a room like this. Not that she'd ever be a grand-prize-winning quilter like Mamm.

A horn blared outside, and Mary ran out of the room to see who it was. "Mailman's here. Be right back."

Rachel finished the wall, then set down the brush and went to the kitchen. Mary had carried in two big boxes addressed to David. One of them was postmarked from Seymour. His boots? Mary set the box on the counter. The other was from Pennsylvania. But not from Bird-in-Hand, so probably not from his parents. Mary set it on top of the other one.

"Anything important?" Rachel gestured toward the stack of envelopes.

"You got another letter from David. Does he write to you every day?"

Rachel grinned as she took the envelope and slipped it into her pocket. She wrote him every day, too. She couldn't wait for a moment alone to read the latest news.

"Go ahead." Seeming to sense her desire, Mary headed into the all-season room, leaving Rachel alone.

She leaned against one of the newly built counters and ripped open the envelope.

Dear Rachel,

This will be short. I'm sad and exhausted. One of the deacons came by and told us that my late brother-in-law's family would probably be by in the morgen to collect what belonged to him. Daed turned a scary color of gray but otherwise seemed to handle it well. Now he says it's for the best.

The deacon said we won't mention Adam and Deborah again. Broke Mamm's heart. Apparently, they did something that got them shunned right before their death. Daed won't tell me what it was. So, it's as if they never existed. But nobody can stop us from thinking of them...or missing them.

I finished cutting the wood and stacking it. Got several ricks ahead. Tomorrow, I suppose, will be spent helping with...well, I'll not speak of that. Just pray for me. Us. And for Gott's will to be made known.

Miss you, miss teaching school, miss Rosie.

Enough of me and my woes. How is the haus coming? Is your daed's new farm nearby? Does Sam like it?

If you can be at the phone shanty on Saturday, I'll call at two.

Love you,
David

Saturday seemed so far away. In reality, it was only a day and a half from now.

She looked up from the letter as Daed entered the room. He glanced from her to the sheet of paper. "How is he?"

Rachel shook her head. "Sad. Exhausted. He's going to call on Saturday." Her vision blurred, and she swiped at the tear that escaped one of her eyes.

Daed nodded. "Don't mention it to him, but if he decides to return, I'll offer him the horse, the buggy, and the livestock that's at the other farm, as well. Don't worry—Gott will work things out. He's in control." He patted Rachel's hand and gave her a reassuring smile.

If only Rachel could muster more than mental assent with his statement.

"How's the painting coming?"

A thump sounded from the all-season room, followed by a loud clatter. A scream pierced the air.

Rachel and Daed rushed to the room to find six-year-old Jenny sitting on the floor, crying, and Mary staring her down, fists on her hips. Both girls were splattered with paint, and the can lay on its side, liquid pooling around it. The ladder had fallen against the wall Rachel had just finished, scraping off some of the fresh paint.

"What on earth happened?" Rachel mimicked Mary's pose, her right foot starting the fast tap that Mamm did when she was close to losing control. "*You're so clumsy*" lingered on the tip of her tongue, but she managed to keep it unsaid. Everyone made mistakes—including her. She was just exhausted from several nights of poor sleep on the floor of the small overcrowded haus. From working at the store and coming home to struggle through an afternoon and evening of more work trying to get the new haus built. Seemed the "adventure" of starting over was wearing on all of them.

"I tripped over the ladder," Jenny wailed. "I'm sorry!" She drew her knees up to her chin.

Daed surveyed the mess, then wiped his hand over his jaw and down his beard. "Are you hurt, Jenny?"

The girl shook her head.

"Okay. Please stop your crying. We have plenty more paint, and everything will be fine. But we need to clean up this mess, jah?"

"How can you say that everything will be fine?" Mary asked him. "See what she did to the floor?" She lifted her foot, as if planning to stomp, but then she lowered it with a sheepish look at Daed.

"I see, Mary. But it's just the subfloor. It'll be covered with tile, so nobody will ever see it." He glanced at Rachel, then turned back to the two younger girls. "It's just like what Christ did for our sins, jah?

Covered them with His blood." Daed smiled. "Excellent illustration. I'm thinking of using it, with your approval, of course, when I preach on Sunday. May I have your permission, girls?"

Sniffing, Jenny nodded. Mary pursed her lips and shot a baleful glare at Jenny, but then she nodded, too.

It was a great illustration. Something Rachel had learned first-hand not so long ago.

"Gut. Then I want you to wipe those tears away and start cleaning up. Accidents happen." He bent down and touched the top of Jenny's head. "It's okay, süße."

Rachel smiled. *Sweetie.* That was the endearment Viktor used for her cousin Esther. So romantic. She shivered as she imagined David saying it to her.

The front door opened and shut. Heavy footsteps crossed the kitchen floor. "Preacher Samuel?"

Rachel turned as Joshua came into the room.

"Wow. What happened here?"

"A sermon illustration." Daed smiled at the girls. "Gut to see you, Joshua. What brings you by?"

"You have a phone call. I was listening to my messages when the call came in." He quirked a smile toward Rachel and winked. "It's David."

Rachel straightened, a grin forming as she started for the door.

Joshua held up a hand to stop her. "He wants to speak to your daed."

Ach.

Daed nodded. "Danki, Joshua." He hurried out of the room.

"Did he tell you what he wanted?" Rachel asked Joshua. She had to force her feet to stay in place.

"He said he'd talk to you on Saturday, as arranged, since he's in a bit of a rush today."

"But he talked to you." She tried not to sound too whiny. "Why can't you tell me?"

Joshua shrugged. "Because it's his news to tell. Not mine." He glanced toward the paint spill. "Let's get this mess cleaned up." He straightened the ladder, then righted the pail of paint. "Sermon illustration, huh? I can't wait to hear it."

Rachel glanced toward the door. Why had David called to speak to Daed?

It wouldn't do any gut to badger either Joshua or Daed for answers. Neither would give in.

She'd likely perish from curiosity long before Saturday.

David surveyed the barn as he waited on the phone for Preacher Samuel to pick up. He was glad Josh had answered when he'd called, and that he'd told him Preacher Samuel appeared to be at the new haus, since his buggy was parked in the driveway. Now he could talk to him right away rather than having to leave a message.

"Preacher Samuel speaking. Hallo, David. How are you? How's your daed doing?"

David pulled in a breath. "Daed is doing well. Still healing. He tires easily but is getting better every day."

"Gut. Glad to hear that. What can I help you with, sohn?"

He'd missed the preacher—and his dochter. "Daed is putting the farm up for sale. Too many painful memories here. He asked me to check into property in Missouri. Could you keep an ear open for some property there?"

Lord Gott, close this door if You don't want us to go through it. And throw it wide open if You do. Help us to be content with Your answer.

Preacher Samuel chuckled. "Jah, I could do that. In fact, I might know of something. Just answer a brief question before I tell you about it."

David ran a hand over the sturdy wall supporting the overhead hayloft where he'd just finished pitching hay to the animals. He turned away as Daed entered the barn, like he'd done so many times before...and soon would do no more. "Jah. Anything."

"Are you planning on courting my dochter when you get back?"

His bluntness took David by surprise. Normally, such things weren't openly discussed. He heaved another breath. "If she'll have me, jah."

"I bought a farm so we'd have a place to live while rebuilding the haus the fire destroyed. I planned on offering it to you if you came back. Everyone here believes I meant it for Sam, but that's a story for another day. The haus is small, with only two bedrooms, but it'd be a gut starter home. You could always add on. Or it'd be a gut dawdihaus. I'll include the livestock, a buggy, and a retired racehorse named Licorice Whip."

A farm? Complete with livestock and more? Gott's gift of a wide-open door overwhelmed him. *Danki, Lord.* "Licorice Whip." David tried it out. He liked it.

"She has an interesting history, too. Her former owner told me that she won eighty percent of her races. Never placed lower than third. But during her second season, in the third turn of the fourth race, the reins snapped. She didn't make the turn but ran wild at full gallop right into the starter gate."

David winced.

"The jockey was thrown into the metal gate and broke his back. Ended his career. Licorice had only some bruising and a gash across her eye that needed stitches. Left a nasty scar. After that, she refused to load into the starter gate, so they sold her. They have trouble loading her into horse trailers, I'm told, and also into narrow stalls. Always nice to know a horse's backstory, ain't so?"

"And a person's, too." The horse's history sounded like a sermon illustration in the making.

Daed came into the room with David and quirked an eyebrow, as if to ask if there were any properties available. David nodded, and Daed grinned. He seemed practically giddy with excitement.

"Jah…danki, Preacher Samuel. That is very gut to know. How much do you want for the farm?"

The amount Preacher Samuel told him was less than half of the asking price for David's parents' farm. David grinned and gave Daed a thumbs-up.

"That sounds doable, Preacher Samuel. Let me give the phone to my daed. He's standing right here. Gut talking to you." He handed the phone to Daed and left the barn.

It was one thing to talk about selling the family farm, but making it a reality hurt more than he'd anticipated. He'd miss this place. Moving away while knowing he could kum back to visit was quite different from letting it go completely.

It would be worth it, though, if Rachel accepted him. He hoped she would, based on the letters and postcards signed "Love...."

If Gott didn't open that door, David might be tempted to move on. But he'd be grounded for as long as necessary to take care of the new farm and his parents. Still, he'd follow wherever der Herr led him.

He looked down at his bad leg.

Rachel could do much better, yet, for some reason, der Herr had opened her heart toward him. She apparently saw past his limp to the heart of her pen pal and friend.

When he returned to Jamesport, he'd knock on that door, as well, and pray it would open. He couldn't ask her the really important question until they were face-to-face.

⌒

Rachel looked out the window at the snow covering the ground and the icicles hanging from the eaves. Somehow, during David's absence, time had marched on. November had turned into December, December into January.

Even though her family had been living in their new home for a little more than two months, they still slept on the straw tick mattresses they'd used at the temporary haus. Still used the makeshift furnishings. Daed was fond of reminding them that things took time—and money—to replace. And with the costs of rebuilding the haus and purchasing the other farm, they were short. The community would pitch in to provide financial help, if Daed asked. But Rachel understood his reasons for keeping quiet. It was hard to ask for help from those who needed the money more.

Instead, he kept telling Bishop Joe that they were doing fine, and that his kinner were learning valuable lessons.

Valuable lessons, such as how to make do with what one has. And how to manage without what one didn't have.

Like David.

But he and his parents should arrive any day now. Their farm had sold quickly, snatched up by a couple who planned to marry in January. According to David's daily letters and weekly phone calls, they'd sorted through everything and followed up with an auction of the items they didn't want to move. David had asked Sam to kum out and drive the rental moving van for them. He'd jumped at the chance. And refused to take Rachel along.

She let out a long sigh.

Sam had been gone for almost two weeks. Two weeks she could've spent with David, even if she probably would have been put right to work packing things, as David had said Sam had been.

Rachel fingered the latest postcard from David, stowed inside her apron pocket. Signed "Love you, David." How long would it take him to get around to asking permission to court her once he got settled in?

She peeked out the kitchen window once more. Nothing moved on the roads, except the blowing snow.

Just to be sure, she went to the front door, opened it, and stepped outside, looking in both directions.

Still nothing.

She'd need to sweep the snow off the porch and the front steps. Maybe she'd do it now, before anyone came in for lunch and tracked snow on the floor. She went back inside long enough to grab the broom and her coat.

As she swept, she glanced at the smoke rising from the chimney of the schoolhaus. She missed having David living right across the street. Her cousin Dory Beachy had been teaching since the first of December.

The wind picked up, and Rachel shivered. She finished the bottom step, then hesitated at the rumble of a loud engine in the distance. Soon a brown UPS truck rumbled past, then screeched to a stop out of view.

Silly of her to imagine they'd drive a full moving van to Daed's farm before going to their new home. Just wishful thinking.

She knocked the snow off the broom and headed back inside, her thoughts on what to fix for supper. Stew and biscuits sounded gut. Warm and filling. She collected some root vegetables from the cellar and started peeling them.

Another engine sounded, but this one didn't sound like a van or a truck.

She looked out the window. It was Sam's old car, which he'd left parked at the bus station when he'd gone to Pennsylvania. It disappeared behind the barn.

Sam was back.

Rachel's heart skipped a beat. David was somewhere nearby.

She put down the vegetable peeler, covered the skinless vegetables in water, and headed outside to demand details from her brother about David and the trip.

Chapter 32

Excitement pulsed through David's veins as he got out of Sam's car. He couldn't wait to see Rachel. To gaze into her eyes. To hold her. To kiss her. After stretching out his travel-weary limbs, he started trudging through the snowy weeds toward the back of the car, sliding his hand over the cold metal exterior of the vehicle for support.

Sam met him at the trunk and took out his duffel bag, handing it to him before slamming the lid. "Gut to be home. And I know I've said this before, but I'm glad you returned, too."

"Gut to be back, for sure. Danki again for all you did to help us." As they rounded the corner of the barn, he glanced at the school. Smoke rose from the chimney. They must've gotten a new teacher. Either that or the regular teacher had returned. He'd miss it.

But not as much as he'd missed Rachel.

Rosie ran up to him, wagging her tail and whimpering. He crouched down to greet the wiggly dog. Then a sound from the direction of the haus caught his attention. He looked up as Rachel darted down the steps and across the snowy yard. David straightened, his heart nearly bursting with joy at the sight.

Sam ran toward his sister, arms open wide. "Missed me, did you?" he teased.

She ducked to escape his embrace, but Sam merely laughed as he continued toward the haus.

So many weeks of waiting.... David grinned and opened his arms. She fell into them and clung tight. "You're back. You're finally back."

∾

"Jah, I'm back." David chuckled as his arms closed around her.

Rachel snuggled against his chest, inhaling the scent of peppermint. "I missed you so much."

250

David pulled back a millimeter. "I missed you, too."

His gaze scanned her face, lingering on her parted lips. She linked her fingers behind his neck, and he groaned softly as his lips brushed hers with a kiss so sweet, it ached. Then he lifted his head and gazed into her eyes. His arms tightened around her, drawing her nearer, as his lips came back and claimed hers once more. She lost herself in the swirling sensation of want and need that his kiss— kisses—elicited. Her stomach clenched, and she trembled, weaving her fingers through his hair. His black hat tumbled to the ground as she poured herself into showing him how much she'd missed him. How much she loved him and needed him.

He eased back. "Wow."

With his arms no longer holding her so tightly, reality began to trickle in—along with a few snowflakes and the cold weather. She reluctantly let him go. Nothing had been settled. She didn't know if Daed had kum out of the barn to witness this reunion or not, but she didn't want to be scolded again for inappropriate behavior. Sam might be watching, too, but she didn't want to look away from David long enough to check.

"I have something for you." He reached inside his coat.

She leaned against the side of the barn. "I don't care what you brought—you're enough."

Grinning, he pulled out a postcard. Similar to another one he'd sent her, it was completely white, except for a pink conversation heart pictured in the center, this one showing the word "Love." He'd added an "I" and a "You" above and below it in pen.

"Ich liebe dich, Rachel." He reached out and gently brushed her cheek with his fingers.

Her heart pounded. "Ach, David. Ich liebe dich, too." She lifted her gaze to his.

He reached back inside his coat and took out another postcard. It had the same design as the first, except the words on this conversation heart read "Marry Me."

Rachel gasped. She blinked, then eyed the postcard again. Then she squealed. "Jah!" Joy bubbled over as she reached for him.

David grinned, but instead of drawing her back into his arms, he reached inside his coat once more.

A third postcard. The conversation heart was blue. "Kiss Me," it said.

She flung herself into his arms. He stumbled backward from the force and fell in the snow. She came down beside him, kissing his cheeks, his eyes, his nose, his mouth....

"Ich liebe dich." She didn't know which of them had spoken, or if both of them had. It didn't matter. The words hung like a shimmering promise in the cold air.

David rolled over on his side and cupped her face in his hands, deepening the kiss. She wrapped her arms around his neck, pressing herself against him. She no longer cared what any possible onlookers might think. David had kum back, and he would be hers forever.

He broke the kiss with a sharp exhalation. The air between them steamed white. "Let's get this wedding planned. And soon."

⌒

The next nacht, David hitched Licorice Whip to the buggy and drove his parents over to Preacher Samuel's farm. It was nice of the Millers to invite them for dinner following a busy day of unloading the moving van and settling into their new home. During one of his rests, Daed had drawn up plans to add on a dawdi-haus so that David and Rachel could live in the main haus after their wedding. And Mamm had taken the time to bake a couple of snitz pies after unpacking the kitchen supplies.

Preacher Samuel had described the farm as small, but compared with their farm in Pennsylvania, it was large enough. David planned to talk to a local nursery about building a greenhaus and starting plants for them. Coupled with weaving baskets and tying fishing flies to sell, it should generate enough money to support a family. Mamm also wanted to put in a large garden and sell extra produce at the local farmers' market.

David pulled the reins to guide Licorice Whip around a corner, and then the Millers' farmhaus came into view. His knee started bouncing involuntarily. He couldn't wait to see Rachel again. To introduce her to Mamm and Daed.

He pulled the buggy to a stop outside the barn. Luther came out and held the reins for David while he climbed down.

"I'll take care of your horse for you." Luther rubbed Licorice Whip on the nose. "Such a fine animal."

"Danki." David turned to help Mamm from the buggy. She handed the snitz pies to Daed for a moment, then took David's hand and climbed out.

Preacher Samuel and Elsie came out of the haus to greet them. Mamm smoothed down her dress and apron, probably to wipe her palms, which were likely damp with perspiration from nerves. Then she retrieved the pies from Daed. "I brought you these—snitz pies. They're a traditional dessert in Lancaster, made from dried apples." She offered them to Elsie.

"Danki." Elsie beamed as she took the pies. "They look wunderbaar. Kum on in and rest a spell while I finish the dinner preparations." She turned toward the haus, and Mamm fell into step with her.

"Nice to meet you, Daniel." Preacher Samuel shook Daed's hand. "Are you feeling well after the move?"

"Well enough." Daed's grin stretched from ear to ear. "I'm glad to be here. David has had nothing but gut things to say about Jamesport."

Preacher Samuel winked at David. "Love has a way of making everything appear bright and sunny. But we're glad he decided to settle in this area. Word of his Bible study has traveled some, so there are bound to be a few more men sitting in on the next one. Sam and even Bishop Joe have expressed interest."

David gulped. Bishop Joe? Really?

Somehow, despite the trepidation he felt at the thought of having his Bible studies critiqued by the bishop, he felt a sense of surpassing peace. He couldn't wait to see how Gott would handle his call to preach.

He looked around. "Where's Rachel?"

"She should be on her way home from work. I asked Sam to pick her up on his way home. He thinks I don't know he's attending college classes." Preacher Samuel glanced at Daed. "The bu is still in his rumschpringe. I won't say anything, but I'm praying that he'll someday return to the faith."

Up the road, there was the rumble of an engine. Gravel scattered as Sam's car drove at too high a speed into the driveway. Sam paused long enough for Rachel to climb out of the passenger seat, and once she slammed the door, he jetted off behind the barn.

David went to meet Rachel, his grin probably rivaling Daed's. He caught both her hands in his, then stood there a moment, gazing into her eyes. "Walk with me later?"

"Jah." She grinned back. "I'm so glad you're here."

"Now and forever." *Lord willing.*

Daed came up beside him with a knowing twinkle in his eyes. "And who is this?"

David answered anyway. "This is my Rachel. My love." In spite of their audience, he pulled Rachel into his arms.

And kissed her.

RECIPE

Apple Snitz Pie

2 cups dried apples (snitz)

1 1/2 cups warm water

2/3 cup sugar

1/2 tsp cinnamon

1/2 tsp. ground cloves

dough for a two-crust pie

Continued on back

Soak apples in water overnight, then cook until soft in the same water. Once apples have softened, mash them, adding the sugar, cinnamon, and cloves. Pour mixture into an unbaked pie shell. Cover with second crust and seal edges, then cut several slits in the top crust to allow steam to escape. Bake at 425 degrees for 15 minutes; reduce heat to 370 degrees and bake for an additional 35 minutes.

Makes one 9-inch pie

About the Author

A member of the American Christian Fiction Writers, Laura V. Hilton is a professional book reviewer for the Christian market, with more than a thousand reviews published on the Web.

Her first series with Whitaker House, The Amish of Seymour, comprises *Patchwork Dreams*, *A Harvest of Hearts*, and *Promised to Another*. In 2012, *A Harvest of Hearts* received a Laurel Award, placing first in the Amish Genre Clash. Her second series, The Amish of Webster County, comprises *Healing Love*, *Surrendered Love*, and *Awakened Love*. A stand-alone title, *A White Christmas in Webster County*, was released in September 2014. *The Postcard* follows *The Snow Globe* in Laura's latest series, The Amish of Jamesport.

Previously, Laura published two novels with Treble Heart Books, *Hot Chocolate* and *Shadows of the Past*, as well as several devotionals. Laura and her husband, Steve, have five children, whom Laura homeschools. The family makes their home in Arkansas. To learn more about Laura, read her reviews, and find out about her upcoming releases, readers may visit her blog at http://lighthouse-academy.blogspot.com/.